TODD GRIMSON'S

WITHIN NORMAL LIMITS

"Sometimes I think, or it occurs to me, secretly, that I might actually enjoy a war or some other big disaster, a nuclear accident or terrorist bomb. Certainly I'd be really, fully alive in my station, my function, dealing with the casualties, rushed, efficient, cool and collected, making flawless snap decisions and ready for anything that might come in. Oh, there are nights vaguely like that, nights of multiple traumas and excitement, but very rarely does it get to that point where it's almost too much, sensory overload, where one is in a fine hysteria, overpowered by the glut of input from all sides."

WITHIN NORMAL LIMITS

TODD GRIMSON

VINTAGE CONTEMPORARIES

VINTAGE BOOKS · A DIVISION OF RANDOM HOUSE · NEW YORK

A Vintage Contemporaries Original, May 1987
First Edition

Copyright © 1987 by Todd Grimson

Published in the United States by Random House, Inc.,
New York, and simultaneously in Canada by Random
House of Canada Limited, Toronto.
A portion of this text originally appeared, in different
form, in *Fiction '84*, edited by Richard Peabody and
Gretchen Johnsen, in 1984.

Library of Congress Cataloging in Publication Data
Grimson, Todd, 1952–
    Within normal limits.
    (Vintage contemporaries)
    I. Title.
PS3557.R496W5 1987   813'.54   86-46192
ISBN 0-394-74617-1

Author photo copyright © 1986 by Beth Eldridge

Book design by Amy Lamb

Manufactured in the United States of America

10 9 8 7 6 5 4 3 2 1

For George Sarant, M.D.

Many thanks to my mother, Kathleen McCullough, Paul Bowles, Joan and Bruce Bartlett, Michael McClure, Bob Colgan, Joel Weinstein, Judy Nordblom, R.N., Debbie Sue Andrews, R.N.

WITHIN NORMAL LIMITS

ONE

Someone screaming wakes me up. At first I think I'm still at work. But then, as I blink, open my eyes, I realize that I'm home in my bed. It's 4:30 P.M. That isn't screaming; it's someone laughing. I recognize the voice as that of Diane, my wife's best friend.

I don't feel good. My senses are too acute, nerves jumping at every sound, eyes restlessly scanning the unmoving furniture. I feel vaguely like I may be in danger, but I cannot plot out why. Maybe I had a bad dream.

I have to be at the hospital at seven. The drive into town takes about forty minutes. I might as well get up and have something to eat. For a moment I stand at the window, looking down at the splashing pool. I see Anna and Diane and her husband, Mike. There are a couple of other people here whom I don't know.

After I brush my teeth, I take a Librium. I step into the shower. I shave. The Librium will render me reasonably immune to most phenomena. Sure, in a better world, or if I was better, I would not have recourse to medication to regulate my organism. For the time being, I'm just doing what I can to stay on a plateau. I don't think too far ahead.

If the tranquilizer makes me too sleepy, or slow-witted, I'll take a Dexamyl. I know what I'm doing. I'm not addicted to anything. I prescribe myself only those drugs with which I'm very familiar, and I never push up the dosage or take something every single day. I'm in control of this situation, believe me.

When I come downstairs, I feel better; I'll be able to get along with Anna's guests. I don't care if they're overly friendly, or drunk. I don't mind. They can be however they want.

Sometimes it would be nice to be invisible, like a bird, flying above everyone without making a sound or moving a wing.

Gretchen, my wife's older sister, is in the kitchen, working on dinner. Whatever she's making smells exotic and good. She is humming while grinding up some spices with pestle and mortar. She sees me and stops humming, looking down at her hands for a moment before saying hello.

I ask her what she's cooking, and she tells me. Three recipes from northern India. I ask her if dinner will be ready by a time that will be convenient for me. She says yes. I'm interested in what she's doing; she tells me about the different spices and ingredients she will use. One dish is already done, simmering on the stove.

"I need something now," I say, opening the refrigerator.

"Just to keep me." A piece of cheese, I think, with a slice of fresh herb bread.

Gretchen has been living with us for the last six months. Although the older, by three years, she seems like the younger sister, and cedes authority to Anna in nearly every matter, thus acknowledging Anna's life of success.

The last job Gretchen had, at a small-time advertising agency, she was fired from after a mere four weeks. She's had trouble keeping jobs, and I'm not wholly sure why. Perhaps she becomes anxious, and subconsciously does not wish to do well; soon she succumbs to various errors that otherwise seem, to those who know her, puzzling and out of character. She's not the sort of person who strikes one as incompetent. As far as I can tell, she's intelligent, sensitive, and hardly lazy—but she can't seem to hold on to her jobs.

Since her divorce, she hasn't met many new men, and has often been depressed. She isn't comfortable talking about her former husband. Anna may know some things here that she hasn't thought I need to know. Secrets. In any case, though, Gretchen has begun seeing a psychiatrist, and I'm hopeful that he can help her feel better about herself.

"Save anybody last night?" she asks, trying to make conversation, repeating the cliché, as I rinse off the knife with which I cut the cheese.

"It was busy," I say, idly, and then remember something. "There was one guy—another motorcycle wreck—who kind of individualized himself to me. He said, 'Doc, no bullshit. Am I gonna live or am I gonna die?' He wasn't very drunk, and he wasn't being overdramatic, and I really wasn't sure. No head injury, but a slight positive return on the belly tap, so we thought he might have a little bleed. But his pressure was good, and he seemed very stable. He started getting worried because no one would talk to him. So I said, 'Don't worry.

They're going to open you up and look inside your stomach, but I don't think that you're going to die.' "

"So what happened?" asks Gretchen when I pause, hearing someone else laughing outside. "Did he make it?"

I turn back to her. "When they got him open, he was full of blood; he had a ruptured vena cava. And his liver was torn half in two. Bill Taylor, the surgeon, came down later and said that they never got the guy off the table. They couldn't pump blood in fast enough to keep up; they put in something like twenty units. . . . He was one we all thought was going to be okay."

I shrug, and she looks at me strangely, as though she doesn't like me, pulling a wayward strand of light brown hair out of her face. She often gives one these funny looks; I don't think she knows how they appear. She's not in control of herself, unlike her sister.

I feel like having a Coke, and open the refrigerator to get one out. I can feel the Librium; I need some caffeine to balance it out. Anna tells me, with justice on her side, that Cokes aren't good for me, and that I set a bad example for my son, but drinking Coca-Cola is a weakness I mean to indulge.

Coca-Cola is an institution, sometimes perhaps the main evidence of America around the world. The red of the signs is the same wherever you go.

Standing drinking the Coke, which is still cold enough that I don't feel like pouring any into a glass with ice, I see Anna come in. She's not wet, but has been wet, her golden hair drying, the short terry cloth robe very loosely belted over her saffron-colored bikini. She's lightly tanned, taking prudent care of her smooth skin.

"You're up," she says, noting the fact, going on down the hall toward her darkroom. Ever since she got two pictures selected for the Sierra Club's annual calendar, she's seen herself as more photographer than part-time nurse. I don't blame her. She's good at photography, gifted even, for all I know, and nursing can get to be a boring, menial profession after a few short years. She just works enough these days to keep up her license, taking classes, meanwhile, in composition and design.

We haven't slept together in a while.

I walk after her. She's right. There's too much sugar and carbonation in the Coke. I feel benevolent, rather affectionate, but not sexually involved. The Librium has something to do with this. She's going to take some pictures of her friends, it seems, at poolside or in the pool.

"Like David Hockney," I say, as she searches for some particular lens.

"What? Oh—swimming pools. That's true. Here, will you carry the tripod?"

"Sure." I'm smiling, but I feel ill-at-ease, out of place. "Who's here besides Mike and Diane?"

"Diane's cousin Sam, and Sam's friend Bob. They're on their way up to Vancouver, and then they're going camping in the province. They may go up to Alaska."

"Who's the girl with them?"

"She's not with them. Her name's Renée; she works in another law office that does a lot of business with Diane's."

Diane is a legal secretary. Mike, her husband, is a stockbroker. They're all right, I suppose. They seem to go on a lot of exotic vacations.

I carry out the tripod, waving to Diane and being introduced casually to these strangers who are going to eat with us. Sam and Bob go to UCLA. Sam acts, and also wishes to direct. Bob is an anthropology major. Both have tight, fit, tanned bodies, and are clad only in swimming trunks, glistening with beads of water in the sun.

"Save any lives last night?" says Diane, half-friendly, half-insolent, and I shrug in response.

"No," I say slowly. "Everybody died. Kids with colds, old men with nosebleeds, sprained ankles, cut fingers—every one of them coded out and expired. Physician error."

Sam smiles at me, while Bob and Mike race in the pool. I dislike and distrust Sam on sight: he's too good-looking, and looks too used to being liked. And he doesn't look stupid, which would mitigate things to some extent.

"I spent a couple of nights as an observer in the ER at UCLA Medical Center," he says to me. "I don't see how you can stand it over a long period of time. What I saw, at least, was a horror show."

I have nothing to say to this, and don't say it. I'm not interested. He's innocent, and sincere, and smart enough, I think, to know how disarming this can be. We have nothing to discuss.

Anna prepares to take some pictures. She's efficient, as always. When I first met her, I was especially attracted by this efficiency. She worked in the Intensive Care Unit. I was the junior surgical resident, which meant that I did all the scutwork for a senior resident I rather despised. I don't think he ever knew how I felt about him; in fact, he seemed to be fond of me, in his way. Because he managed to mess up a few surgeries, and a few patients' post-surgical care, I was in ICU all the time, trying to keep the poor souls here on earth. I got to know Anna, who's five years younger than me, and I liked it that she wasn't transparently trying to hook a young doctor, as were so many of the other young nurses I saw.

When I became senior resident myself, I could be more authoritative, showing myself in a better light, and we started to go out. She had been living with a musician, but had broken up with him and moved in with another nurse, and the arrangement wasn't working out.

The musician kept coming around, also, trying to get back together with Anna, who didn't want to have anything more to do with him. He confronted the two of us once when we arrived there, in the morning, after having spent the night in my quarters at the hospital. I was bigger, and he changed his mind about wanting to fight. A good thing, too, as I was terrified I would embarrass myself, though I glared as good as I got.

Anna told him off in no uncertain terms, and he seemed to see there was no chance, looking even more unhappy than he had been—and he never bothered her, to my knowledge, again.

After this, Anna seemed to trust me more, and we began depending on each other for most of our emotional and social support. I was the one who wanted to get married. Anna was wary, wanting to live together instead. I said that if we got tired of each other, we'd get a divorce. It didn't have to be a big struggle, I said.

When I decided to leave surgery and switch to emergency medicine, she didn't oppose me, although this move has meant a lot less money coming in over the years. I was tired of cutting, tired of feeling like a glorified TV repairman or plumber, tired of using my hands. I hardly miss it, I think. There were fun aspects, just like in anything else. Sure, sometimes I diagnose someone with a hot appendix or some such thing, and feel like going in myself—but that's a momentary urge, and it's passed by the time I drive home.

At first Anna didn't want any children, and I wasn't sure, more than willing to put it off; she had a sudden change of heart and got pregnant with Roger after we'd been married less than a year. I was happy at the time, but by now, when Roger's seven years old, I almost wonder if he's mine.

He's a crybaby, and a little coward, with a stubbornness I detest. He's stubborn about being dumb, for example, stubborn about not wanting to learn how to read or count or play sports or go to school. Anna's spoiled him, and sticks up for him, but I don't really think that, in her heart of hearts, she's any more pleased with him than I am. I wasn't like him when I was a boy. I can't see myself in him at all.

This weekend he's at his grandma's again. (Anna's mother, not mine. My parents are in Connecticut.) I have little idea how he spends his time there. Eating a lot of sweets, I suppose, and talking baby-talk with his "gram." He leaves me cold. Whatever guilt I may feel about this only moves me to dislike him the more. I can't help it.

If I didn't have to go to work, I'd take a Percodan and cool out for the evening. Feel no pain. I don't like watching Anna take pictures of these people. Democratically, she's including them all: her real interest, though, I think, is in the body of Sam. He must know this, although the rays of her attention are discreet. She's never tasteless. Neither, I sense, is Sam. He's narcissistic, however. He holds himself too well.

The other bodies are imperfect. Diane's is too skinny, with no real breasts. Mike, who comes over to bore me with talk about the economy, is slightly overweight. They're drinking frozen daiquiris. Bob, who seems shy, is fit but nondescript. Renée looks all right. Her breasts and hips are bigger than I might choose for her, but her waist is slender and her thighs are firm. She's wearing the most revealing swimsuit. I find it somewhat vulgar. I have to say, objectively, as a stranger, that I'd still pick Anna. She still holds my attention. I can't help this, either.

I don't think much about what I look like. I can't describe

myself. I don't notice my face when I look in the mirror to shave: it's all mechanical. I'm vain, though, anyway, I suppose. I need glasses, and won't do anything about it. I'd like to see better, I guess, yet I don't want to have glasses all over my face. It may just be the idea of making a change.

There are plants all over, hanging and in planters and tubs. More plants than we need, inside and out. Mostly green, occasionally blossoming red, white or yellow, purple or blue. Gretchen takes care of them. They're Anna's idea. You never know when she'll come home with a new one. They'll add some atmosphere to these photographs.

Dinner is excellent. The actual food we eat, I mean. I don't like it when Diane pretends something's too hot; I don't like it when Mike says the flavors are strange; and I don't like it when Bob and Sam are polite and praise Gretchen's cooking, comparing it favorably to that of Indian restaurants in Los Angeles. And Bob has been to Pakistan, India and Nepal. He tells us about these places. Gretchen is pleased. When she feels confident, she resembles Anna somewhat, if Anna's face was less well-defined and she had brown hair.

When I have to go, it seems sudden. Anna walks out with me to the car.

"What time did you get home this morning?" she wants to know.

"I don't know. Late. Ten or so. I had to give that talk on intubation to the new residents."

"That's right. I forgot about that."

I'm not sure what's on her mind. I can't believe she might think I've got something going on with anyone else, even though, as always, it would be easy. I look at her, and I don't know what she's thinking.

"Did you play tennis?" I ask, just to seem interested, although I'm fairly sure she did.

"I got beat," she says, gazing off into her memory. "I got in a match with a Japanese girl I'd never seen before, and she ran me all over the court. It was good exercise, of course. Are you coming home tomorrow morning? Straight home, I mean? I'll make breakfast if you are."

"Okay. I'll be here."

"Okay. I hope it's not too busy."

"Well, Dan's on, so it'll be backed up when I get there; everyone will be in a bad mood. If someone has CHF, he thinks they have pneumonia. If they have pneumonia, he thinks they have CHF. You know. Oh well; I'll see you in the morning then."

"Yes, I want to talk," she says. "Have a good night."

She kisses me on the lips, coolly, and waves as I pull out of the driveway in my car. I have a Fiat Spider. Black. Polished and clean. I can push it on the curves as I wind my way down the hill; my nervous system and muscles know this road by heart.

On the freeway, I left-lane it all the way, as usual. I'm not really speeding outrageously, although I'm over the limit. This car likes to go fast. I never turn on the radio because I like to hear the sound of the engine and what's happening with the other traffic on the road. I don't think the Librium slows my reaction time to any significant degree. I go more carefully if I feel stoned. Tonight I'm pretty straight. Numb.

I'm trying not to wonder too much about what Anna wants to talk to me about. Maybe there's something wrong with the filtration system for the pool. Or, she may have the desire to go someplace faraway for a vacation, emulating Mike and Diane. I wouldn't mind spending a couple of weeks in the Caribbean. Maybe something's wrong with Roger. Or, it's possible she's mad at Gretchen for some reason, and thinks we ought to kick her out and make her find a job.

There was a time, when Anna and I still worked together, when we couldn't keep our hands off each other. It didn't have to be necessarily sexual contact—even a held hand was enough. We'd give each other foot massages, back rubs; and we were always play-fighting, like kids in fourth grade who don't know how else to flirt.

I remember once, I was going through the chart of an old alcoholic/smoker who had an incredibly long and complicated medical history, and I was sitting in the ICU, at the central console, about ten-thirty at night. All of the nurses seemed busy with their patients, quietly changing I.V. solutions or noting down hourly outputs, when a slightly hefty, rather sluttish but reasonably attractive respiratory therapist came in, to check on the respirator of some patient, and she started talking to me, talking in a sweet soft voice that contrasted with her brassy laughter. Her name was Mary Louise, and she had coppery red hair. I didn't realize that Anna was watching us talk and smile at each other; I thought she was busy with some poor post-op shotgun-to-the-chest. Mary Louise left, called off by her beeper, and I started going through the reports again, when Anna came over and said, in our "play-fight" voice (which I found irresistible), "So I'm not sweaty enough for you, huh?" and swept all of my reading matter violently to the floor. I laughed, but I had to pick up the papers and put them back in order again, all by myself.

We'd punch each other on the bicep. We also liked to wrestle: I'd let her pin me down, which she enjoyed, and then I would take back the upper hand when she'd begin to torture me. I'd torture her in turn. She always liked it when we'd simply act, communicating physically, on a basic level, child-within to child-within, a level on which supposedly we could not lie.

When I get to work, it's as I expected. Patients have been

waiting an hour or more to get in, and are irritated and testy, while Dan's still taking his time, joking with the nurses, eating an apple, making detailed, time-consuming notes on a chart dealing with a straightforward, simple case. Dr. Dan Petibon. "Petty-bone." From Louisiana. People generally like him; some like to imitate the way he talks, the cornpone expressions he can come up with. I like him a bit less, though I can get along with him well enough.

I change into scrubs and start seeing patients. I'll be here for twelve hours, until 7:00 A.M. A resident will be here until midnight, having begun his shift at noon. Two residents per month do this rotation, trading days on. There are four of us on the ER staff; five if you count the head of the department, who only works (as a real doctor, instead of as an administrator) two or three days a month. I work about three shifts a week, but sometimes as many as seven or eight days in a row, following this with a good number off. I make a lot of money, I suppose, by some standards. By others it's not that much at all.

This hospital has perhaps the busiest Emergency Room in the area. There's some controversy over who's really the local Trauma Center, but, as far as I can tell, we're it. The hospital is in the black part of town, such as it is, and most of the city's violent crime seems to happen in our vicinity. There is also a helicopter that brings us traumas from the rural environs, mostly from car or motorcycle wrecks, with an occasional suburban shooting or industrial accident, a logger losing his leg or some such thing.

Tonight, once we're rid of Petibon, we start to get some patients in and out. Quickly, like at a hamburger stand. Greg Hong is the resident, and I let him have the more seemingly interesting cases, rather than making him do all the boring kids with colds, because I like him and he's bright.

"Hi, I'm Dr. Patterson," I say, with or without friendliness. "What kind of trouble are you having tonight?" One must always ask, because sometimes the patient will give one story to the admitting interviewer, another to the nurse, and then come up with something completely different when they're finally presented with the physician.

History of Present Illness. Past History. Social History (neglected; or taken in at a glance and the inference developed as the person speaks). Review of Systems. When patients say, Yeah, they've had problems with every organ in their body, you've got to cut them short. Control the interview. Lead them to tell you only what you need to know, not their whole life story.

A young white welfare mother is back in with her six-month-old child. I recognize them from last night. The child isn't any better, she says. I gaze in the open, half-buttoned blouse at her fresh, dumb breasts. It turns out that she never got the prescription filled. Even though, with her welfare card, it's free. I tell her to get it filled. The hospital pharmacy is open now. She seems grateful to me for straightening this out.

A sixty-eight-year-old woman, white, is in again, a frequent guest. She comes by ambulance, bringing her suitcase along. The first thing she wants to do is go to the bathroom. She's no sicker than usual. She's lonely. I don't like her. Still, I order a chest X ray and EKG, just to cover myself. I won't admit her unless there's something new.

At 9:30 P.M. an ambulance brings in a trauma; the Trauma Team is activated and on hand when the patient arrives. I hardly have to do a thing, nor am I interested. The guy was riding a motorcycle, typically without a helmet, and typically missed a curve. His pupils are fixed and dilated. Blood seeps out of one ear. Swastikas are tattooed over his nipples. He doesn't look like a very nice individual, from my point of view.

Soon he's out of the department, gone to CAT Scan, and then to ICU. The cops have arrived, and one of them asks me if it's likely to be a fatal. If it is, they have to do more reports.

"Eventually," I say. "Maybe not tonight. Maybe tomorrow."

Dr. Hong asks me if I know a housekeeper named Clarence Cantue, who works here at the hospital. The nurses have warned Hong that Clarence is a malingerer.

"What's wrong with him tonight?"

"Back pain," says Hong. "He says he hurt it bending over to pick up some boxes."

"Give him Motrin," I suggest, knowing that this will leave Clarence disappointed. Motrin will help legitimate back pain, in time, but it does not have any psychotropic side effects.

Some Laotians have brought in a child who is ill. A three-year-old. For the most part, the Southeast Asians' English speaking skills have steadily improved: this group is either newly arrived and without an interpreter, or simply an exception (also without an interpreter).

"Baby sick."

"How is he sick?" I ask them.

"Baby cry," one of them announces, perhaps the father, after deliberation.

But the baby's not crying now. He's smiling. No temp, no cough, no dehydration. And he looks like a generally healthy, plump baby boy. I'm nice to the family, explaining that he looks all right to me, trying to talk to them without too much condescension.

Of course, a certain amount of condescension from me is expected. Nobody wants their doctor to be too humble. And I'm cocky enough, in my own way, most of the time. I'm better off here, I function more confidently and efficiently here than I do anywhere else.

It's eleven o'clock. The new shift of nurses has come on,

to work with me until seven in the morning. Sandra, Lucy, and Michelle. The evening crew lingers for a while, rehashing gossip and new events. Complaining about day shift.

I go back to my room, where there's a TV and a bed. It's slow now. I feel like working on my article. I take a Dexamyl and then, seized by an impulse, pick up the phone and call home. Gretchen answers on the third ring.

"Oh, hi Darrell," she says, sounding happy. "Are you having a busy night?"

"Not so bad. In fact, right now it's kind of dead."

"That's nice. I'm just watching TV."

She starts to tell me about some movie on the cable film network. The light on my telephone comes on, which means they're trying to reach me, that something has come up. I tell Gretchen I have to go. She understands. I walk out to the nurses' station in Room 6 to see what's coming in or already here.

"We're getting a Trauma Code in about three minutes," says Sandra. "Multiple gunshot wounds. Chest, abdomen, neck."

A Trauma Code means that the patient is probably dead or dying, that the EMT's can't get a pressure and/or the patient's stopped breathing on them.

I'm ready, standing in the Trauma Room next to the stretcher, while the nurses get out the supplies they anticipate will be called for. The rest of the team, including the surgeon and the surgical residents, get here just as the EMT's come rushing in with the patient on their gurney. Everything goes quickly now.

The gunshot victim is a very well-built young black male, probably around twenty-one or twenty-two. His hair is cut short, and his complexion is very dark. The holes are about the size of pennies, without exit wounds in the back. There is one hole in the right upper chest, one in the left lower quadrant of the abdomen, and one in the throat. The throat wound is bleeding out. The others are not.

We've got to get some blood in him; at the same time we might as well go for it aggressively, open his chest and try to get his heart going again. The Respiratory Therapist holds the ambu bag over the patient's mouth, a tube going down into the trachea, pumping it like a bellows to force air down into the lungs, to keep him oxygenated. Rick Briscoe, the Trauma Surgeon, makes the incision to crack the chest. Rib spreaders, as the sternum is cut, open him wide so that the heart is easily accessible.

Michelle is suctioning out the blood; I hold the heart up in my hands, giving it squeezes to contract the muscle and get it going. Then we zap it, and it starts beating on its own. Briscoe looks for the bleeder, poking around, as the lungs inflate and stand up, spotted, free of the constricting ribs. I find the bullet. It has pierced the right ventricle. The heart muscle stops. We zap it again.

Security has had trouble with the family, who have arrived in force. They have been unwilling to go down to the conference room to wait for a doctor to come talk to them. One black guy in particular is highly upset, demanding to see his brother. He doesn't think that anyone has any right to stop him. The security officers present at the moment are among the least effective ones on the payroll—white fundamentalist Christians who turn red when somebody calls them a name.

Washed up, I go down to talk to the family. On the way (they've finally agreed to go to the conference room), I stop to ask Charlotte, the clerk, what the patient's name was.

"Raymond. Raymond Minnieweather. They call him 'Scooter.' "

There are ten or twelve black people gathered to hear me tell them that Scooter is dead. I think they know before I speak.

"I'm sorry," I say—and immediately one woman, perhaps an aunt, calls on God and starts to sob—"he didn't make it." I'm speaking primarily to the mother. "We did all we could."

"All you could?" exclaims Scooter's putative brother, whom I've glimpsed earlier, menacing the security guards. "Where was he shot?"

"He was shot three times, but the one that did it for him," I point to myself, expressively, "was right in the heart."

A pretty, teenaged girl cries out, "No! No! It can't be!" really hysterically. Someone moves to hush her. Scooter's brother smacks his fist against the wall, hard, and starts talking about killing Eddie Ray Green. The mother seems very upset by the fact that the bullet went into the heart.

"His heart? Oh my God. I thought he was just shot in the neck. His heart? Lord, Lord."

The on-call hospital chaplain, Reverend Williams, who is black, with a deep voice, comes in, and I let him take over.

Charlotte called him a while ago, and as I go by I thank her for her prescience. There are police all around, but they're talking to Rick Briscoe. The plainclothes detectives are indifferent and sleepy-looking. I feel sorry for Scooter as I look in on him; the nurses are cleaning him up. Everything's quiet in there with him now. There is still a lot of bright red blood all over the floor. Somebody will shortly be mopping it up.

I see other patients. I order X rays for a very dirty twenty-five-year-old white guy who fell off a loading dock at United Parcel Service. He hurt his back, and because of his general demeanor I think he's legit.

Sandra assists me while I do a pelvic on a seventeen-year-old black girl, thin and attractive, who says, "My vagina, you know—it hurts like there's knives down there." Draped, her feet in the stirrups, she stares up at the ceiling.

"Ow," she says, loudly, when I touch her, separating the labia to examine the vestibule and clitoris. I carefully insert the speculum into the foaming aperture. The red papules, bright red inflammation and yellow discharge lead me to believe that she has both trichomonas and gonorrhea. She complains again, unjustifiably, that I'm hurting her: Sandra tells her to be quiet and lie still. I like Sandra. She lives on a farm, and she's big and healthy, with brown hair and freckles. She takes the slides; we leave the girl still lying there with her knees up, now crying.

A white guy has brought in his black girlfriend who's having a headache. Security has been called, because apparently the man became abusive when Charlotte wouldn't take the woman back to lie down right away. Charlotte meant to have her register first, but the woman, sitting in a wheelchair, pretended to faint and fell down onto the floor. Michelle, who had come out to see what was going on, popped an ammonia ampule in front of the woman's nostrils. She pushed it away violently. So now she's back in a room, and the boyfriend's mad that he's not allowed to be back in with her, holding her hand, giving us all a hard time.

The chart says her name is Natalie Brown. She's slender and rather pretty, twenty-nine years old. Her dark brown eyes look long-suffering and neurotic. It's rare to see a biracial couple in which the man is white.

"Isn't there a woman doctor I can see?" she says, turning her face away from me. "And could you please turn out that light? It's bothering me."

"I need to examine you before I'll turn down the light. And

no, there isn't a female physician who'll see you here for this. If you have a private doctor you'd like to call, you're free to use the phone in the waiting room. So tell me what you want to do. If you want to be seen, I'm happy to see you."

"I've got a terrible migraine headache. I've had them before; I know what they're like. Can't you just give me something for the pain?"

"Not without examining you."

I'm irritated, the more so perhaps because she is attractive and seems to dislike me on sight. I look and sound cold, however, in command of myself, relatively nonjudgmental and fair. I'm sure of this. I've acted the part so many times. You just use as your premise the idea that the patient is not responsible for whatever he or she does, and, on the surface at least, withhold all blame.

Natalie allows me to check her. I palpate the carotid artery for pulsations and tenderness, and the bones of the cranium and face for tenderness or irregularities of contour. I look into her sullen eyes. There's no distension of the superficial temporal artery. Its pulsations are the same on either side of the head. I turn the light down (it has an adjustable dial instead of a binary switch), and leave the room, going down to the nurses' station to write on the chart.

"What are you going to give her?" asks Michelle.

"I don't know. Oh, go ahead and give her seventy-five Demerol, twenty-five Vistaril."

I could try a placebo. An injection of normal saline. Some people have been miraculously "cured" by this in the past. Or I could just give her fifty of Vistaril, which would have the effect of a mild tranquilizer, inducing drowsiness (as well as getting rid of any nausea she may have)—but I don't care, I'll give her the benefit of the doubt. I think that Natalie is having a fight with her boyfriend or some other kind of emotional strain, and that that's really why she's here. In any case, the Demerol will make her feel better.

Another motorcycle wreck. This guy's less damaged—and comes in fighting the EMT's. He's yelling at us. Howling like an animal. He has to be tied down in restraints.

There are cuts on his head. His other visible injury is an obvious broken leg, tib-fib, so I can dump him on the ortho resident, Chuck Brady, whom I don't quite like.

"This guy's a real bozo," I tell Brady on the phone. "It looks like he might also have broken his wrist. The belly tap's negative. We're still waiting on the Blood Alcohol. See you."

Maybe Roger will grow up to be a biker, or a rapist, or simply an unsympathetic homosexual. I've seen many seemingly nice parents come in to find out what has happened to their thoroughly obnoxious, worthless offspring. Of course, Roger may change in a few years. I can't anticipate how he may turn out. I shouldn't be so negative.

It's 2:30 A.M. I'm sewing up the arm of a strange twenty-two-year-old female, white, who says she cut it on some glass. However, it's deep and clean enough that it must have been done with a knife. I'm trying to figure out if she's a prostitute. She's tall and kind of fat, dressed all in black, with heavy eye makeup that is smeared from tears that she's cried. She's wearing high heels and black stockings, a hole in one at the knee, the white flesh showing through in a way that, somehow, I find attractive.

"I'm a model, you know," she says, as I put the first stitches in and Lucy cuts the threads for me. "Have you ever seen me? Teena Overstreet."

I don't say anything. Teena, lying down, continues to talk.

"Mostly I've been in these magazines, you know: making love, going down on somebody, stuff like that. This guy hypnotized me, and then took pictures of me. I was in a coma for like a year. His name's Pierre, but that's just one of his names. He's also named Dean, and Alexander, and Johnny Young. He's a black guy, you know, and he really hates whites — How many stitches are you putting in? What was your name? Dr. Patrick? No, Patterson. That's it, isn't it? Patterson."

"That's right. I think you're going to end up here with about twenty."

"Twenty. Oh, could you make it twenty-one? That's a better number. Seven times three. Is that all right? It's kind of important. Numbers with a five in them are bad, you know. Especially at night. Like a pentagram."

"I can make it come out twenty-one."

"Thank you. You see, I have to be extra careful, 'cause I know about a murder that no one else knows about, and I never know when Johnny Young might get worried that I'll talk. Can you keep a secret? I should tell someone, in case sometime I get killed, you know?"

"Sure."

"There was this girl named Laurie, okay, and Dean got mad at her, I mean he was calling himself Pierre then. He got mad at her 'cause she was holding out; and he killed her and cut her up. I found this pool of blood in the closet that's still wet: it'll never dry. Pierre had the pieces of her cremated, and he keeps the ashes in an urn under the bed. And so, one night I was sleeping there, after making love with him, and I had this vision. Laurie came up through a hole in the mattress, all bloody, and she was telling me that I had to kill Pierre with this ax she said was downstairs in the basement. I said, 'Laurie, I'm not killing no one for you! You're dead now, so just leave me alone, 'cause I'm alive!' "

"Stay still, okay? I don't want to make a mistake. Don't move."

"I'm sorry," she says, and lies quiet for a while. Lucy and I exchange glances. I raise an eyebrow, and Lucy has to smile.

"Say, do you believe in Jesus?" asks Teena Overstreet.

"Yes," I say. "I'm Jewish, though." I'm not.

"What does that mean? Don't Jews believe in the Lord?"

"We think he was a great prophet, yeah."

"The Jews killed Christ," she says, as if just remembering this fact, wanting to see how I'll handle it.

"No, we didn't," I say. "The Romans did."

She thinks about this, and then says, "Can I stay here until it gets light out? I'm scared to go in the dark. When you're out in the darkness, that's when demons can enter your body. When the sun's out, I'm protected. Praise the Lord. The Lord is my shepherd, I shall not want. There's more demons on earth now than ever before. There's millions of them now. You go out into the darkness and it's just swarming with them. It's horrible. I've had trouble with them before."

In the nurses' station, while Lucy is still down bandaging the sutured arm, I tell Sandra and Michelle some of the things that Teena said, making them laugh.

Then I go into the little lounge next door in the hall and put some whole wheat bread into the toaster. When I come back out into the hall, my toast toasting behind me, I'm confronted by a scowling, scruffy-looking blond guy, whom I gradually connect with Natalie, who's still lying, I think, down in Room 9.

"What kind of a doctor are you, anyway? You haven't done a damned thing for her, and she's *hurting*. Nobody's even been in to check on her for the last half hour. She could fucking *die* and you guys wouldn't even know. I hear you laughing and talking, making jokes—Natalie might have a brain tumor, and all the nurses are sitting on their asses, smoking cigarettes, listening to you make fun of people. You're supposed to be here to *help* people."

"I've examined her," I say, taken aback and temporarily intimidated by his passion and the factor of surprise. "She's had a shot for pain, and I've written her a prescription she can get filled in the morning."

"For Tylenol *three's*," he says, scornfully. "Those don't do a thing. They don't even *touch* it."

They're junkies, I think then, and wonder why Security let this guy get back here to bitch at me like this.

"If those don't touch it," I say, getting back my composure, smelling my toast, "then she should see the follow-up doctor, maybe get a neurological work-up. We don't do those in the Emergency Room. There are other drugs for migraines besides narcotics."

"All you're telling me is that she's going to be in pain. That's all you're telling me. And you're supposed to be a doctor."

I'm waiting for him to take a swing at me. The smart thing would be to just take it and fall down, pretend I'm really hurt, have him thrown in jail—and then harass him with my lawyer.

"If you're not satisfied," I say, "take her to another hospital."

"You should write her a prescription for something that will *work*. She needs something to help her pain."

"I'm not going to give her anything stronger. I don't write prescriptions for heavy narcotics," I say, lying, amazed that he'd either be so dumb, so desperate, or think that I would be so weak. I'm getting really mad at this fool; I feel like popping him one, see what happens after that.

Security intervenes, called by the nurses, and they tell the guy to leave. He calls me a few names while talking to them, and then takes Natalie out, pushing the martyr in a wheelchair. I discover that I've burned my toast. I go to my room and take a Librium. I sigh and slow my breathing, surprised that I'm so stricken by this commonplace event.

I leave my room, after glancing at the television, flicking through the channels without sound. I'm restless. I want to drink a Coke. There are still some voices raised down in the lobby as Natalie finally leaves. Lucy is calling the other ER's in the area to warn them of what to perhaps expect.

It's slow now. I go to the cafeteria and buy a twelve-ounce Coke in a can. I like the red and white design on the cold aluminum. Lee, a black security guard whom I like, is just taking his break from the Information Desk. I eat one of his french fries with catsup.

I ask him about the latest scandal. The safe in Patient Accounts was recently robbed of eighty-five hundred dollars. All of the security officers have been asked to submit to lie detector tests. Junior, Lee tells me, whose father, Senior, was fired a month ago for coming to work drunk, and who is a prime suspect—Junior, possibly to cover his father, has refused the test and thus has been suspended without pay.

Life is so complicated for everyone. I promise Lee that I won't spread all this around.

Back in ER, I see a guy who says the cops beat him up. He's white, with a big mustache and a long ponytail.

"Where do you hurt?"

"All over, man."

"Show me where."

"All over," he repeats, as though I'm stupid and he doesn't have time for me. "They really did a number on me, man, and I'm gonna file a report."

"Where do you hurt the worst?"

"I want you to X-ray my whole body. I'm hurting all over. And in the meantime, can't you give me something for pain? I'm dying, man, I can't stand it."

"I can't do anything until we narrow it down a little. You walked in, so I can't believe that they've broken every bone in your body. Now tell me what hurts you the worst."

"My back. My back and my head. And my arm. I think they broke my wrist."

When it's getting close to seven, I change back out of scrubs into my clothes. I wonder what Anna's got on her mind. I wonder what she's planning to make for breakfast. Gretchen won't be up. She sleeps in, most days, until eleven.

Dr. Flanagan arrives, a few minutes early, with some banana bread that his wife made. I tell him about the cases of the night.

On my way out, I see Teena Overstreet. She's smoking a cigarette and looking at a bus schedule. I'm surprised that she's still here. She must have convinced Security that there were demons in the dark.

"Do you have fifty cents?" she asks, not as if she recognizes me as the guy who sewed her up. "I think I'm going to try and take the bus. I tried to get a ride, but no one will come get me. I want to stay with my sister, but I don't want to wake her up."

"How far is your sister's?" I don't know why I say this. Her eyes look really crazy and confused. I should head straight home.

"It's up on Thirty-fifth," she says. She doesn't seem to expect me to give her a ride, even to imagine that it's a possibility, so I tell her I'll give her one. I'll drive her to her sister's. She accepts this without thanks.

I feel funny walking out with her, saying hi to other doctors who are arriving, ready to attack the new day in their lab coats and suits, parking their cars in the convenient, exclusive doctors' lot. Teena, when she's in the passenger seat, asks me what kind of car this is.

"I used to have one just like it," she says. "I cracked it up on my eighteenth birthday. I only had it for a day."

As we blend into the traffic, I can smell her perfume and perspiration. She asks me if I mind if she smokes a cigarette. It's going to be a hot day; there are a few thin clouds, but they're the kind that should burn off before noon.

"I was sitting there praying," says Teena, elbow out the window, "and I suddenly thought: how can God understand me, when He's never been through what I've been through? Know what I mean? *God* never gets beat up. He's the All-Supreme. No one can beat up on the Lord. No one."

She talks all the way to her sister's house, which we have a little trouble finding. She's not very good at numbers. I'm rather relieved when she finally says, "That's it. Over there."

"Do you need some money for breakfast?" I ask her, neutrally, when I've pulled over to the curb.

"No, I'll be okay. My sister's got a lot of food in her house. She's a lot fatter than I am. I didn't used to be fat before I had the baby, but they took it away from me. That's back when I was a model. Do you want to come in for a while? You could make love to me. I don't mind."

"Thanks, but I've got to get home. My wife's making breakfast for me; I'll probably be late as it is."

"You better go then."

"Take care of yourself," I say. "Good luck."

I like to wish people good luck. Everyone can use some. As I drive away, I look in the rearview mirror, and see Teena Overstreet walking on down the road. That must not have been the right house after all.

TWO

I like where we're situated—the nearest neighbor's more than a mile away, with woodlands in between. I like our house. I like its sky-blue exterior, with cream trim.

The house I grew up in was nothing so fine, though hardly representing any great material deprivation. I've done much better, financially, than my father, whom I'm not close to, and who, in a very real way, resents my success. He may boast to his buddies at Hartford Copper Works that I'm a doctor, but he feels much more comfortable with my older brother, Jack, who's part owner of a tool-and-die shop.

I was my mother's favorite; she would almost always stick

up for me when my father would attack me for alleged sloth or conceit, or for being a prima donna about one thing or another. Of course, it's true that I took advantage of whatever I could get away with, and as time passed I could get away with more and more.

I was even a better athlete than Jack, at least in baseball— I didn't want to go out for football, where Jack, in any case, hurt himself a lot and achieved only the most moderate success. Then he screwed around with college, dropping out, drinking a lot, getting some nowhere job: I wasn't friends with him, I always felt like he disliked me for the competition I furnished; and I in turn resented, I suppose, the bond between Jack and my father, their joy in working on an old motor and getting dirty together, painting the garage, cutting down branches or whatever, all activities in which I wouldn't take part, even at the cost of a scene.

My studies became important. I could please teachers and get good grades, and I had no fear at all of taking tests. It was a game, and I liked competing with the kinds of kids who played 'cellos or bassoons, beating them on what they thought of as their predestined turf. If my father never gave a damn about National Merit Scholarships or the like, and would just shrug, unimpressed, and ask when I was going to mow the lawn, my mother would be proud of me, even if her advocacy sometimes wore thin on my nerves.

I didn't like it when she'd get emotional, when she'd hug me tight and wet my shoulder with sentimental tears. If she had troubles with my father, I didn't want to know about them. That was their life, not mine. I made it plain I didn't want to hear. After all, what could I do?

And so, while going to college, I didn't have to work, as my brother did, and I took pre-med and excelled. I worked hard, even at things that were repugnant to me, like biology.

I put a kind of anger into my discipline, and I've kept up my force of will until it's become habit, and then decayed from habit into something else, something I don't quite want to really examine or try to name.

But I'm the star of my family, in a way. As such, I can forget or ignore Christmas, birthdays and all that. I haven't been back to Connecticut in three or four years. Anna ends up talking on the phone to my parents (my mother) more often than I do. I'm a physician, I'm busy, my time is important, I can't be bothered.

I pull into the driveway and stop, get out of my car. The fan goes on, making a noise. Fiats do this. The brilliance of the yellow morning sunshine dazzles me. Birds are singing, bees are buzzing here near some blackberry bushes, and I hesitate for a moment: it's too much for me. I'm not equal to it.

I look around, and then go into the house. I'm about forty-five minutes late. However, Anna's seemingly in a fine, practical mood, and if she's been waiting for me she says nothing to that effect. She looks nice, in a vivid cobalt blouse with one big horizontal yellow stripe, a gold cross on a chain around her neck. I gave her that cross a couple of years ago, though its symbolism means little to either of us; but she likes it, and likes it when someone assumes from it that she's a Christian of some sort. It amuses her, and she docs not disabuse them.

"How was your night?" she asks, as I go with her to the patio, and I seize the opportunity and say it was terrible, I'm exhausted, I haven't had a chance to sit down all night long.

She's too poised and composed. I have a bad feeling about what she's going to say to me—I want to try to slip by or delay it if I can.

Actually, I am quite sleepy, I'm not exaggerating, the Librium I've ingested does lie heavy in my head.

When Anna asks me, pleasantly enough, what kind of cases I saw, I start to speak and then stop. I can't recall a single one.

"Wait, I think we had another motorcycle accident—yeah, and a stabbing. No, excuse me, a gunshot wound. A black guy, gunshot to the chest."

"Did he make it?"

"No," I say, for an instant remembering the hole in the ventricle, shrugging, not feeling like going into any detail: it wasn't that special a case.

Fresh croissants, raspberry jam, and Sumatran decaf (in deference to my having to get some sleep). Anna baked the croissants and they're very good. She isn't as noted a cook as is Gretchen, but I think that's only because she doesn't try as often or as hard. Anna can do anything she puts her mind to. I am confident of this.

"It's a nice morning," she remarks, conversationally, and I follow her gaze over the glossy aqua water of the pool to the flowering bushes, green lawn, and healthy upright trees. A bluejay hops up mechanically onto the rim of the birdbath, and then douses himself, shaking furiously. I agree that the weather's very nice.

"Darrell," she says after a while, following, no doubt, her program, "are you very happy these days, the way things are going?"

"Happy?" I say. "That's a funny word." I think there's some sticky jam on my face, next to my mouth. "Why? Do you think I'm not happy?"

"No," she says, after looking at me, as I wipe my cheek clean, "I don't think you're happy at all." And then, when I don't argue or offer any comment, "Neither am I."

She can probably read something in my expression, perhaps I roll my eyes a bit, involuntarily, or otherwise seem to show some reluctance, for she presses ahead, saying, "I know you don't want to talk about it, Darrell. I understand you that far, at least. But it's not easy for me either. We haven't talked, you know, really talked, for an awfully long time."

"I suppose we haven't," I admit. "Well," I say then, "what's your plan?"

She shows some displeasure, despite her poise, at my choice of words.

"I guess my plan is that we should . . . let some air into our marriage for a while."

"What does that mean?"

"I don't know. Maybe an open marriage . . . maybe that's` what I mean."

"Sounds more like something Diane would think of. But sure. All right. Whatever will make you happy, Anna. Whatever you want."

"Don't be sincere, then," she says. "I'm not going to blame myself. I'm not responsible for the way you've been, the way you've been to me. This way," she continues, "we won't have to lie to each other. We won't be hypocrites."

"Good," I say, after a moment, a moment spent in consideration of her, mouth open, eyes shut, moving under what I remember of Sam's tan young back. "We won't have to lie to each other. That's important."

In a few moments I get up to go to bed. I don't know if Anna wants to talk some more or not. She's a stranger to me—past intimacies only making the degree of strangeness more severe. Did it really matter how I reacted? She must think that I'm in pretty sad shape. The problem with this is that I trust Anna, I trust her judgment: I think she's sensible and knows me very well.

I can't get to sleep, although I'm very tired. I'm not rehashing the events of the recent past; I'm not rehashing anything. Sometimes I almost slip away, and even start to dream, but then I catch myself, and pull back, nearly panic-stricken, as though in surrendering consciousness to sleep I shall give myself to Death.

I'm uncomfortable. I'm too warm, and then, after I kick off all the covers, a breeze coming in through the window makes me too cold. It's absurd—it's sunny out, it's a nice morning in May, and here I am, thinking my feet are cold. I don't feel good.

Finally, I get up and go into the bathroom: if I don't get some sleep, I'll be miserable at work tonight. I take a Nembutal, and then go back and jump into the covers like a cowboy (or a child). *Now* I'll sleep, I'm sure, and I try to think of something pleasant, so that I'll drift into a good dream.

I suffer through a grotesque nightmare instead. I'm in a very crowded, shabby department store that I somehow know is in Manhattan, and I'm several floors underground, trying to crowd into an extra-large elevator (there seems some necessity of getting upstairs and out into the air), pushed and shoved this way and that by grayish shoppers.

Then I'm somewhere else, but the feeling of dread is stronger. I'm being given a tour of a creepy, underground prison, lit with yellows and golds that give way to very dark shadows, lit like a film—and I see numbers of blond young men, New Wavers and punks, all quite young, all naked, chained to stone slabs, lying on them, chained so that they cannot move. Iron collars around their necks. None of them makes a sound. Some try to wiggle a bit, but the only real movement comes from the pulsations, the metabolisms of the brown or gray leeches that are feeding on their tender forms. I think I'm watching a weird, terribly morbid film, their bodies are so pale and white. I'm thinking: They go too far; this is too repulsive.

I wake up. I go to the bathroom, wash my face and look at

myself in the mirror, viewing that same impassive mask, and then I go back to bed, sleepy, hoping that I won't have any more ugly dreams.

Gretchen is up. I hear her moving about. Then I'm back asleep, deeply, and the alarm wakes me up all too soon. I could easily keep sleeping for hours and hours, perhaps all through the night. I feel like it's all I'll ever want to do.

They could put me in suspended animation for a hundred years. Any time. A thousand years. It'd be fine with me to wake up in the distant future, a stranger to everyone, disconnected, probably a moron by the new standards that would be in effect—it would be okay. I'd be happy just to see how things will be.

Obviously, I'm a sentimentalist: I'm not imagining waking up in a nuclear wasteland or in an oppressive, electronic mind-control state; rather, through rose-tinted glass, I see some kind of a technological yet health-oriented utopia.

In college I used to think about utopian and socialist idealism a great deal. I wrote a big paper in which, in somewhat cursory fashion, I designed the rudiments of an ideal society; and, for a year or so, all my leisure reading dealt with such social schemes. Was I an advocate of behavioral engineering, à la Skinner? Yes, I suppose I was. It seemed better than all this disorder.

I take a Dexamyl. Then I shower.

At dinner, Anna is breezily cheerful, talking mostly to her sister. Gretchen knows something's up. Whether Anna has confided in her or not is another matter. I'm sure she will; and this intrusion of another party makes me angry. I'm outnumbered, and I don't like it.

The less Anna and I talk, I guess, the worse our conflict is. There's so much going on, wordlessly, and it's mostly negative.

It's an exaggeration, I suppose, to say we hate each other; but if I were going to casually describe our feelings right now I'd say she hates me, probably has for some time, and I, in turn, half out of shame, hate her as well. I hate myself in the role I've ended up in; I hate being the way that I am.

Anna asks me if I want some iced tea. I say yes. And that's all I have to say.

THREE

A security guard whom I like, Tom, is telling Patricia, one of the evening shift nurses, about a regular who came in the other night, a black alcoholic named Rotheree Moore.

"He kept calling Suzi"—another nurse—" 'Vanilla Ice Cream,' and naturally he couldn't wait his turn. It's the third time he's been beat up in ten days. When they asked him where it happened, he said, 'On the moon.' "

"That's Rotheree," says Patricia. "He always says that he lives on the moon. All he knows anymore is the moon."

"I know," Tom says, smiling under his mustache. He's interested in Patricia, who wears her dark brown hair in one

long braid and lives out on a farm with an unexciting, pre-
maturely balding orthopedist. Tom, who is handsome and
going to school, in his late twenties, doesn't have a chance.

"His brother beat him up again?" exclaims Patricia. "I thought
his brother was dead."

Tom shrugs, deadpan. "Everyone's his brother."

Later on in the evening, Tom comes back to the department,
and wants to talk to me, alone. I sense what's coming up. He
used to play football, at Michigan State, until he injured both
his knees. Now sometimes they ache. He wonders if I could
give him anything for pain. I'm silent, then offer him a scrip
for Tylenol 3's. Tom thanks me, and I make it seem like
nothing, though I don't like it when employees of the hospital
come to me with these personal appeals. I believe, I guess,
that Tom's knees really hurt, but I imagine that it's pain he'll
just have to live with, though I don't really mind giving him
the pills.

A mother and father bring in their daughter, sixteen, an
OD. The history I get is that the girl ingested a bottle (approximately thirty) of aspirin about two hours ago. She told
her mom about this only a short time before now, when she
started feeling ill. Her name is Tammy, and she's not very
attractive: a skinny, jumpy, pale-skinned blonde. I ask her,
away from her parents, if she was trying to kill herself.

"I don't know," she says, holding herself rigid on the stretcher,
fists clenched by her sides, defiance mixed with hysteria, near
loss of control.

"Well, what did you think this was going to do to you,
then?" I ask, a little bored. None of us have much sympathy,
normally, for OD's. There's certainly a school of thought which
dictates that one make the "suicidal gesture" unpleasant and
unrewarding, so that the perpetrator will not gain the desired

rewards (sympathy, attention, drama) and thus may not be as likely to repeat the performance in the future.

"I don't know what I thought," says Tammy, half-smiling now, viciously, as though she likes it that I'm not friendly or affectionate. "I've done it before. I did it last month."

A nurse gives her a large, shiny, stainless steel bowl to hold in her lap; then, some Ipecac to drink, which will make her vomit up all the contents of her stomach in fifteen minutes or less. I've ordered one blood test, a salicylate level, to see how much aspirin is presently in her bloodstream. The test will have to be repeated in four hours or so, when the drug's action is at its peak.

The parents, when I speak to them, seem to have a very bitter attitude: I have the impression that they wish to dispute my authority for some reason.

"She's having some blood drawn," I say, and I explain just why.

"The same old thing," says the husband, nastily, to his wife. They're both obviously in a higher socioeconomic stratum than are our usual run of customers—I wonder why they've brought their daughter here, rather than to a hospital which has a Psych Unit.

"She's done something like this before, I gather," I say, and the mother nods, seemingly angered that I've found this out, as though, absurdly, I have been prying.

"Yes, Doctor, she's done this a few times before. She just got out of Lakeside a couple of weeks ago. They apparently didn't do too much for her, did they?"

"I don't know. Who is her doctor?"

"Her psychiatrist is Dr. Johanson." The same mad, malevolent gleam is in her eye as was in the eye of little Tammy.

"What are you going to do, Doctor?" asks the father, as though he doesn't think I have a clue.

My plan is to call Dr. Johanson; otherwise, I'll simply admit the girl for observation, assigning her to whoever's on call for Medicine. If her salicylate level is high enough, her kidneys could shut down. If I wanted to be extraordinarily aggressive, I could have her dialyzed; however, this seems rather extreme under the present circumstances—if it becomes necessary it can be done later on.

I wonder if Tammy's parents want her dead. From their affective behavior, one might think that they do. If Tammy really means business, she ought to visit her grandmother (supposing she has one) and get hold of some Digoxin or Lanoxin, or other heart pills . . . a few of those and she'd be gone in a short while. I remember one black girl, only fourteen, who had been raped and then, when she went back to school, found out that everybody knew—she took some of her grandma's Digoxin. By the time we got her, via ambulance, she was quite dead, but, because of her youth, we ran a Code on her all the same. She had such beautiful skin, she looked so pretty even in death.

Others have been unsuccessful even at shooting themselves. One guy, using a shotgun, simply blew off all of his face. No eyes, nose, or the upper half of his mouth. Other than that, he was fine. No brain damage, nothing critical. But he did succeed, I guess, in radically altering his life.

I see a kid with asthma, for whom I order some aminophylline and a breathing treatment; a cute black baby with an ear infection; a sixty-five-year-old white man with congestive heart failure (CHF), whom I admit to CCU; a softball player with a sprained ankle; a lacerated palm; a seventeen-year-old with PID (pelvic inflammatory disease); and a prostitute who was given some "strange" marijuana by a customer, and now thinks that her heart is beating too fast and feels dizzy and scared.

"It'll wear off," I tell her. "How long ago did you smoke it?"

"About an hour or so."

"It'll wear off. The effects last, usually, about four hours. I tell you what: I'll give you something to calm you down, and you can wait here until you feel better. Try to breathe more slowly, all right?"

"How do you know it don't have PCP or some shit like that in it, huh? It might've been poisoned, you know. I've smoked a lot of shit, 'n' this is different: I feel *weird*, you understand?"

One of those white girls who talks blacker than black. Who'd want her for their date? Who patronizes these girls, anyway? Nineteen and looks easily twenty-five, could pass for thirty. Tight red pants, a silver sequined top, spike heels. Ridiculous makeup on a freckled, ordinary face. I'm doing her a favor by giving her some Vistaril: the nurses don't really approve.

I'm not sleepy. I feel fine. I'm a professional. I do my job. I'm where I'm supposed to be, doing what I'm supposed to be doing.

The resident tonight isn't Greg Hong, whom I like and who's very competent, but a blond, red-faced guy named Martin Chamberlin, who's arrogant and slow. He lifts weights and jogs a great deal, and, although it's still early in the season, he's deeply tanned. Maybe he managed to slip away to Hawaii for a week somewhere along the way.

In the closed world of the hospital, Martin Chamberlin, who is not exactly handsome, but who comes from a rich family and is going to be a cardiologist, is said to be doing very well with the nurses, who see in him quite a catch. He knows this, and it shows.

When I have to correct him, he hates it, and his face gets redder than ever. One of the nurses tips me off that he might not be pursuing a sufficiently aggressive line with a new patient; when I go to see what's going on, I find that she is right.

Clinically, the patient has wet-sounding breath sounds, his skin is moist—pulmonary edema (fluid in the lungs). Chamberlin is just kind of standing around, evaluating the guy, when he ought to be ordering Lasix (to move out some of that fluid), morphine and aminophylline. I suggest this course of treatment, trying to be diplomatic, and he has no choice other than to demur and do what I've said. I can see that this makes him unhappy, and that he'll perhaps hold it against me, but I am clearly in the right. I presume that he realizes this, though I don't know. Seeing someone in ER is different from seeing them in clinic, where they're not acute and you can take your time getting the history and proceeding with your work-up of the case. Here, the patient needs treatment right away, he could very easily go bad on us. Now Chamberlin sulks.

It's slow, really, for a Saturday night. No big traumas. I feel restless. I'd just as soon have some excitement. It's after 1:00 A.M. Tomorrow I'm off, and for the three days after that. I don't know what I'll do. One plan that occurs to me is to spend more time with Roger, as in doing so I may discomfit Anna a little. I'll have to see how I feel.

A black guy named Brice Jeter comes in, with a minor laceration on his throat. He's very black, really ebony, handsome, in good shape, but too naturally antisocial, I think, to channel his energy into something constructive, even by his own standards, such as I can judge. The nurses and Security dislike him. He intimidates Charlotte, the black admitting clerk, he won't answer any of her questions. It's a cheap satisfaction, but I reach a rapport with him. The element of real, physical danger is what gives it the kick.

"Who did that to you?" I ask him, interrupting his rage about how this hospital can kiss his motherfuckin' black ass.

"My *brother* did it, man. Is that right?"

"No," I say, looking concerned. "Shit. Your brother? What's wrong with him?"

"He's crazy. He had no reason—hey, is that right? Try to kill your own brother?"

"It's fucked up," I tell him, knowing that "fucked up" will put him more at ease. It's got to be said right, though, with a certain grace. Brice's shirt is off, his black chest gleaming, blood streaked on his dark blue nipples.

"Damn right it's fucked up. Blood walk in, blood see me talkin' to his lady, blood pull out his blade—and *ssst*, just like that." He's acting it out, in front of me and a few others, there in the hall. "If I hadn't jumped back, you know, man, I'd probably be layin' there dead on the floor. You believe it? That was my *brother*, man. Shit. I was just standin' there, you know?"

There's another side to this, I'm sure. Brice Jeter gets in too many fights to always be just an innocent victim. Besides, he looks too tough and mean to always lose. I wonder if he really means his brother, or one of his friends.

"Is my throat cut bad? Am I gonna be okay?"

"Let me look at it. Well, you need a few stitches, but it's no big thing. I can close that right up. Take me about twenty minutes."

"Twenty minutes? Okay, man. All right. Where you want me to be?"

It's easy after this. He's still indignant about the injury that has been done him, but he lies down on the stretcher in Room 4 and lets Lucy numb him up. He even answers Charlotte's questions, so she can fill out his form.

I'm expecting a plea for pain pills, but when I'm done sewing and am telling him who to see to get the stitches out, Brice seems content with the treatment as it stands. Before he leaves, he shakes my hand, thanks me again, and tells me to be cool and have a good night. I tell him to take care of himself, which makes him laugh.

"The whole family's crazy," Lucy tells me, after he's gone. She tells me about a scene Brice caused the last time he was here.

"He seemed okay to me," I say, just to tease.

Two twenty-one-year-old girls are brought in who were apparently hit in the parking lot outside some popular bar by a guy who got mad. These girls are wearing tight jeans and look like nice, wholesome, pretty girls—with blood on them. They're not drunk; they seem mostly embarrassed and upset. One has a laceration just above her left eyebrow, which has bled all over her nice blouse, and she's crying, worried about having a scar. I want to get a facial X ray to make sure none of the bones around the orbit of her eye have been fractured. I try to reassure her about the laceration.

"It's a clean cut, so I should be able to do a good job. It's not very long, either, so the scar should be pretty tiny. In a year you won't even notice it; it'll fade away until it's just a tiny little line."

The other girl has a broken nose. Michelle has given her an ice pack to hold on it: Michelle once had her nose broken while skiing, so she tells the girl about that and makes her laugh. They seem like pleasant girls, and I ask this one, who seems less upset, how the whole thing happened.

She starts to explain, but I never get the story straight. I have to go see someone else.

Early in the morning, a young white male comes in at a time when I'm standing out with Michelle and Charlotte by the triage desk. When Michelle asks him what's wrong, he says something that sounds like he got in a fistfight.

"Where do you hurt?" I ask him, seeing no obvious bruising or blood.

"I got fist-fucked; where do you think I hurt?"

"Oh, yeah, I see." I keep a straight face. Elaborately. So do Charlotte and Michelle. I guess I'll have to put a scope up him, look around to make sure that his colon isn't perforated.

Charlotte pretends not to believe that people really do these things. Back in the coffee room, when Michelle tells Lucy, we all start to laugh.

When I talk to the patient again, though, I'm perfectly neutral and even sympathetic. He's in pain.

FOUR

I think it's a father's obligation to teach his son how to catch and throw a ball; it's also incumbent upon the son to enjoy the exercise and have fun. Roger's not doing this. He catches the ball cleanly one in four times.

He doesn't have any enthusiasm for this game. He performs dutifully, but with ill grace. I can't help recalling how much fun I had, at such an age, discovering how to play games that involved balls. I wasn't good at first, but I liked playing. I had a friend named Jimmy, a year older, who was better, but patient, and who led me on, teaching me the lore, as he understood it, of the world of sports. It seemed a valuable initiation, at the time and for years after. I suppose one is like a young dog or cat, but at that age it's wonderful, I think, to run and jump and throw things, all with a concentration that is never again matched. Fatigue was so temporary, a mere fleeting interruption of the play.

No doubt such comparisons are unfair. If Roger seems sloth-ful, lost in fitful contemplation of I don't know what, then perhaps it's our fault, we've raised him wrong, failed in so many ways, and that's that.

I was a great pitcher all through Little League, Babe Ruth, and American Legion, even, at one time in high school, think-ing that I wanted to be and was capable of becoming a profes-sional ballplayer. I suppose this has made me a particular kind of American snob.

Roger's grandmother feeds him too many cookies; he's a little soft. I see a bit of myself in him, in his face or his expressions, and this seems like an additional vulnerability I have exposed. I'm responsible for him, for what he becomes, and I feel like I've already lost some crucial opportunity, some moment or time when I might have applied force at a given point and pushed his personality toward some semi-ideal ver-sion that I'd find more admirable. A new, improved version of myself.

Roger can't catch the ball. And he whines, he complains. He wants to know if Gretchen's going to make any cookies.

"Daddy, what's Gretchen doing?"

She babysits for him so much, she might as well be his nanny. I don't know what he wants her for now, besides food. We go inside.

I'll call Paul Swanstrom, who I suppose qualifies as my best friend. I intended to call him earlier, but I was distracted. When I first woke up, at about two o'clock, I wanted to go swimming, but I felt reluctant to be caught at it by Anna. She wasn't around, but her car was still here. I don't like the idea of my untanned body being compared by her to Sam's. I could be more fit, I could be less pale. It occurred to me that I could take steps, beginning today, but then . . . I got distracted.

I need to talk to Paul. We've fallen somewhat out of touch: I don't think I've actually seen him in person now for two or three months. He's a pediatrician. We went through med school together, and since then have stayed in touch.

He can quickly tell from my voice that things aren't going well. I confess, in a moment, that Anna and I are having some problems.

"We should talk," he says. "You really sound down. Do you want to come over here? Why don't you slip away, come and have dinner with Julie and me. Is that possible?"

"Sure." I'm glad to have someplace to go. "How soon should I come? It's four-thirty."

"As soon as you can get away. I'll make Julie do the cooking, for a change; you and I can talk. I've got some new Japanese beer."

Off the phone, I go to the kitchen looking for Anna or Gretchen, finding Gretchen, who looks a bit strained (so that I'm sure she's been the recipient of some confidences from her sister—and thus able to understand my present mood).

"I'm not going to be here for dinner. I'll be home later. See you, okay?"

"Okay."

I get in my car and take off. I have a Percodan in my pocket. I took a Librium before brushing my teeth. What stops me from taking the Percodan is the thought that Paul would certainly be able to tell if I was high. Librium is not nearly so apparent, or such is my belief.

Paul Swanstrom lives close to Lake Washington, in a house with a nice view. It's not that big, because he doesn't wish to waste either energy or space. He heats his water partially through the use of solar panels, and doesn't own a TV. He's a vegetarian, and doesn't drive a car.

We don't sit on chairs, we sit on the floor, on bamboo mats. Not everything Paul does makes sense, but I do not and have never really cared. He's a devotee of avant-garde art in every medium, much less skeptical than I am, for instance, but I've found this openness of his to be useful to me, even if on occasion it has caused me to suffer through some very tedious, annoying performances and films. Paul takes all these artists at their own word. If something seems, to the layman, stupid or childish, Paul will as often as not furrow his brow and say, ingenuously, that he doesn't think he understands it. He'll give anything a chance, the benefit of the doubt.

He became a pediatrician in order to stress early nutrition and preventive care, to educate the parents of his patients as much as he possibly could. "Getting them young," he used to say, "before they're all screwed up." The better educated and more middle class the parents, the better they respond to him. It's his continuing frustration (though less and less so, I think, as the years go by) that he does have some trouble with the poorer, more ignorant parents, who can't, or won't, understand or believe much of what he has to tell them. Still, he makes allowances for their way of life. They have so many pressures, he says, that the rest of us don't understand.

Children like him. He performs for them, raising his voice and simplifying-exaggerating his responses, unself-conscious and thrumming with vitality. He knows how to make kids laugh. And he's quite competent, unlike some of the pediatricians one sees. Most of the kids, of course, aren't that sick. The ones that are—well, that's what he was trained for. That's when it gets interesting, when it's a good case.

"I saw a six-year-old the other day," I tell him, after a good swallow of the beer. "He'd been sick for a week, you know, with a cold, but seemed better, only now he wouldn't walk. Wouldn't stand up; had to be carried. Said his legs hurt really bad."

"Post-viral myositis," offers Paul, with confidence, and I nod.

"Right. His CPK was over six thousand." CPK is an enzyme, secreted when the muscles of the body are under unusual stress. Normally, CPK's run between 35 and 230.

Paul in turn tells me about a diagnostic coup of his—he diagnosed a four-year-old as having acute lymphocytic leukemia from a mere palpation of the child's not-very-enlarged little spleen. I admire his expertise, and after reviewing another case or two we've disposed of the preliminary small talk and can get around to real life.

Paul has been married twice, without children. Now he lives with this girl, Julie, who is only twenty-one. He's thinking of having a vasectomy, which, I admit, seems strange, given his job. But he's pessimistic about the future of the world.

A few months ago, I tell him, when I was working a lot of nights, and when Anna was strictly on a day schedule, I began sleeping in the guest bedroom, so as not to bother her and to be able to find peace during the day. What began as a part-time thing, a convenient arrangement, has gradually become full time. I now call it "my bedroom" instead of "the guest room," and it's become a rare thing for me to sleep with Anna instead of by myself.

Paul asks, "When are you two getting together, then, you know . . . ?"

"We're not. Not for a while."

"Are you seeing anyone else?"

"No. But, recently . . . Anna has been. I can't blame her, I suppose."

I'm silent, thinking, and Paul changes the record, from some kind of slow amorphous electronic musings to an African jazz band with plenty of drums; then Julie brings in the first tray of our dinner.

The first time I met her, six months ago, she said I looked like I needed a massage. Warm smile, blue eyes, and short brown hair. A yellow, tunic-style top over loose white pants. Sandals. No makeup. She's into yoga. Paul met her when she joined the percussion ensemble he belongs to, in which he plays the marimba. Julie plays some bells and a set of gongs. Paul smiles at her, appreciative, under the spell of their shared sensual serenity. He's told me that the sex with her is better than it's ever been before, in his life, with anyone else.

I'm not comfortable discussing my personal affairs in front of her, no matter how close she and Paul presently are. I rather resent it, in fact, when he asks me, "Are you considering anything like a separation? Maybe to get some space in between you, see where you stand." He waves his hand, laughs helplessly. "All these clichés!"

"I'm not considering anything," I say, beginning to eat. Broccoli with tangy sauce; eggplant with garlic. We use chopsticks, which is all right with me, though I'd prefer to have a fork. The Vietnamese don't use chopsticks, they use metal utensils (perhaps because of the French): for some reason this seems to me a compelling argument for Americans to use their forks.

Julie starts talking, in an enthusiastic way, about some person in the percussion ensemble with whom she's disenchanted: she thinks he's too conceited, puffing himself up because he used to play drums in some band.

"All he wants to do is show off how fast he can go. But" (in between bites) "just playing *fast* doesn't have anything to do with the beauty of these rhythms. It's like—in reggae, or in funk, they don't play fast: the really funky stuff is always slower than you might think. That's why, when white people try to play it, they just don't quite get that feeling. Because . . . they can't really relax. You need to relax with the beat; and if this generates speed, then it's a natural progression, and sounds right, not like something forced, like some machine."

"You don't like machines?" I ask, raising an eyebrow, meaning to get her going, which I do. No, she doesn't like machines. Her theories are admirable, no question about it. Who would disagree?

She's very pretty. I can see why Paul enjoys himself with her. She looks prettier to me all the time.

We drink jasmine tea. Paul tells me that I ought to start playing a percussion instrument. Julie emphatically concurs.

"Get a marimba," Paul says. "Beat the hell out of it. Best thing in the world for you."

"Maybe you're right," I say, and Julie proceeds to give me detailed and explicit instructions as to where I can find a particular shop which has, according to her, the largest selection of percussion instruments in town.

As I drive home, I reflect that it's just as well I didn't talk more, in greater confidence, with Paul.

I can see why, from the standpoint of pure sensation, Anna might like someone young. Young, tight, tender flesh. Anyone can understand that appeal.

When I arrive home, I'm hoping that Anna will be up, so that I can talk to her, but it seems that she's asleep.

The house is quiet. Outside, I hear a far-off dog bark, and then, much closer, the hoot of an owl.

I'm wide awake.

FIVE

At one time I thought that medicine was the perfect philosophical subject, that in knowing the limits of human knowledge about the human body I would come to the edge of all we really know, objectively, about ourselves—the human body = the physical world, and to know how this works and what it is *in situ* is to know all that it is truly possible to know.

The intimate, inner workings of the body—pumping of the blood, gray material of the brain, secrets of birth and death—all other subjects were "soft," were overly subjective and interpretative; or else, as in the case of pure math, too often mere gamesmanship, or the amassing of knowledge (theoretical physics) that is turned, in its application, to destructive ends.

If knowledge is quantifiable, that is, measurable—as in, "How many facts do you know?"; and the more facts, the more knowledge you possess—then wisdom is something beyond that, quality over quantity, and it was this, in the red recesses of the body, that I wished to pursue. I desired to become, in short, wise. A Wise Man. Yes.

After all, who knows Death if not the physician? So I reasoned. And is not the problem of Death the central and great problem of all religion and philosophy, the question without an answer, inconsolably so from the dawn of time? Think of the Pharaohs, wrapped up as mummies, dreaming of their wonderful, fanciful afterlife. Think of Jesus and his supposed resurrection, with all that has been drawn forth since from *that*. Think of each individual on this planet's painful or insensible end, with or without a pretense of acceptance or significance, taken by illness, accident, violence, or the simple decay of age. No one is immortal, and I thought that I might figure out, if not the why, the how.

Through the Finite (the corpse) I would come to some apprehension of the Infinite (the living body). Or is it in fact Death that is Infinite? Is Zero an infinite quantity? Is "everything" contained in an absence, a lack, a void? I cannot say. The living body can be quantified, in many respects, and yet something about it remains beyond reach of exposure or expostulation. And, though I believe Death to be finite, an Absolute Zero, as it were, perhaps it is not. Perhaps it is something. I would love, for instance, to be reincarnated or some such thing. It is finitude that I fear; my dread is of the lack of *anything*, anything at all—which, literalist that I am, I see in the figure of the corpse. The corpse just lies there. Cut it open and you reveal not a thing. The corpse just lies there, and says nothing, does nothing, begins to decompose, and that is the extent of its powers. That is all we are.

This banal and hardly brilliant insight is all I've come to. I have nothing enlightening or comforting to say to the person dying, say, of cancer. "Goodbye." As a resident on the wards, I shunned such patients. Let the Death specialists, who speak of going through light and have an entire approach, a menu, so to speak, that may well be true as not—let these people speak to the corpse-soon-to-be. I can offer only my own horror and fear. I do not see how they can stand it. I do not understand how someone could be led out in front of a firing squad or to a hangman's noose and not fight, screaming and kicking and biting, every step of the way. I don't think that Death is noble: therefore, there can be no such thing as a "noble" death, except perhaps to the onlookers, who can pretend that the death is not real, that it is something else (martyrdom, an end to suffering, a "tragedy" such as we have known in literature and films, and so forth).

I've seen so many people die. Most of the time, in the Emergency Room at least, they seem to experience little enough conscious pain. When they're badly injured and dying, or in the throes of some acute medical condition, usually they're too out of it to know very immediately what's going on. Only a very few times have I ever been particularly touched or affected by one of these deaths. Children, I suppose, traditionally are the worst . . . though sometimes, because one is supposed to feel bad, one doesn't. I've had the experience of seeing a child who was caught in a reaper-harvester or accidentally shot by its brother or some such thing, and just feeling that the child was unlucky, such things happen, I'm left cold. The child was doomed. Otherwise the child would have been saved, or narrowly escaped, or . . . "Doom" is of some comfort, as you may see.

I'm in no way in awe of the corpse itself, as it lies there, heavy and cold, blood caking in its wounds. I go and eat (after washing my hands); the Medical Examiner or funeral home representatives come and take the body away, swathed in white, to be autopsied or embalmed.

People who are seriously injured in big car wrecks seldom remember much of anything about the crash. It's all a blank. Shock-induced amnesia. They may be yelling and struggling when they're brought in: they remember nothing of this later on, when they are recovering. Perhaps it's the profoundness of the surprise. It's too big. Their systems are overwhelmed. They've got too much to do, in a sense, to have time for normal, "social" consciousness.

That may be the best way to go.

My problem is that I don't have a job I'm wrapped up in, as I did throughout medical school and residency. I think I'm a task-oriented person; I need work I believe in to keep me interested in the disposition of my days. My job now is just a job. Not all that different from being a car or TV repairman. There's nothing new; it's the same thing every day.

And, on my days off, I no longer know how to spend my time. I used to read a lot, I used to read a lot of history, for instance; but now I don't know what to read. I don't know what I need to know.

There are a lot of different ways to live. Being a physician and having a wife and child seemed like a good, almost unbreakable circuit to be wired into: I was always so busy, and the few times I had time to think seemed like a luxury, and so I thought I'd wait, that I'd have time later; and, basically, that matters would, in and of themselves, become clear.

Maybe they have. Maybe things are clearer now than they ever have been before. I'm not sure. I'm not sure how much I should trust myself at the present time.

Sometimes I think, or it occurs to me, secretly, that I might actually enjoy a war or some other big disaster, a nuclear accident or terrorist bomb. Certainly I'd be really, fully alive in my station, my function, dealing with the casualties, rushed, efficient, cool and collected, making flawless snap decisions and ready for anything that might come in. Oh, there are nights vaguely like that, nights of multiple traumas and excitement, but very rarely does it get to that point where it's almost too much, sensory overload, where one is in a fine hysteria, overpowered by the glut of input from all sides.

I used to think that I loved Anna so much that I would feel a great tenderness upon seeing her grow old, that she would never lose her attractiveness for me, that the signs of vulnerability and mortality could only endear her to me all the more. I told her once that even if she was in a car accident and left para- or quadriplegic, I would push her around in her wheelchair and take care of her, that I would stick with her even if she were badly maimed by burns.

Now I still think I'd stick with her, that I'd push her wheelchair or whatever, and I still almost look forward to seeing her grow old—but I no longer know quite why. There are no "reasons" anymore.

SIX

Gretchen answers the phone, about noon, and then comes to tell him that Roger has been hurt. Some other little boy has hit him on the playground at his school, it seems.

Anna is gone, taking pictures somewhere. By this time, according to the itinerary that I understand, Sam and his friend Bob ought to be in British Columbia, camping out beneath the stars. So if Anna is practicing her open marriage with someone else, I wonder if it's anyone I know or have met. The possibilities are not very clear in my mind.

I drive to the school to pick up Roger. As soon as I see from his face that he's been crying, I feel, involuntarily, a bit disgraced, though I try, of course, to show nothing of this. Why couldn't he either win the fight or take his beating stoically, as I would have done? I know it's wrong to think like this, but I can't help it.

The principal is terribly apologetic. "Dr. Patterson" this and that.

"These things happen," I reassure him. "No big harm has been done."

Am I being cold to Roger? I feel ashamed, and hug him, somewhat awkwardly, looking more closely at him with a professional eye. He's going to have a black eye. That, and a scrape on one of his hands, seems the extent of his injury.

In the car, I ask him how he feels.

"All right."

"You okay?"

"I'm okay."

"Well, how'd it happen? What's the other boy's name?"

Roger hesitates, looking down into his lap. I shift into third. It's a gray, cloudy day, muggy, with no wind.

"Gary Potter."

I nod, acknowledging him, and then, with a look, urge him to continue.

"He just started picking on me," Roger says, and then adds, as though this will explain it (which in fact it does): "He gets into fights all the time."

"Is he tough?" I ask, trying to visualize the whole business, unhappily seeing a picture of some stocky little kid kicking Roger's ass.

"Yeah. He beat up Bobby Adamson."

"Uh-huh. So, anyway, what happened with you and Gary? He hit you first?"

"He started shoving me." Roger's getting a bit excited, losing some inhibition, even as he begins to stammer slightly. "And so I—I—shoved him back, and told him to leave me alone—and then he started slugging."

"What'd you do? Did you hit him back?"

"Yeah, I guess so. I grabbed him, and we fell down. Then pretty soon Mr. Fredericks broke us up and took us to the principal's."

I reach over and pat him on the shoulder, giving him a smile of complicity, as if he did all right. I am pleased that it sounds as though he tried to defend himself. And he isn't whining. Perhaps later, with Anna, he'll fall into his usual pattern of complaining about every little scratch, but for the moment, because of me, or because of the fact that a fight at school is a social event, he's being solemn and composed.

We'll get some ice cream. But first, I have an errand I might as well do in town. Roger doesn't ask where we're going. He's looking out the window at the scenery, absorbed in it, or, more likely, absorbed in a replay of his playground battle. It looks like he really will have quite a black eye.

We pull up to Barry's House of Percussion and go inside. Roger tags along, and I tell him that I just want to look at some of these instruments. I don't give any reason why; another one of those inexplicable grownup errands, that's all.

Actually, I feel a little funny in here. What do I know about drumsets or marimbas? I can look at things, but I don't know what questions to ask in order to appear knowledgeable, and I don't like being ignorant.

It's not my field, however. Conga drums, bongos, tablas, African drums, shiny cymbals, bells, glockenspiels, vibraharps, xylophones, even triangles—I have no preference, no choice, no real interest at all.

Luckily, the proprietor is busy, having a serious conversation with some other man, someone who presumably knows his drums. They're fooling around with a drumset. First one and then the other sits down behind it: the main object of their inquiry seems to be the bass drum pedal.

Thud, thud.

Roger has found a black upright piano, and is softly, tentatively tapping out something that strikes me, for the moment at least, as strangely close to euphonious, primitive music. I am diverted, and put down a cowbell and go over, which has the effect, as soon as Roger notices he's drawn my attention, of making him stop. Since he doesn't want me to be, I'm intrigued.

Thud.

"Where'd you learn to play the piano? At school?"

He's ignoring me now, looking at a display of blond drumsticks, touching one gently with his fingertips—but he answers me, all the same.

"Gram's got one."

"Oh? Is she teaching you how to play?"

He shakes his head. "No," he says. "She doesn't like me to touch her old piano; she's afraid it'll break or I'll get it dirty or something. One time I was playing it kind of fast, and she got really mad and made me stop."

I buy nothing in the shop.

On the way home, we stop at an ice cream parlor, and, as we order, it strikes me for the first time that from the look of Roger he could be taken for a battered child. I might be buying him an ice-cream cone in order to placate him, feeling guilt after my rage.

The ice cream boy comments on the shiner as he hands over the cone, asking Roger if he ran into a doorknob. Roger doesn't get the joke.

"No, I got in a fight," he says, and starts to lap at his ice cream. We go outside, but I suggest that we stand around and finish our cones before getting into the car. Fussy of me, I think, and am amused at myself for a while.

When children have been abused, usually you can get some clue from the way they interact with their parents or with the nurse or with you as examining physician. The child may cling and not want to let go, or be seemingly stricken dumb when he ought to be able to speak. The nature of the injury itself may be suspicious, or the explanation given may seem not to make sense. Sometimes the injuries are obviously inconsistent with what has been described as having taken place, like, for example, clear horizontal marks of a belt across the back when it is said that the child has fallen down. Old bruises, burn marks or a history of broken bones are all signs of a possible pattern of abuse.

The parents may both come in with the child, and if only one is the abuser there may be palpable tension between the parties, and they may contradict each other when explaining what has happened to their child. What we do, when we suspect an incident of abuse, is call the children's services division of the police, and they send someone over to investigate. The child may be taken into custody of the court right then and there. These scenes are always uncomfortable, always a strain. One feels naturally righteous and indignant, but somehow this does not seem to be enough. The people involved are often so pathetic that they nearly disarm one of all rage.

Anna is swimming in the pool when we come home. Gretchen marvels at the purple swelling of the eye, and Roger seems proud of his injury, an attitude which is fine with me.

"Well, what would you like for dinner?" Gretchen asks him. "We can have anything you want."

"Hamburgers," says Roger, pleased with his power.

He has to describe the fight all over again for Gretchen,

and then for Anna, when she comes in, hair wet, having showered and changed after her swim.

I haven't had any medication all day, incidentally. I'll see how I feel, but at the moment I don't think I'll take anything. I don't want it to be a problem. I don't think I'm really capable of an addiction.

Hamburgers. Anna says that she and Gretchen were raised on them. They didn't have the middle- to upper-middle-class upbringing that one might suppose, judging, that is, by their present appearance and affect. Their father was an alcoholic, and would often turn ugly—sometimes, when sufficiently drunk, hitting his wife or one of his "smart-ass" daughters. When he died, twelve years ago, as far as I can judge he died unmourned. Predictably, he had a GI bleed. After his death, my mother-in-law (to-be, at that time) received a reasonably sizable insurance settlement through his company, and shortly thereafter inherited some more money, though not a great deal, from a long-forgotten aunt. Consequently, she's been better off since then than she ever was before. Her daughters feel some kind of loyalty to or solidarity with her because of all the years they spent together putting up with dear old Dad.

Anna feels that, in comparison with me she had a difficult, deprived childhood. She refuses to believe that growing up in Connecticut could have been anything but privileged and plush. I know some Ivy Leaguers, after all, and might have been one myself if I had pushed. Thus, although she says she prefers the West, she's somewhat jealous of the East. "Of its pretensions," she would say.

After dinner, I say to her, very innocently, "Tell me about Mike and Diane. Where are they going for vacation this year?"

"Why do you ask that?" Anna responds, with some mistrust. She's putting the dishes in the dishwasher. I have decided to make an after-dinner drink.

"I want to know, that's all. I'm curious."

"No you're not," she says, closing the dishwasher and then turning it on. "You don't give a shit about Mike or Diane."

"How can you say that?"

"Oh, come on." She's amused, but bitchily, joining my bitchiness. "What are you making there?"

"A drink." I show her: a concoction including Frangelico, brandy, Tia Maria, and milk, with ice. I don't think it has a name. Anna decides she wants one too.

"Okay," I offer, after a sip. "Forget Mike and Diane. Tell me about Bob and Sam. What are they doing now? Are they having a good time up in the Canadian Rockies, camping out under the stars? Are they both sleeping in the same tent, do you think, or do they have separate ones, little pup tents, like Boy Scouts?"

"Come on, Darrell. Stop it."

I can only laugh, briefly, in disgust. She resists me.

"What was that boyfriend of yours, you know, Giorgio or something, who used to take you camping all the time? I was just thinking about him a little while ago."

"Were you? You must mean Jerome. You never even met him, I don't think."

"Is that Giorgio?"

"Yeah. That's Giorgio. You don't want to go camping, do you?" She sees that I do not, and adds, after a moment, with an expression of annoyance, "I don't know anything about their fucking tents."

Gretchen comes in then, smiling, and I think she's overheard this last bit and is embarrassed, believing that she may be interrupting—but she's not.

"Roger's tired of keeping the ice on his eye," she says, and then goes to the refrigerator. I don't see what she gets; I leave the kitchen and go through the dining room and on outside, finishing my drink in a long swallow and putting down the glass. I'm not mad. I'm perfectly content. It's not even dusk and the birds are making noise, getting ready for sleep. I can smell the lawn, and the faint perfume of cherry blossoms in the breeze. I feel like playing croquet or going golfing. We don't have a croquet set. I've never learned how to play golf.

I could speed somewhere in my car. But I need a destination. A mission, or sense of same. I walk into the shadowy woods, watching my footing but not staring at the ground. When I glance up, I see the moon. The sky has cleared.

I could murder someone without remorse. What do you feel, anyway, when the body isn't yours? You leave the room: they're on their own. And you're on yours. You go to sleep.

On my way back to the house, returning by a different trail, I come out by the garden, where I see Anna, attending to the peas. I hear the soft hiss of water running into the soil. Where's Gretchen? I don't see her.

"Anna," I say quietly, so as not to startle her. She stands up straight then, and I walk down the row to her. She's not so overtly attentive as all that, she's trying not to appear so, but she's highly aware of my presence as I near.

I thought that I was going to say something, but I don't: I touch the back of my fingers to her cheek. She doesn't look at me. I withdraw the hand; then, letting gravity pull it down, I touch her breast through the fabric of her blouse.

"Don't," she says, as if I'm about to hurt her—not physically—

I unbutton one button, then, moving closer, I slip my hand against the cool swell of her flesh, familiar nipple hard against my thumb. I'd like to hold on for a while, outside of time, blank and without thought, but after a few moments of docility Anna moves, putting her head on my shoulder, and my hand is now somewhat cramped. I step back and remove it, watching her with some intensity. She gazes at me with what I take to be sad affection. It's getting dark.

I examine the peapods, and wonder aloud how soon they may be picked.

"You know," I go on, "that conference I signed up for is coming along in a couple of weeks. You still want to come back East with Roger, see my folks? I could just go to the conference and come back, we could tell them that something has come up. Or, I could stay in New York for a while."

"We've already got the plane tickets, Darrell. Why don't we just stick to our plan."

"Do you really want to spend a week with my parents? That's seven days. I know I don't. I'd rather just fuck around in New York."

"I don't see any way you can go to the conference and not see your family, when you're so close. Besides, they want to see Roger. They haven't seen him since he was three. We've been over all this, you know."

"I know."

"Are you getting cold? I am. Let's go in. I think there's a good movie on cable at nine, I can't remember what. Gretchen knows."

Roger wants something for dessert. He's whining. Anna gives him some ice cream. Gretchen is on the phone to some-one. She has few friends. They never come out here, as far as I know. She meets them in the city.

Anna's very nice to Roger. Patient. To some extent, surely, she's simply playing nurse. Gentle but firm. Warm but slightly cool. Efficient. She explains to him (again) about the bag of ice. If he understands, he's unimpressed. He doesn't like the ice.

I have an impulse to tell Anna about the piano, but I control myself. The impulse comes from the same source as the earlier desire to feel her breast. I'm full of urges. I'm starting to feel jumpy, like I might go on a talking jag or otherwise embarrass myself. I feel vulnerable and unpoised. There's a muscle twitching slightly in my shoulder.

Roger's put to bed. Gretchen tells me about a book she's been reading, and I have the impression that in so doing she's rebuking me for not reading much anymore. The movie starts. It's set in northern Africa. I see the desert. The desert sky. I watch the good-looking people on the screen. The local color. I hear the music and then the voices talking. But I'm not thinking about this film. Actually, I'm reviewing what pills I've taken in the last few days, trying to assess dosages and patterns of use.

I'm uncomfortable. My stomach feels funny. I have a little headache just behind my eyes. My mind is getting kind of blurred—I'm going over the same data, circularly, again and again.

Anna seems to be wrapped up in the world of the movie. Gretchen has seen it once before; she tenses and draws in her breath when something exciting is about to occur. A young man and a young woman are kissing. I guess they're in danger.

The screen is bright with life.

SEVEN

Every Thursday morning at 7:00 A.M. a meeting takes place, in a conference room on the fifth floor, called "Trauma M & M." Morbidity and Mortality. As many as forty or fifty people may attend, depending upon the number and nature of the previous week's cases to be reviewed. The more garish the cases, the more people will show up, even those who were not directly involved in the patient's care.

The emergency room doctors, trauma surgeons, ER and ICU nurses, surgical residents, all of whom are of course rather familiar with each other, assemble and share coffee, orange juice and a choice of donuts or rolls.

I'm very sleepy and dull-witted this morning. I drink some of the predictably bad coffee just to get an edge on; I eat a donut, hoping to receive the benefit of a sugar high. I'm sitting between Steve Gold and Michelle, both of whom worked all last night.

Besides myself, the other ER physicians are Dan Petibon, the oldest and dumbest, Peter Flanagan, and Steve Gold, who likes me, likes to gossip and joke with me, the youngest and most abrasive or controversial of our little group. Matthew Vandermeyer, Director of Emergency Services, is the doctor who works no more than two or three days or nights a month.

Steve Gold is very Jewish-looking, with curly black hair and a fairly well-trimmed beard and gold-rimmed glasses, not very tall, spontaneous and outgoing and energetic. He's thirty-two, and trying to have sex with as many women as he possibly can. One day, not long ago, he came up to me with obvious excitement, took me aside, and burst out, "I fucked four women in thirty-six hours!" After laughing, I shook his hand—he was so pleased with himself. I wasn't about to offer a critique, even though I disapprove, not only of Steve's attitude toward women but of promiscuity in general. I asked him if he'd washed. In between, that is. He assured me, even through his amusement, that he had.

"Just like a bumblebee," I said then, "flying from flower to flower," and he agreed. A CCU nurse; a medical transcriptionist; a blond, plump phlebotomist; and Marcy, the Chief Trauma Surgeon's secretary. Steve has something approximating a "relationship" only with Marcy and also with Beth, the phlebotomist. They're jealous of each other, these women, and don't know about the others on the line. Steve had a vasectomy a year ago, after he got two different women pregnant at the same time.

"Busy night?" I ask, as he devours his second chocolate-covered donut.

"Kind of. But it was all just shit. Only maybe one or two needed to come in. All we saw were fakers and drunks. Can you believe, sometimes, how many really stupid people there are in this world?"

"I know," I say. "And they all come through our doors."

It's true. People come in with the most minor cuts, like they've never seen a Band-Aid before, and then complain loudly when they're not seen right away. "What would you do if someone was dying?" they ask, idiotic and indignant. Or someone gets really drunk and passes out, and this person's buddies bring him in and act hysterical—or try, inexpertly, to do CPR on someone who's just asleep, breaking his ribs by pounding on his chest. Or someone with a laceration that could use stitches comes in, acting very concerned about it, very dramatic, and then just refuses to be stitched up. If you ask the person, then, why they came in, they don't know. Or mothers who call an ambulance for a child who has a runny nose. And then, of course, there are those who think they can be admitted to the hospital, just on their request, because they think they need to take it easy for a while.

In other words, a good percentage of our time is wasted trying to explain simple facts of life to naturally stupid and sometimes willfully ignorant people of all ages and persuasions.

Donald McIntyre, the Chief Trauma Surgeon, arrives with his secretary, the aforementioned Marcy, and the meeting begins. The surgical resident who was on presents the case, and McIntyre and whoever was the attending Trauma Surgeon feel free to interrupt with comments, questions, or advice for future similar occasions. Any problems? Anything that might have been done differently? If the patient died, was he at any point viable, and, if so, why did he fail to survive?

"At the scene, the patient presented apneic, with a pressure of . . ."

Numbers. Lab values. Technical jargon, data, and details. One thing that always comes up—getting lines in too slowly. When the total blood volume of a patient is replaced one or more times, the patient is bleeding out at such a rate that speed in replacing the lost blood is essential, and sometimes sufficient cut-downs (slicing the skin open to plug into a vein) are not undertaken right away. How stable is the patient? There are all kinds of objective parameters within which to judge this, with percentages of survival given such and such an injury, and so on, but there's still a large subjective element, and, while one wishes to stabilize the patient before further traumatizing the body with the invasive scalpel, I myself still have enough of a surgical mentality as to think that one knows very little until one has opened up the form and looked inside.

And so on and so forth.

John Woodbridge, who was the Trauma Surgeon on when a bad MVA came in one night last week, a seventeen-year-old girl who had her liver nearly severed (and yet survives), says, during the review of that case, "Let's tell it like it is: Steve had trouble getting that chest-tube in. When it finally was in place, we got out a liter of blood, just like that."

Next to me, Steve shrugs, but I'm sure he's furious. For one thing, he doesn't like Woodbridge; nor does he particularly respect him in regard to the latter's management of trauma. John Woodbridge has the nickname, among some, of "Jack the Ripper"—he's reportedly blown a good few surgeries. He tends to act very authoritative and give loud orders when he's in charge of a critical case. I don't like him either, though he's never yelled at me.

A secondary matter is: everyone fucks up a chest-tube now and then. It's not that easy, cutting through the flesh and the tough intercostal muscles, spreading these and sticking in the tube—sometimes you can get a lot of blood coming out through the tube, and think you're in, when you're not, you've merely ruptured one of the good-sized vessels in the muscle mass. What with Jack the Ripper yelling orders left and right, asking for something and then immediately bullying the nurse, saying "Where is it? Come on!" before she's had a chance to move, the atmosphere can quickly get everyone rattled. Dr. Woodbridge is tall and thick, fifty or so, very rich and conservative, with curly, iron-gray hair and red skin.

At eight-fifteen Steve Gold and I walk down the hall, heading for the hospital library, where I need to look up some material for an article I'm writing about Munchausen's Syndrome. Steve is really mad at Woodbridge for criticizing him about the chest-tube.

"That does it. As far as I'm concerned, from now on if he's on trauma call I'm not even going into the room."

"He's an asshole," I agree, shrugging. What else is new? It's not that big a deal. Steve hasn't really lost any face, unless he thinks he has.

In a few moments he seems to realize this, and changes the subject; we get to the new president of the hospital administration, who's been selected by the board to clean things up. Already, three vice presidents have either resigned or been fired, or asked to resign. The administration's in turmoil. Every department is wondering if they're next.

"If I was Matthew," says Steve, "I'd be worried about my ass. Too many people are asking, 'What does he *do*, anyway?' "

"I know," I say. "Nobody ever knows where he is or what he's doing. It doesn't matter, either: the department runs itself. If they're really going to cut costs, and they're looking at unnecessary administrators . . ."

"Don McIntyre'd like to get rid of Matthew, from what I

get from Marcy. Though she won't tell me much about what he says, the bitch. Pisses me off." He shakes his head. Usually, what he tells about Marcy is, "All she wants to do is fuck. I like that." She and Steve smoke Thai, snort coke, and get kinky. Anna, by the way, can't stand Steve Gold.

"Have you seen the new nurse?" I ask, and when he says no I make a pantomime to indicate someone fat. "Like a refrigerator."

"Oh shit. Another fatty, huh? What's she going to work? Day shift, with the other fatties?"

"I think so."

"You know, they just hired this nurse up in ICU, you should see her. She's Hawaiian: wait until you see her. She's incredible."

"What's her name?"

"I'm not sure. Teri or Tina or something. Well"—he checks his watch as we reach the library—"I've got to go. It's my one day a month to watch those old farts swim at the Y." For which he gets a free membership. "Then I'm having lunch with Beth."

Steve Gold grins. He pats me on the shoulder as he says goodbye. He likes to put his hands on people.

After about an hour of taking notes I leave, saying goodbye to Suzi the librarian, a notorious doctor-groupie whom I'm not attracted to at all—she wears too much makeup, and acts too animated and grateful. She seems a touch melancholy today, having to force herself, perhaps, to be as friendly as usual. Oh well. The new crop of residents will begin their rotation here in little more than a month, on July first.

When I get home, I see that the piano has not yet arrived, and I puzzle Gretchen by moving a chair and a large potted plant out of the living room to create space.

"Where's Anna?"

"She's having lunch with that woman who runs the gallery," says Gretchen. "And then I think she's playing tennis." She can't quite bring herself to ask me what I'm doing. She's wearing a green T-shirt and jeans. It's been a while since she's gone out on any interviews for jobs, but I don't mind. She comes in useful; it's probably better that she's here.

"I bought a piano," I tell her. "This is where it's going to go. What do you think?"

"Are you serious? Well. Why do you want a piano? Do you know how to play?"

"It's for Roger."

"Oh," she says. Clearly this deserves some deep thought. I'm sure she sees that Anna doesn't know, and she's not sure what position to take as a result. If Anna is angry, Gretchen doesn't want to be caught in the position of having encouraged me, of being, so to speak, a co-conspirator.

"The deliverymen are supposed to be here sometime in the early afternoon. I'm going to go swimming—if they come while I'm in the pool, just come and get me and I'll sign for it."

I didn't know I was going to swim until I spoke. I don't really want to, but, since I said I would, I will.

The water's cold at first. The sky above is white, with vague patches of pale blue. I'm a clumsy swimmer, splashing a lot, expending more energy than my progress would seem to warrant. Still, I'm not slow. I'm determined. My muscles aren't used to this, though, and I feel momentarily exhausted when I climb out. Weary, though there is exhilaration in this weariness.

The piano arrives after lunch. I don't know what Gretchen eats, for she's in her room listening to music, but I have a mango, some green grapes, and a piece of home-baked bread.

Just as a piece of furniture, I like it. A baby grand. Black, of course. A good brand, used rather than new. I like it. It looks good in here.

When Roger comes home from school, dropped off by the bus, he seems rather worried by what I've done. Is he happy? He doesn't show it.

"Who's going to play it?" he even asks.

"You are," I say, as if to imply, what could be more natural, he should take it for granted as his destiny and be glad.

"Go ahead," I urge him. "Try it out."

But he's very reluctant. He feels pressure, I suppose, and thus becomes self-conscious. He thinks I'm trying to pull something. He doesn't trust me. Maybe he's right.

EIGHT

Tonight Anna is also working, in an ICU in another hospital, and I liked seeing her this afternoon once again dressed all in white. It gave me a pang. She probably looks better now than she did when we first met. She has a good bone structure; I have no reason to think that she won't look fine all through her thirties and beyond.

As for me, I'm just beginning to feature a few gray or white hairs amongst the brown. I look distinguished. Especially tonight, when I'm wearing a tie and white lab coat instead of scrubs. It scares me, though, to think of being forty, much less to go much further on.

The piano hasn't angered Anna: on the contrary, she's pleased that Roger has shown some enthusiasm for something, and only hopes that this will endure. She did ask me why I hadn't consulted her, since a piano isn't exactly an insignificant purchase, and I didn't really have any ready response.

"I don't know what you're doing, or what you're thinking," I said last night, to which she shrugged and said that all I have to do is ask. But to ask, I realized, I'd first have to be clear on how much I wanted to know. And so I withheld my questions, and we were shy together, some of her composure seemed somehow to have temporarily worn off. Or she was tired. I don't know. We slept together, though. We were talking, and it was late, and it just seemed rather false to me, a gesture that would mean more than it should, for me to leave her and go to my other bed. For a moment I thought about trying to have sex, since I don't think that I'm impotent, and the prospect was somewhat attractive, but the negative factors converged and combined with the long-term residues of various barbiturates and narcotics to send me easily into a mock-exhausted sleep.

I've been thinking lately about this problem of my use of medication. Every time I take a pill it crosses some part of my mind that I'm being weak, that I'm thinking short-term effect, and thus giving in to a stimulus-response pattern that could worsen to the point of real danger and embarrassment over the next few months or years. I don't want the situation to deteriorate to the point where I might conceivably end up at the Center for Impaired Physicians in St. Louis. I don't want any problems or questions of irregularity to ever come up; this means I have to be careful and conservative in what I allow myself to ingest.

There was a resident in the program at this hospital last year, a bright, pleasant guy from Indianapolis, who got into

Demerol and cocaine. He was careless. It got so that he was ordering cocaine in solution when he was going to put down NG-tubes, presumably to numb the inside of the nose against the invasive tube, and then I guess he'd just do some sleight-of-hand to keep the cocaine, but ordering it to pass an NG-tube made the nurses on the floor very suspicious—no one orders it for that. And I heard that he was writing some loose prescriptions, which his girlfriend would cash in, but you can't do that with the heavy narcotics, Demerol and Dilaudid, for instance, and not expect to have your practice, sooner or later, closely examined. He was suspended from the residency program, and then his license was suspended, and I think he lost it—he'd had some trouble earlier on. David Briggs. By now maybe he's a pharmaceutical salesman. Sure. That's what happens. The drug companies snap these guys right up.

Everybody wants to feel good. Monkeys and baboons nibble poisonous roots to get high; when introduced to alcohol, once past the taste the whole primate family loves to get drunk. And, needless to say, every primitive society, as far as I know, has had some intoxicating beverage or substance, whether sacred or profane. From the Sumerians to the Aztecs to the Druids.

I happen to prefer certain other chemicals, generally, to alcohol, though sometimes alcohol is very nice (and tastes good too). However, no matter how precisely I may calculate my doses and effects, these pills remain toxins, and there's no way I can tell myself they're harmless and good. There may be mysterious interreactions, cumulative residues, unexpected idiosyncratic side effects or reactions, and so forth.

Still, the euphoria induced by selected medicines is a real "product," tangible and possessed of a value which is variable insofar as is the severity of the patient's need. Pain can be killed, or ameliorated, or at least postponed. This is something that falls into the category of the possible, and temporary lessening of pain or anxiety may be a very blessed state indeed.

Anyway, I'm checking myself for any signs of physical addiction: I haven't taken anything for three days. I don't notice myself going into withdrawal. I'm neither tremendously nervous nor physically restless and uncomfortable, though I do feel rather . . . officious, perhaps, or desirous of respect. Tonight I'm really into playing the role of doctor: I feel like making pronouncements, judging, "saving lives."

Anna is working three to eleven, while I'm doing the seven to seven all-night-stand. After Anna left, this afternoon, I asked Gretchen what our "open marriage" meant to her: what did she understand by the term and what did it in fact represent? Gretchen was unhappy that I'd brought this up.

I said, "Basically, she wanted to do that kid from UCLA . . . and she did, I guess—but now he's gone. He's not a constant factor. So who else is she doing, or is she just looking around, open to offers? I know she knows other men, and has maybe had lunch with guys from her classes, or people she meets at the athletic club. I just want to know if Sam was an exception or a symptom of a whole new kind of disease."

"Darrell, I can't answer these kinds of things. I don't know. Anna doesn't confide in me that much, she never has. You know how she is."

Gretchen seemed hurt, somehow, that I'd pressed her, and I felt like a jerk. I also didn't like the idea that she might think I lacked the strength to attack Anna directly on these points. I don't know why, when I think about it, I haven't insisted on knowing everything all along. Or rather—I do know.

Lately, Gretchen's been reading science fiction novels and letting herself get kind of slovenly, putting on some weight.

She needs to get organized. She ran into some scheduling problems with her psychiatrist, I gather, and so hasn't seen him for a couple of weeks. I think they need to talk.

Steve Gold worked day shift, so when I got here the patients weren't backed up like they get with Petibon. If anything, Steve is sometimes accused of seeing patients too quickly, or sometimes of not listening long enough to their complaints. He's friendly, assuming a facile familiarity that really endears him to some, but others, patients who take themselves and their conditions very seriously, are sometimes offended and don't think that he cares. Oh, he can be serious, he's by no means flippant when someone's gravely ill or dying, yet still, some people react badly to him.

We get rated all the time. The nurses rate us, turning in a questionnaire designed by Vandermeyer, and we're given scores evaluating every phase of our job. As the residents rotate through, spending a month each in the department, they are given a chance, after the month is done, to rate us as teachers of emergency techniques. And, of course, if we make a mistake, it usually comes back to haunt us. All the X rays, for example, are reviewed by radiologists the next day, and if we've missed anything the patient is called back in.

I'm rated number two in warmth and rapport with the patients: "compassion." Dan Petibon, with his southern accent, is rated number one. His competency and speed, certainly, are rather lower—though the nurses all like him, and put up with his ordering unnecessary lab tests and also taking time to eat his meals, stopping working, that is, even when there are many patients waiting to be seen. The residents like Petibon much less. Their favorite is Peter Flanagan, who likes the teaching aspects, and who is more conscientious in that area than anyone else finds the time to be. I confess I tend to be a little cold to the residents: I'm not interested in them, really, as a class of people. They come and go, and they're younger, and I just don't want them as new friends. But I don't think I'm threatened by them, as is Petibon, who falls back on a kind of patriarchal southern formality to try to avoid being second-guessed.

"Mike Williams was here," said Steve, as he followed me back to our room to give his report. "You know him, don't you?"

"Sure," I said. "What's wrong with him today? The last time I saw him he'd tried to strangle his mother and then his stepfather hit him over the head with the leg off a coffee table."

Mike Williams is a twenty-three-year-old white male who was in a bad car wreck when he was nineteen, in which he sustained some brain damage, and he talks like someone angry and retarded and has a permanent case of the shakes, for which he takes Librium. He drinks alcohol, mixing it with the Librium, and then gets in fights. Sometimes I feel a kind of perverse affection for him, even though he's always a problem to see.

"Today he got in a fight at the barber shop," said Steve, "and the barber threw him through the window, so he was all cut up—some really good lacerations. When the EMT's brought him in, around five, he was already in restraints, screaming that he was going to kill us, spitting at people. It's the worst I've ever seen him."

The thing is, Mike starts all these fights with people, acting belligerent, but he's so physically fucked up that he can never win. He's got scars all over him, bad scars, and he just keeps getting cut. When I see him, I get the feeling, like watching Boris Karloff as Frankenstein's monster, that there's some part of him that knows how messed up he is, and is ashamed of the slurred speech and minuscule attention span, and that this remnant of the pre-accident Mike is what makes him so bitter and combative. I genuinely feel sorry for him, and try to be nice to him: but he's hard to have around.

It's eight-thirty, and, while it's been steady, nothing significant or challenging has come in. There's a finite number of diseases and injuries. Mostly it's routine—nothing special, nothing hard. And then you get so you dislike seeing something strange.

A sixty-one-year-old white woman was assaulted, knocked down, when her purse was snatched an hour and a half ago. Her wrist hurts a little, and one knee is scraped, but her main problem seems to be anxiety. I talk calmly to her and dispense two Vistaril to help her sleep, one to be taken now and another in four hours or so if she still feels uneasy at that time.

I see a twenty-two-year-old black female who complains of chest pain, seeming very agitated. Her heart sounds fine, though I have to tell her to slow down her breathing so she won't hyperventilate.

"I think your heart is fine," I say. "So has anything been upsetting you lately? Have you had any unusual stress?"

There is a kind way to ask this, of course, just as there is a brusque, "superior" way that belittles the patient and evinces little sympathy for whatever her failings may be.

"Well, my boyfriend and I . . . just had a big fight. He said somebody told him they saw me at the disco with Leon, this guy who lives by me, when Bobby was out of town."

"Bobby's your boyfriend?"

"Yeah. So he got really mad, and he wouldn't believe me. . . ."

I see a screaming two-year-old with a very red inner ear. I don't enjoy examining screaming, uncooperative kids. It's better when they try to be brave. Maybe they feel better, though, when they scream and let it out. This kid's really loud. He doesn't like doctors, his mom explains.

Out in the hall, Tom comes by, smiling, and says, "What were you doing to that kid?"

"Torturing him," I say. "Sticking pins in him to test his lungs."

"That's what I thought," says Tom. "Hey, you want to play basketball some morning when you get off? It seems like we were going to do it a long time ago. Now that the weather's nice, maybe we should. Cooper Park is just a couple of blocks away, and I've got a good ball."

"Okay," I say. "Sure."

Yes, I remember talking about it once before, during basketball season. Football was Tom's sport, in of course a much larger way than baseball was mine. I'll play him, one-on-one. He's an inch or two taller than me, and both bulkier and I'm sure stronger, but I can use the exercise. I'm not naturally clumsy, so I shouldn't make too much of a fool out of myself. I am a little uneasy, though, I will admit, about seeing Tom outside of working hours—I hope he won't push it, because I don't want to have to freeze him off. Is this pure snobbism, classism? Not quite, I don't think, though that's an element, a factor in my machinations that I cannot deny.

Somebody has vomiting and diarrhea. "Vomicking," they call it. A dancer from The Starlight Club, which I think is topless, has a sprained ankle, purpling, for which she wants Workmen's Comp. Yes, definitely topless. I have the feeling she'd look better under different lights.

An obese white man, fifty-nine, is brought in as a Code 99 (that is, cardiac arrest), and he's blue and dead by the time he comes through the doors. One of the EMT's is doing CPR, pushing the chest way in, but this guy's DOA. A Code has been announced over the hospital's paging system, and the room is full of residents, respiratory therapists, the works.

"Why don't you stop now?" I say to the EMT. I listen to

the guy's chest one more time, just for the sake of form. The monitor shows a straight line. "Does anyone have any objection to us stopping now?" I ask, and nobody does. The fellow's wife has arrived, I'm told, so I go down to talk to her in the Quiet Room. There are other relatives present as well. They seem prepared, though the wife is a little shaky.

"I'm sorry," I say. "He's passed away." A nurse will come in to talk to them about funeral homes and all of that; and the Medical Examiner will be called, though it's likely that on this kind of case he'll pass on the opportunity to take a look.

The family wants to see the departed before they go, so the nurses clean him up and drape him down in Room 7. They're weeping discreetly, walking slowly, as they come up the hall.

I go into Room 4 to see Rashad Hankins, a thirty-two-year-old black male who wears a crash helmet day and night, everywhere he goes, because of his fairly frequent, only partially controlled seizures. I've seen Rashad many times: he's not as spaced out as he may appear. He never gives anyone any trouble, though sometimes it's hard to get him to talk with any precision about what is bothering him. The Dilantin and phenobarb he takes for his seizures are meds that can, as a side effect, cloud the mind a bit, and Rashad occasionally gets confused about how many he's taken in a day. Tonight he's sitting on the stretcher, still in his crimson warm-up jacket and scuffed blue crash helmet: his expression is sullen, but I know Rashad and he knows me (or at least I think he does).

"How are you doing, Rashad?"

"Oh, I don't feel so good, Doc."

"What's the problem? The nurse told me that you think you took too much of your medicine. How do you feel?"

"Funny."

He's not willing to speculate on when he might have taken

his last dose; once he tells me that he can't remember, that's all he wants to say on the matter. He just shrugs and looks away. I decide to have some blood drawn: a Dilantin level and a Blood Alcohol (ETOH), since I think I smell some of the latter on his breath.

Rashad's older brother, Marcus, was a boxer, a middle-weight, who about ten years ago actually fought for the world title. He got knocked out in the third round, after looking pretty good; now he drives a truck for Dr Pepper. He came in here once when he fell and hurt his back.

I don't think Rashad has ever had a job. I don't know who would employ him, or what he could do. Like Mike Williams, he's kind of a lost soul. Some people are on welfare forever, and they deserve to be: there's nothing else that they can do.

Rashad looks so sad there, in his crash helmet and high-top, beat-up tennis shoes, like a very melancholy, abandoned child. An almost sweet resignation, resigned to life without hope of more.

The Hear System sounds its tone, and then the report comes on that we're getting two patients from an MVA. One is critical, with a head injury; the other one is combative and in restraints. We alert the Trauma Team, via all their beepers, and within a minute or so they're all assembled and waiting, some getting gowns on in the Trauma Room. The Trauma Surgeon, tonight, is James Cavender, who is as handsome as any movie star, as arrogant, and who is strongly rumored to be gay. He's not effeminate. I get along well with him; I always have. He's tall and tan, quite slender, with short, curly golden hair. Like a Roman emperor on a coin.

The first ambulance arrives, with the head injury, whose legs are both obviously fractured, as is also his right arm. He's young, maybe just twenty. Very pale white skin. Unresponsive, pupils fixed and dilated. The right leg is turned completely inward, until it faces the left, so it looks as though he may have a fractured pelvis as well, which certainly opens up the possibility of internal bleeding, though his systolic pressure is still seventy-five. The only motor response is some extension to induced pain.

He was the passenger: the car ran into a telephone pole at a speed of approximately fifty mph. David, the evening clerk, digs out the patient's wallet and finds out that the name is William Freeman, age twenty-one.

When the next ambulance comes in, I go to take care of this patient, the driver, whom we put in Room 5. The EMT's, one male and one female, look angry, disheveled, and serious. This patient is also young, and is struggling, writhing, speaking in a loud abusive voice.

"Let me up, will you? Will you assholes let me up? Don't touch me, man, get your motherfuckin' hands off me. Listen, if you try to poke me with a needle I'll go into convulsions, you hear me? I'm allergic to needles; you stick me with one and I'll sue your ass off. I'll own you. You hear me? I'll *own* you, I'll own this whole fucking hospital."

"We need to start an I.V., and we need to draw some blood to make sure you're not bleeding internally," I say to him, right above his face, professional, calm, and cold. The smell of ETOH is ugly and strong. His clothes are dirty, expressive of a certain prole life-style one might, down South, call "white trash." Facial hair that one can't call an attempt at a beard, merely a day or so without a shave. Dishwater blond longish hair.

"Call Kaiser," says Jeff (that's his name, according to the EMT's). "They'll tell you about me. I'm allergic to needles— the last time they tried to stick me I passed out and almost died."

If he's not lying, then obviously it's a hysterical reaction;

I'm inclined to stick him and let him throw a seizure, if that's what he wants to do. He's in restraints already: there's not much harm that can be done. Let him faint. We can't evaluate him if we don't start finding some things out.

Lucy, aside, says to me, "Why don't we call Kaiser, have them check his record? That way we cover ourselves."

I say fine: call Kaiser. Meanwhile, I go back down toward the Trauma Room and see that Anna is out by the triage desk, seemingly hesitant to intrude. She must have just got off work herself. I am, involuntarily, very pleased to see her. I go to her for a second and say, "You came at a good time. Hang around for a few minutes and you can see what's going on."

In the Trauma Room, they're trying to keep the guy stable—the surgical resident has performed the belly tap and got a positive return, which means that William is bleeding inside his abdominal cavity. The catheter, however, has not brought forth any blood, so at least at this point his kidneys and bladder would seem to be intact.

Wayne, the Japanese anesthesiologist, is intubating him so that his breathing may be controlled via a respirator. Having confirmed the belly bleed, Cavender is having blood products pumped through the two peripheral lines.

Anna, white pants and shoes beneath her navy-blue long coat, steps in the doorway just to take a look. While Cavender is looking at an X ray, I tell him about Jeff, the clown in 5.

"If Kaiser'll take him, I think we should just dump him on them. He's stable enough to be moved, and God knows they've dumped enough on us. Anyway, if they don't agree to take him, I'm going to order bloodwork and an I.V. in another two or three minutes."

"You know what I bet he's thinking?" says Cavender. "He must think that if we don't draw blood, there'll be no proof that he was drunk. I bet he's trying to sneak out of Vehicular

Homicide. Pretty low, isn't it? Kills his buddy and he's already trying to beat the rap."

"He's a real scumbag, all right."

"How's his pressure?"

"A hundred."

"Good. Ship him out. If they don't want him, then let's work him up. Is CAT Scan ready yet?"

Yes. CAT Scan is ready. And now Ben Weiss, the neurosurgeon, has arrived. The police are all over the place. One of them tells me that, according to witnesses, Jeff and Bill were celebrating Bill's birthday, and then went out racing in Jeff's souped-up car. They were racing another car, with two other friends who did not crash. Apparently Jeff blew through a red light, just missing a car going through the intersection, lost control, and went right into a pole. The policeman I talk to, Andy, who comes in a lot on nights, bringing donuts and drinking our coffee, really wants a Blood Alcohol drawn on Jeffrey Burns.

"He's got a bench warrant out for failure to appear on another case of Driving Under the Influence, so he's driving with a suspended license. If his buddy dies, I think it's safe to say we might have Jeffrey locked up for some time."

"His buddy's going to die," I say. I point my right thumb down. "No question. Just a matter of when."

I talk on the phone to the ER doctor at Kaiser. To my surprise, he agrees to accept Jeffrey Burns. So we call an ambulance to perform the transport.

"Where's Billy?" says Jeff. "I want to see him. What're you guys doing to him? You fucking assholes, what're you doing to Billy? Untie me—you can't keep me tied up like this. I got a right to see my friend."

I feel like telling him something to the effect that Billy's going to die and you killed him, but I say nothing. I write on his chart, making careful note of the circumstances of the transfer to Kaiser, and then relocate Anna, who's in the now-empty Trauma Room, talking to Gabrielle as she cleans up and restocks. There's blood on the floor, still wet, to be mopped up. Gabrielle loves trauma; that's why she took this job.

Anna comes with me back to my room. On the way, we pass the EMT's coming out of Room 5 with Jeffrey Burns. At last he has shut up.

Rashad Hankins's Dilantin level has come back within normal limits, and his ETOH level indicates that he's only moderately drunk. I tell him that I think he needs to get a good night's sleep. He gets up, as though this is all he's been waiting for, and is ready to leave.

"I just thought I'd stop by and see how you were doing," Anna tells me, in my room. "You look nice in your tie. All I did tonight was suction and check gases. It looks like you're having a wild night."

"You just timed it right," I say, standing there in front of her, and then, in a moment, she puts her head on my shoulder and hugs me, and I stay kind of stiff because I don't know what's going on. I have an impulse of mistrust that contradicts my earlier pleasure upon seeing her, perhaps generated by the vague idea, which I can't help but see as a legitimate hypothesis, that she may be on her way to see another man. A fellow photographer, or someone else she may have met in connection with the gallery that's scheduling an exhibition of her works. What brings her to me, then, in the interim, may be some perversity or perverse sentimentality. And then, as I feel I may understand her after all, I kiss her on the mouth, and our mouths are hot and familiar and strange.

The telephone in my room rings. Another ambulance is on the way, bringing in a young woman found in a park, unconscious, possibly the victim of a rape.

Anna comes with me, coat on, saying hi now to Lucy, whom she likes, and the patient is delivered into Room 5. She's a punk, with blue hair in an aggressive cut, heavy, smeared eye makeup, and bloodred lipstick, with a studded dog collar around her neck, a grass-stained white T-shirt with a black design that looks like a Rorschach test, and no pants: she's nude from the waist down. This is why the police and EMT's worried about rape. She was apparently let out of a car on the edge of a park, where a neighbor across the street happened to look out, see her, and see the car speeding away. So this bystander called the police, who arrived and then summoned the ambulance.

We lie her on her side to keep her from aspirating: I examine her head for any sign of injury, looking in her ears for any bleeding, but my immediate notion—since I don't smell any ETOH on her breath—is that she's an OD. Heroin, most likely, from her pinpoint pupils. Her breathing is shallow, but her pressure isn't too bad. I inject her, under the tongue, with Narcan, even as Lucy is starting an I.V. and Gabrielle is putting in a Foley cath. Narcan counteracts the effects of opiates, and if that's what she's been doing she should start to come to within a minute at the most.

"Let's give her an amp of D-fifty," I say, just in case she's in a diabetic coma.

She has a very thick growth of dark pubic hair and large firm breasts. She starts to wake up; she groans and tries to roll. We'll give her some more Narcan through the I.V.; get a drug screen, a smear, and some lytes. Since she's coming around, it doesn't seem necessary to stick down an NG-tube or get blood gases. We'll have to keep an eye on her for a while: Narcan is short-acting, whereas it takes heroin a good long while to wear off.

"Do you know what happened to you?" I ask her. "You're at the hospital now."

"I don't know . . . I did some dope. . . . What happened to me? Who brought me here?"

She's so young. She still sounds loaded, blurry, like a very sleepy child. Somebody's daughter, probably still lives with her folks.

When I find Anna again, she's curious about the practice of injecting Narcan under the tongue. She's never heard of that before. Of course, in ICU, it's not likely to come up.

Other patients have arrived. A sick baby and a guy with a lacerated hand.

"I'd better go," says Anna, though some part of her seems reluctant, as if maybe she doesn't feel quite right about her tryst. We kiss goodbye, somewhat more coolly, now.

"Tomorrow," she says, "Gretchen and I are going to bake some bread. I guess I'll see you by dinner."

I can't tell what's going on. I say goodbye. She may be a little scared of me, though that hardly seems to make sense.

Before Anna and I got together, I think she was somewhat promiscuous or "wild," and this hint of unpredictability and even wantonness was one of the things that contributed to my attraction. She didn't go with doctors, she was too proud, but one had the feeling that she might decide to do anything. She seemed so strong-willed, self-possessed, and, to my imagination at that time, enigmatic even in her sensuality.

I remember the first time we made love. I was anxious, trying to be smooth, but somehow my anxiety was overridden by my sensing in her that, once she had determined to be generous, to give herself, that henceforth her generosity knew no bounds. I remember a kind of vertigo, a feeling of floating above the bed with her. It was almost like being doomed lovers, in that the doomed, illicit love is more intense, possessing *fatality* . . . while the licensed, sanctioned, safe love loses intensity by its very lack of boundaries to be transgressed.

I felt like our time together was stolen time, like it might end at any moment, like the fates were against us; if we went through the motions of an ordinary romance, it made no difference, it was a charade we hardly needed acknowledge, because, ultimately, our love was tragically doomed.

If things have gone wrong now, it's not in the way I would have imagined. Nor would Anna, I don't think, have predicted the way things have turned out. It's not my fault, I don't blame myself. Neither do I think Anna is to blame. Separate from either of us, it seems, a third force has impelled us, and this third, "outside" force must be simply the passage of time.

I wonder what Anna sees. I feel that it would be so easy for her to judge me and find me lacking, viewing me dispassionately and not necessarily without mercy. I wonder what she sees.

The blue-haired girl, Kris, is feeling much better now. There seems to be no question of rape. Her stretcher is moved to the hall, I.V. kept open, and we let her smoke a cigarette, an ashtray in her lap. It's one of Lucy's Kools.

"Hey, Doc," she says. "A lot of people get killed here, right?"

NINE

In a few weeks, there will be an exhibition of Anna's photographs at the Shadow Gallery, a gallery that specializes in photography. The exhibition has been arranged now for some time, and Anna has met several times with the exhibitions director, a woman named Claire, and with the owner, a very rich sixty-some-year-old architect with a big reputation in his field.

I am disappointed when I find out that Anna is going out to dinner tonight with the preparator, the fellow, that is, who actually hangs the exhibits. I've heard his name mentioned before, but I did not know that Anna was particularly friendly with him. I may even have met him at the gallery and not realized it.

At any rate, when I ask her where she's going, and with whom, she tells me, and explains to me the importance of the preparator to the showing's possible success.

"Christopher does environmental installations, you see, which aren't exactly very marketable—though he had a well-thought-of exhibition space in Boston last fall. It's in a sense the purest kind of art, since he doesn't produce a commodity, but what he does isn't easy to show, either, so he works as a preparator to get by. He's very good at it. We need to talk about the dividers; and I think the walls will have to be painted, since I know that they'll be soft gray for Edward Moebius's show, which is all black and white. I might be better off with stark white." (Anna's photography is in color.)

She and Christopher are meeting at a new little French restaurant that just got a rave review in the paper. It seems that Christopher and the owner-chef are old friends.

Anna's being so open and is so innocently excited about her exhibition that I feel it's gauche of me to suspect anything sexual—though, were I to ask, perhaps she'd tell me exactly what her plan is.

Gretchen is gone. Roger is being babysat by Diane. I eat some bread, a cold breast of chicken, and a papaya. I watch part of the news before I drive to work.

All the way, in the sun, I'm thinking that I ought to seek out someone new to fuck. I hardly know any women other than at the hospital, and I go over, in my mind, any that might possibly respond. It's not a question of pleasure. There's one nurse, in CCU, on nights, who's seemed to like me, though I haven't laid eyes on her for some time.

I'm in a bad mood, and suture the leg of a skateboarder, a

fifteen-year-old, with suppressed irritation, disliking him but nevertheless doing a good job.

Then, a short time later, we get a Pediatric Code, with less than a minute's warning from the Hear System; and, as the EMT's run in with the infant, doing CPR, I feel total panic come over me—I don't know what to do, I can't remember dosages for a one-month-old, I feel like I'll really have fucked up if this baby dies.

As the anesthesiologist hasn't yet arrived, the fucking bastard, I try to intubate the child myself, and have Patricia start an I.V. through the umbilicus. Bicarb, epi, atropine—I'm radically guessing at the numbers, converting so much per kilogram instantaneously, without time to look anything up. I think I've placed the tube, and the anesthesiologist takes over. I don't know, the baby's breathing, we're making it, and I guess we've saved it, it's pink and well-suffused. . . .

I go to talk to the parents, who are there with some other woman, and all three are crying, though the husband seems somewhat composed, trying to be strong, I suppose, his whole body poised for the worst. Even he, however, starts to sob when I tell them that the baby is all right. I say that it's a good thing they acted quickly, that the speed of the treatment is what made all the difference.

They tell me their story, and I listen, even when parts of it are repeated again and again.

Sally, one of the helicopter nurses, has come down, probably because of the Pediatric Code, and takes the opportunity to ask me, in the hall, what I think of tanning booths, whether I think they cause skin cancer or not.

The child is in the care of the pediatric residents, on his way up to Peds ICU, the chief resident, Linda Weatherspoon, talking to the parents as she walks up with them, showing them the way.

I tell Sally that, as far as I know, they use ultraviolet light, so yes, skin cancer is a risk. I'm not interested in this subject. I think Sally is crazy.

When she first started working here, two years ago, she was pleasant and somewhat chubby, a naïve Christian girl just off the farm. I remember her working in ER and saying one night, in amazement, that no one had ever called her a bitch before in her life. She didn't think she could adjust to the attitudes of our clientele.

After she started working with the helicopter, I'm not sure what happened, other than that I understand she broke up with a boyfriend, but she started dieting furiously, and jogging, and got braces on her teeth.

She's terribly thin now, and, with her new hairstyle, she's almost pretty at a little distance, but up close she looks unwell. I've heard stories of stormy tears and even faints, and I don't want to have anything to do with her. I wonder what she'll need after a tan. (And I wonder why she can't just go outside.)

I'm still in a state of nervous tension over the infant, who could just as easily have died as hung around, and I'm really annoyed when I go in to check out a drunken Indian named Joseph Bearghost whose girlfriend, a fat and ugly white girl, says he got hit on the head last night and has a headache: he needs something for his pain. She wears thick glasses and is belligerent; she won't let go of Bearghost's arm. Somebody doesn't smell good in here, somebody's not very clean.

I look at Joseph's head. He seems very, very drunk—when he answers any of my questions, his words are so slurred that I almost always have to ask his girlfriend what he said. I see now why the nurses let her in: to translate. She's had a few drinks too, judging from her breath. Cheap wine would be my guess.

There's a bump there. No laceration. Joseph pushes my

hand away when I try to look back in his eye. Normally, anyway, we don't give pain meds to head injuries for at least the first twenty-four hours, so as not to mask symptoms which might present and indicate a worse injury than was evident upon initial exam. In this case, given the alcohol that's obviously been ingested, to mix this with pain medicine could result in an OD.

I explain this principle, perhaps in a bit of a superior manner, and the girlfriend gets angry. She starts telling me off, but Joseph Bearghost just gets up and says, "Let's get out of here." He tears his arm away from her grasp and starts to go the wrong way, into another patient's area, until I go to the door, open it, and show him the way out.

"If you think we're paying for this shit, you're crazy," says the girl, as she follows her boyfriend out into the hall.

I'm not going to argue. I write my findings on the chart and then, seeing that Sally is holding forth to the nurses in the coffee room, telling them about some guy losing his legs in a logging accident, I decide I don't need to hear and go back to my room. They can call me when there's someone new to see. Martin Chamberlin is doing a couple of kids with colds.

We've got some samples of Soma, a muscle relaxant for low back pain, and I take one of these and watch some show on TV for about twenty minutes before I feel any different than before. There are more psychotropic side effects than I would have predicted, which means I'm getting slightly high.

Around midnight, I take a Valium, half of one rather, only about 2.5 mg. I'm tired of Librium. Nothing's going on. I could maybe even take a nap.

Instead, I go to the cafeteria and steal a coconut macaroon. I eat it on the way back.

Then I go up to CCU, telling Lucy where I'll be, making a show of checking on the patients, doing "follow-up," though nothing could be further from my mind. The nurse who likes me is on duty; I have to see her name tag to remember who she is. Kathy.

I look at the chart of a patient she's taking care of, some relatively young MI, and she tells me how he's doing, speaking as though he is her friend.

"Listen," I say, "do you want to get together sometime? We could have lunch or something. I hardly ever see you up here."

"Sure, we could have lunch. But what about your wife? I don't want to, you know—"

She's not a real beauty, though I like her as a nurse. I like her manner. She's taller than Anna (which means she's pretty tall), with short dark hair, kind of tomboyish, with a few freckles across the bridge of her nose.

"We have an open marriage," I say. "Anna's out tonight with a guy named Christopher, an artist who does environmental installations. So, you see, there's no problem. We each have our own circle of friends."

"Dr. Patterson," says one of the other nurses, from the unit console, "Michelle just called from downstairs: there's a new patient for you to see. She said, though, to tell you it's nothing big."

"Okay." I turn back to Kathy, looking at her expectantly, waiting for her to speak.

She realizes this, and says, "How about next week? I'm off on Tuesday. If it's nice, maybe we can go out on the water."

I don't want to go out on the water. I take her telephone number, though, scribbling on the prescription pad I always have. I smile, and then leave the beeps and blinking lights of CCU behind.

The corridors of the hospital at night are generally empty, though there are people working in the lab, and in Housekeeping, and in Food Service, as well as taking care of the sleeping patients on the wards. I am at home here; I've been walking down these halls for years.

Back in ER, a couple of cops have come in to have coffee, and are sitting in their blue uniforms, walkie-talkies at the ready, talking to Lucy and Michelle.

"Do you remember this girl?" asks Lucy, handing me the chart.

"Overstreet, Teena L."

"Yeah, I remember her. What's wrong with her tonight?"

Some kind of an infection in her vagina. Great. Wonderful. I really don't feel like doing a pelvic right now, especially on someone whose personal hygiene let's just say that I suspect.

I'm sleepy now; I don't feel like listening to any more confusing stories. I don't want to be entertained. Right at the moment, I just don't have that need. I was in a good mood a couple of minutes ago, but I felt serene, I wanted some peace and quiet for a while.

Piss and shit, vomit and pus: I don't like these substances any more than the next person. I hate to get puked on, or to have to closely examine someone's shit. Oh, I'm detached, I know what to look for and all of that, but nobody says I have to like it.

Blood I don't mind. Blood's different: it doesn't smell bad, and it's a predictable color. There's something almost festive about it. It excites some primitive emotion, I guess.

But Teena Overstreet's not dirty. Indeed, she smells, not too heavily, of perfume, musk I think, and her skin seems fresh and maybe even recently washed.

I can't tell if she remembers me or not. She may be pretending not to. Her answers to diagnostic queries are terse and vague. She's not elaborating or digressing. She seems depressed, a bit sullen and abstracted, thinking about something other than her immediate circumstance.

"How long have you been hurting?"

"I don't know. A few days. A couple days."

"Have you had any discharge?"

"I think so. A little."

"Any trouble when you urinate?"

She thinks it over.

"No," she pronounces, frowning, "I go just like everyone else."

Lucy assists while I do the pelvic. Teena's uterus is tender and inflamed. Probably PID.

"Doctor, how many—how many times can a girl make love, you know, before she gets stretched out?"

"Stretched out?"

"You know what I mean. So that your pussy isn't tight anymore. You know."

I wonder: has the whole examination been incidental, the discovery of the infection a mere side effect, almost an irrelevance—is, for Teena, this question of whether her pussy is still tight the main reason she came in? I don't doubt it. Someone must have said something to her: insulted her, and it's been preying on her mind. I don't know what to say to her. I turn to Lucy, who's barely smothering a smile, and plead with my eyes for help.

Which I am refused.

A tall black guy in a brown shirt and yellow pants comes down the hall, looking for me, having passed through the NO UNAUTHORIZED PERSONNEL double doors, and I catch his eye and don't flee; I'm not surprised when he asks me, glowering, about Teena Overstreet.

"She all right?"

"Yes. I'm just waiting for some lab tests to come back."

"She gonna be okay?"

"Well, it looks like she's got an infection, so she'll have to take medicine for it, but it's not serious."

"Not serious?"

This seems to piss him off. It figures that he'd be crazy too. Lucy rescues me this time, telling him that he can wait with Teena in Room 3. She shows him the way.

I sit down and listen to the cops. One of them (Elliot) is explaining to Michelle the difference between Traffic and Prowl.

After a few minutes of this, I go to my room, looking first at my watch as if I've got something to do. I try to read an article in *The New Physician* about chest trauma, but I can't concentrate, so I look at the pictures instead, flipping, looking vainly for the quiz. All these magazines have a quiz.

The results of the smear are positive for GC (gonorrhea). I write on the chart an order for 2.4 million units of procaine penicillin. Then I notice that Lee and Carol of Security have shown up, looking not as if they're after coffee but ready for action, and I'm on the verge of asking what's going on when Teena's boyfriend comes out into the hall, whereupon Lee and Carol accost him.

"Let's see what you have in your pockets, man," says Lee, and the other black just waves and turns his back, walking quickly away. Lee and Carol hurry after him, not about to let him escape.

"Keep your hands off me, Tap Dance," the guy says at the triage desk, very angry now, turning. The cops stroll out of the coffee room to see what's going down.

"He took some syringes and stuff," Lucy says to me. "He was sneaking all around. Stevie saw him." (Stevie is the archetypal gay orderly.)

Teena comes out into the hall, barefoot, in her open-backed hospital gown.

"Dexter," she says, "what're they doing to you?" Then she turns back, toward me, and toward the curious, advancing cops, who saunter as they put on their black gloves. Teena looks distraught.

It's still like she doesn't recognize me from before; but, as the cops pass her, on the way to hassle Dexter, I come to her and touch her on the shoulder, as if to guide her back into Room 3, out of harm's way. She seems ready to burst into tragic tears. I wonder, though, if she's on Stelazine or something, because she seems so much less animated than she was the other time.

Dexter, if he's cool, could just give back the syringes and probably go home, if he could manage to smile and confess his error—but, instead of acting with discretion, he keeps complaining, acting indignant, trying to stand on his "rights."

Then, suddenly, he swings his fist and hits Carol smack! in the face. Pointlessly. Right in front of Lee and the police.

They have him down on the floor and handcuffed in no time. He's yelling, but now Dennis, the bigger of the cops, yells at him even more loudly, close to his face, telling him that he's going to jail and that he better just shut up.

The implication is: or get thumped.

Dexter quiets down.

Next to me, by the stainless steel drinking fountain, Teena is crying. But she hasn't flown to Dexter's aid. I'm glad and surprised.

"There's nothing you can do," I tell her, calmly, and she seems to realize this, to understand, but does ask me, "Will you get the cigarettes from him for me? He's got all the cigarettes."

I say sure, and she goes back into Room 3 without even looking down to see syringes being pulled from every conceivable hiding place in Dexter's clothes.

I have to check Carol, whose lip is bleeding. She has graying hair, and looks tough, very butch, like the prototypical lesbian that she is. She needs two or three stitches in that lip.

I do my job. One might say that the Valium steadies my hands.

Maybe I should go back into surgery. At this point, it might be restful. Ear Nose & Throat (ENT), for instance. Nobody dies too often from having their tonsils taken out.

Elliot, who's stayed behind while Dennis is making the pinch, talks about the other night, when he responded to a "gunshot heard" and ended up having to protect a black guy from about fifteen others, who were throwing him out of a party because of something he supposedly said to someone's lady, and who had then allegedly gone out to his car and fired off his gun a few times, just to scare them or something, make them take him seriously. Now the gun was gone, thrown into the bushes most likely, and the partygoers were terrifically enraged at the undesirable, trying to get at him, and Elliot says he even took a punch in the face while trying to keep himself in between, the undesirable not making things any easier by yelling back at those who were now calling him names.

"Finally, I got him in the car, and then I had to try to cool everyone down—"

He shakes his head, bemused. I try to picture it. No partner, all by oneself. At night, in the dark.

"You don't ever draw your gun and fire in the air, anything like that?" I ask, to bring him out.

"No," says Elliot, smiling a little. "I don't pull my gun unless I think I'm going to shoot it at somebody. You can't just go pulling your gun all the time. If you do, pretty soon you're going to be killing some citizens. When you don't need to."

Lucy comes in and tells me that Teena wants to ask me one more question before she goes. Lucy's taking a little advantage of the fact that I'm not as "official" as, say, Dr. Flanagan. I assume that Lucy tried first to deflect Teena and send her on her way, and that for some reason this has not worked.

I go down to see Teena, and she's dressed now, in a black dress, and she has the concentrated, serious look that crazy people sometimes get as she asks me, straightforwardly, "Can you give me something for my nerves? Something to help me sleep? Please, Doctor!" Her fists are clenched, up at her temples. Her buttock must still ache from the megadose of penicillin, which is thick stuff and needs to go through a big, thick, hollow needle.

"Have you ever taken medication for your nerves before?" I ask, not cruelly at all.

"Lots of times. But I don't have anything at home right now."

"Okay," I say, and take out my pad. I write her a scrip for Valium, 5 mg, to be taken at bedtime. I make it for twenty, nonrefillable. And then I go back to the med cabinet and get one Vistaril, 50 mg, individually wrapped, to dispense to her tonight.

"Here you are," I say, and watch as she reads the prescription. "Don't give these to Dexter, all right?"

"Dexter'll probably stay in jail for a while. I think he's got another warrant, once they figure out his real name. You're really nice to me, you know," she says, looking up. "I remember, once you gave me a ride in your BMW. Here, I want to give you something." She digs in her purse. "This'll keep you safe from spells." She hands me a cheap-looking ring, which I accept. "But you got to wear it all the time." She seems resigned to the fact that I will not.

I just nod, listening, and don't mock her. Then I tell her to check on the culture in three days.

TEN

I play basketball with Tom. It's a gray, very cloudy morning, and I don't really want to, but I said I would; if I say no now he'll think it's because I'm a doctor and I'm pulling rank, saying that my time's more valuable than his, and all of that. Besides, he really wants to play.

I put on tennis shoes, and we each drive the short distance to Cooper Park, which is deserted and dewy and green. The basketball is a dark shade of burnt-orange. It's very bouncy.

I haven't shot baskets for years. Not since I was a resident, when I used to play with a tall left-handed neurologist named

Dave, whom I would usually beat. We played loosely, casually, though, and the outcome hardly mattered. I just could make more shots.

My brother Jack and I played all the time through high school, and I did all right against him, the games were always close, though he played on the school team, was a year older, and both slightly bigger and somewhat stronger. We played hard. I was just a little bit quicker, while he could make fancier shots. This tendency to attempt difficult moves worked against him, even though he might occasionally do something so cool we'd both just stop and laugh.

I'm somewhat out of shape now, of course. And Tom doesn't seem to be too slowed down by his knees. I feel sluggish and wonder, momentarily, if I'm slowed down by the lingering effects of certain drugs. Or, alternatively, maybe I should have taken a Dexamyl. I simply didn't think of it.

We start to play one-on-one. Tom's two or three inches taller, six years younger, and much more huskily built. I'm surprised at how aggressively he chooses to play—if this was for money, I'd think I'd been set up. I thought we'd play loosely, so that neither of us would have to work too hard. Instead, he's driving right at me, bumping, taking more than three seconds in the key, dribbling and dribbling and backing in until he can use his height and strength to hit a short shot without much grace.

I never played like this when I had an opponent whom I knew I could beat. I'd lay back, giving them a chance, letting it stay fairly close. A friendly game is a friendly game, even on the playground against strangers.

When I get the ball, Tom is all over me, trying to steal it off my dribble, reaching in, smiling, trying to make me look inept. I'm infuriated that I'm not better, that I haven't practiced, that I'm not in better shape because, under other circumstances, I think that I could win. His shots are kind of stiff, lacking arc or touch.

I hit a couple of shots from outside, then, when he comes out, I drive by and am viciously fouled, his forearm striking my wrist. It hurts, and makes a big red mark.

"Foul," I say, and he shrugs, and I take the ball out of bounds. I fake, then miss a jumper, and feel the main thrust of my adrenaline drifting away. I'm puzzled now, as I catch my breath, at Tom's hostility. I wonder if he's made advances to Patricia and, rebuffed, correctly deduced that a security guard is not quite the hot prospect that a doctor is—and he's taking it out on me. I'm a surrogate for Osborn McCrae.

I let Tom score, making less of a pretense of guarding him. He's content to run up the score, to slaughter me. If I thought I could, I'd like to beat him up. He must sense that I'm irritated, though I try to act more like I'm just tired and don't care.

He acts as if it's my problem if I can't keep up, if I choose to quit.

We rest, and I'd just leave now but I'm too tired, I need to catch my breath. I've stretched all kinds of dormant muscles.

Tom says, "I went out to visit Patricia's farm the other day."

It takes a moment, but then, despite my annoyance, I'm interested in the confidence, and say, "Oh? What was it like?"

He laughs, briefly. "Eighteen goats. Three big dogs, ducks, chickens, geese. Maybe eight or nine cats out in the barn. Does that give you a picture? Patricia really likes the animals, I don't know. You know Osborn, don't you? Do you like him?"

"I don't know," I say, feeling like there's a lot, for Tom, behind this question. At a great distance, I feel some sympathy for him, for he seems sad, but the distance is too great, my real indifference is insurmountable. "He's kind of dull, I suppose," I admit, just to throw him a bone.

"Cindy"—one of the other evening shift nurses—"calls him 'Mr. Excitement,' " says Tom, savoring this for a moment.

Then, for some reason, we play once more, and Tom is less rough, though I still haven't forgiven him, and then we part. The drive home seems endless: I'm relieved that I don't have to work again for a couple of days. Little drops of rain have started to fall.

Roger is at school. Anna is reading the paper. Gretchen is in bed. I'm thirsty; I want a Coke.

"Tough night? You look like you've been through hell."

"I played basketball with one of the security guards, a guy who used to play football at Michigan State. He beat the shit out of me."

Anna smiles. "And now you'd like to kill him, wouldn't you?"

"Why do you say that?" I sigh. "I'm not like that."

"You don't hate to lose?"

"I don't *like* to lose. You exaggerate my faults."

"No I don't."

"Then you must have a very crude picture of me. I'd hate to hear what you say about me to Diane; you probably make me sound like some kind of predictable, fucked-up robot."

"Well," says Anna, very coolly, as I drink some Coke, "how do you want me to see you? If you think that you act like a robot—hasn't that been your ideal? To run yourself like a machine, turning it on and off, fast and slow, changing your chemistry—you're the one in command, the All-Knowing: you do it to yourself.

"You don't need me," she continues, getting warmer and warmer, "you don't want to need me. You don't want anyone, you don't love anyone—you don't even love yourself. Yeah, I think you're trying to be a robot; I don't know how you can think that things can just go on like this—for years, forever. . . unless it's supposed to be some kind of machine heaven. Whenever you think you're starting to slip, that you're getting too human or something, you take another fucking pill. Then you're leveled out, you're back in your zone, you think you're back in control—but you're not. You know you're not."

"No," I say, quietly, after a moment, "I'm not." Anna's staring at me. She's not crying, though for a moment it seemed as though she would. Something she rarely does. I'm unable to respond, I'm a million years away.

I don't know who she is or who she's been talking about. I really don't.

"I can't talk now," I say, finally, over a mass of feeling that has built up in the room. "I understand—" But then I can't go on.

I go take a shower. Under the water, washing all over, my mind is blocked up like a frozen motor. Not even a click.

Lying in bed, the door closed, I feel terrified, as though I'm holding myself together with a fraying, ancient string. I'm too tired. I feel like calling out to Anna like a child, an infant; but I don't. Her reference to my "chemistry" still scares me, and seems unjust, though it is not. The injustice and the justice together smite me down. I'm suffering but I'm numb. I've got to calm down and be numb, and then I can feel what I need to feel. I'll be okay. I need to add things up. I need to talk to Anna some more, and I want to, and I will.

ELEVEN

My brother Jack was always more popular with girls than I was, because, I suppose, he was more outgoing and maybe better-looking: his very success, in fact, served to inhibit me—during high school, at least, if not later (when a certain reserve had no doubt become habitual). Jack thought nothing of approaching strange girls and immediately talking to the cutest one, asking questions and introducing himself, with a charm served well by his authentic air of not really caring if the encounter proved fruitful or not.

Later on, this somewhat indiscriminate friendliness would lead him to spend a lot of time in bars, and he never seemed to get the very best or classiest girls for himself, partially, certainly, because of his reputation of going from one girl to the next. Still, I envied him, and he rubbed it in, somehow sensing whenever I felt vulnerable and he could embarrass me by saying, "Hey, Candy, my brother here really likes you, you know, only he's shy," or some such thing. Sometimes he'd call me "the Brain," which he knew I hated, and which misrepresented me, too, as I wasn't at all some wimpy, sissy bookworm—but of course he wasn't trying to be *fair*.

It wasn't until I was a senior in high school (with my brother gone away, temporarily at least, to college) that I "went steady" and also was initiated (or initiated myself) into the world of two-party sex. The girl's name was Laurie, and she was outgoing and very striking, an actress in the school drama department, who had also done some small-time modeling— she was a perfect size "N" or something. She was high-strung; she didn't have any close girlfriends; her other boyfriends before me were all college guys, one from Dartmouth has gone on to gain a seat in the U.S. House of Representatives. I ran for and, somewhat to my surprise, easily won the office of senior class president, mostly to impress Laurie. I had been aloof, a loner, etc.; now I suddenly was popular. I'm sure I thought myself then, walking around with Laurie, to be just about the coolest guy in school.

I helped Laurie rehearse her parts, feeding her her cues, and watched her play Nora in A *Doll's House* and Ophelia and *Miss Julie*. She won some award at a festival, and of course wanted to go to New York to act on the stage.

I knew she was a little egocentric and opinionated, but I suppose I forgave a lot simply because of her loveliness, which was of a sophistication far from the cheerleader or Mamie Van Doren type that Jack always went after. Even when Laurie wore an absurd outfit (in the interests of high fashion), I accepted her without qualification. She was a snob, and I aspired to be one—her parents were impossible, for instance, affected and fake-aristocratic, but I pretended to like them, to admire their culture and taste.

And all the time, I was fucking Laurie probably an average of ten times per week. She was as overheated as I was. I'm not sure, in view of subsequent events, exactly what was going on, I mean in regard to her "transports of passion"—when she left me, in a year, after an abortion and then another few months of constant companionship, she left me for a half-failed playwright, ten years older, who was seemingly bisexual and quite possibly gay. Laurie told me then, when we had a fight, that all her orgasms with me had been fake, that she had just been "acting," and hadn't she been good? I didn't believe it, but there was nothing I could say.

Through college and med school, then, there were long periods of time when I didn't go out with anyone at all, for months, or then I went out with someone only once and never called her back. I'm very picky, or particular, or have specialized tastes, I don't know—but not that many women appeal to me. I wasn't holding out for someone without flaw, a dream-girl, either. A couple of times I was infatuated for a week or a month, but either the young woman wasn't interested, wasn't interested enough, or I myself lost interest once I found out more clearly who she was/what she was really like. I went through a period, as a resident, when I was confident of my status and my looks: I felt like women had no reason not to find me attractive, and I was hurrying around enough that I had no time to be shy or slow. I had a nice affair in my first year of residency, with another resident, from Iowa, named Karen Green (who was going into anesthesiology). We weren't in love, or madly passionate, but we were in proximity, and we got along well together, we liked to share meals and so on, and so it was often convenient to sleep together too.

I've never been totally confident sexually; what Laurie had said to me, however I rationalized that she'd just been trying to hurt me, made me a little skeptical of extravagant displays.

The implications of sexuality as a biological imperative simply to reproduce the species, ad infinitum, our only form of immortality—these implications are not lost on me. However much pleasure may seem product rather than by-product of this activity, it's side effect, then, rather than relevant effect.

Before Anna and I leave to meet Mike and Diane somewhere to play tennis, I get a telephone call from Steve Gold. He's at work, doing day shift on a Saturday. Anna's already out in the car, or looking at flowers, talking to Roger and Gretchen. Gretchen, our perfect babysitter. I think lately she's been smoking too much pot.

"Hello, Darrell, how are you doing? Listen, do you remember a guy you saw the other night . . . Bearghost?"

"Yeah," I say, after a moment. "Drunk; got hit on the head, wanted pain meds. What about him?"

"Well," Steve says, "it looks like he had something. The story we get is that he kept drinking for his headache, and then he went to sleep and his girlfriend couldn't wake him up. So he came in this morning, by ambulance, comatose. We got a CAT scan, and the guy had a subdural."

"Shit."

"Right."

A subdural is a bleed inside the skull: as the blood gathers, its volume presses on and damages the brain. Mostly fatal. So I missed one.

"Where's he now?" I ask. "Surgery?"

"No, he's out of Surgery, gomed out in ICU."

"Fuck."

"Gomed out" means: in a terminal coma.

"Head injuries who're drunk and uncooperative are tough," Steve says, to console me. "What can you do? From your charting, it sounds like the guy was an asshole."

"He was," I say. "Wouldn't sit still—you know. How well did I document it? I can't remember what I might have written."

"Just a minute; I don't have it right here, hold on a second, okay?" He puts me on hold. It must not be busy there today. He's back quickly: "Darrell? Basically, you wrote that he was 'uncooperative, strong odor of ETOH—impossible to evaluate. Left before treatment completed after being refused pain meds.' I don't know . . . just one of those things. Anyway, I thought I'd let you know, because the family is raising a fuss. His brother and some guy from the Urban Indian Council are saying that you were prejudiced, and that they're going to sue. I don't see what else you could have done."

"Yeah. Okay. Thanks for calling, Steve. I'll probably call Matthew later on."

As head of the department, Matthew naturally worries a lot about any malpractice suits or other legal matters. He worries a good deal about PR, about how the department *looks*, how it *appears* to be functioning. . . . He's given talks about all the quality control measures that are in effect, and how very few errors ever get past them. He gives lip service, at length, to the notion that the physicians in ER should be caring and compassionate, seeing the patients as human beings rather than as "cases"—that whole syndrome—equal treatment to all. Always, in theory, it sounds very nice. Always in theory.

The tennis rackets and tennis outfits are in the car. My Fiat Spider, which is slightly dirty today. Dusty: I could write my name with my finger on the hood. Anna gets in beside me, in a good mood that I can strongly sense but not return. I start the car, and then we drive away. Gretchen and Roger wave goodbye.

"Richard called Gretchen the other night," Anna says, as we descend a long curve. Richard is Gretchen's ex-husband. "She said she didn't know what he wanted, but I think he just likes to upset her. Every so often . . . remind her that he's still around."

"And then she broods for a week," I say, knowing the pattern, a bit impatient with it at the moment. I pass a pickup, accelerating mightily, leaning into it, and then whip through the next curve, between vistas of trees and fields and over a small bridge that goes over a creek. "Gretchen would do a lot better," I say, "if she didn't have so much time on her hands. She needs to be working, seeing other people, interacting with the world."

"I know," says Anna neutrally, withdrawing a bit. I'm on the verge of telling her about Bearghost, but somehow I just don't.

"Asshole," I can't help saying, honking my horn at the driver of a red car that has done wrong, hindering our progress by the mistake.

Expressing anger at other drivers isn't a particular sign of any strong feeling on my part; it's something I do all the time, something I even enjoy. It's part of driving. The anger goes out of me in an instant, like running water.

I want to, though, say something to hurt Anna's feelings. Like ask, in an offensive way, for a divorce. Something along those lines. It wouldn't bother me to do it. There's a risky, spiteful pleasure involved, which I put off. I want to do it, and it wouldn't be hard—but I'm postponing it until later. First we'll play tennis with Mike and Diane.

We're meeting them at the estate of David Fairchild, a rich

client of Mike's. Fairchild owns some property downtown, and
he's behind one development or another, here and there,
throughout the Pacific Northwest. He's in his fifties, Republican, very fit, barrel-chested, with white hair. He has two
tennis courts on his property, in addition to a stable, horses,
swimming pool, sauna, and billiards table just in off the sun-
deck.

Anna and I have been out here before. Twice, actually.
Fairchild's all right, I guess, for an egomaniac. He doesn't try
to arm wrestle or anything. I'm surprised, in a way, that he
finds a use for Mike. I would think that he could find somebody
brighter. But then, I don't understand much about the stock
market. It's possible that, in his field, Mike could be brilliant
(though I'd be surprised).

I drive through the gate and up toward the big house. Really,
this is a little out of my league. If I were a cardiovascular
surgeon, or even a successful psychiatrist who'd written a book,
then I'd be in the proper economic bracket—then we could
talk. As it is, well, ER physicians have traditionally been losers
or fly-by-nights, and even if that's been changing in the last
few years, particularly at the bigger hospitals, we're still not in
the upper echelons, not by any means. Some physicians have
even been known to say that we in the Emergency Room don't
practice medicine at all. Snobbery, you see, because we don't
do follow-up, we do the initial evaluation and treatment and
that's all. That's not subtle enough for some.

Fairchild doesn't have an excessively younger wife, thank
God. She's in her forties, and she doesn't play tennis. Fairchild
does, however. He and his daughter (from his first marriage,
as I understand; nineteen years old) play doubles against a
handsome Middle Eastern young man and his partner, a very
skinny girl who might also be nineteen.

They've already started. Mike and Diane are warming up,

trading groundstrokes, in the other court. Anna and I aren't late, I don't think, but it feels like it. Since playing basketball, I've been doing more swimming, and I feel stiff; my muscles are tender as I start to get loose. I'm not a very good tennis player, generally, though I am a bit better than Mike. He, however, has obviously been practicing. Diane has seen to that.

We begin our match. My reflexes aren't bad, and I have some notion of where the ball's likely to go, but I tend to overhit and miss the lines. Anna can patiently beat the hell out of me.

The sun's out, and it's hot, with just a little breeze. We play. I'm thinking about Bearghost. Nearby, Fairchild and his daughter are gradually losing a hard-fought, pretty skillfully played match. On this court, though, the Pattersons are annihilating Mike and Diane. Both Anna and I are making one splendid, ungettable shot after another. Everything's going right for us. I can watch Mike's spirits sink, visibly, despite his usual attempts at good humor. Diane is playing below form, and I detect some reserve in her behavior toward Anna, which may or may not have to do with the matter of Anna's seduction of Sam, Diane's cousin, the pride of UCLA.

The winners of the other match want to play us next. Haziz (little mustache, handshake, British accent) and slender Caroline (legs taut as a ballerina's). Anna and I smile at each other, sharing the intelligence that we're in over our heads, still savoring the athletic harmony of our earlier win.

Haziz is intense but courteous, with a terrific serve. Anna runs well, but at one point lunges too far and falls, slightly skinning her knee. She doesn't make a big deal out of it, but it makes me more competitive, and I manage to get lucky at the net. Caroline calls a couple of close ones out that look in (on her side), and then argues about one of hers that's clearly six inches too long. In a tantrum that surprises us all, after hitting an easy shot into the net, she throws her racket down and yells, "Fuck it! Just fuck it!" Then she picks up her metal racket and just plays on. Haziz gives me a little smile, as if he's embarrassed. Anna calls one out that looks in: in retaliation, I realize, hearing the coolness of her voice. I'm glad that she's capable of doing this, of playing the bitch. Caroline, clearly furious, asks Anna if she's sure. "Yes," says Anna, and after the next point (which we win) she gives me a covert little smile, perspiration glittering on her brow.

Fairchild's house is interestingly constructed, long and low and turned back against itself, much bigger than it at first appears, different levels and wings materializing unexpectedly; the kind of place where one might need a map at first to find one's way.

Anna and I shower together, not without self-consciousness despite our weariness from the match. But it seems absurd to take turns, one waiting for the other to come out. We *are* partners, after all. We're pleased with ourselves, as tennis players, as a team, even though we didn't ultimately hang on for the win.

Mike and Diane were in this bedroom before us, but they didn't mess anything up. The place is spotless. As I dress, I feel exhilarated and relaxed.

Because I'm relaxed, I don't have any inhibition about telling Anna the story of Joseph Bearghost.

"I fucked up the other night," I say. "You know, that phone call I got just before we left the house? That was Steve Gold, telling me about it. I missed one."

Anna's still essentially feeling good, but she's serious, she looks at me, she wants to know how bad it is. Her hair is dry: she's just wearing pink panties and bra. She comes to me, holds me as I sit upon the bed. She hugs me, kisses my neck.

"What happened?" she asks. I lie back, and she comes with me, touching me, smiling a little to show that she trusts me, as a doctor at least, that she's on my side.

"I missed a subdural on a drunk. He'd been hit on the head, but I didn't think he was hurt very badly—he was obnoxious, and he didn't smell good, and right away he was asking for pain meds, so I didn't end up giving him much of an exam. I mean . . . I didn't exactly formally check all twelve cranial nerves, or even equal grips. When I tried to look in the fundus, he shoved my hand away. I don't know. I didn't like his girlfriend either . . . but I suppose I could have been nicer to them or something, sweet-talked them into staying. You see, they got mad and left, and then the guy went into a coma the next day. Or no, I think there was another night in there . . . I'm not sure."

"How's he doing now? Is he dead?"

"Not yet."

"Oh, Darrell, you shouldn't feel bad, you can't CAT scan every drunk who gets hit on the head. You just can't."

"I know. But I guess—Steve said the family's saying they're going to sue. Claiming I didn't give him as good care as I would have if he had been white."

"He was black?"

"No. Native American. Indian. Joseph Bearghost. Usually, if anything, I think I go out of my way to be nice to Indians and blacks and Vietnamese. The ones I don't like are the dirty, trashy whites."

"I know what you mean. They're the worst." Anna knows, from relatives visiting the patients in ICU. ICU has its security problems too, just as in ER.

"The thing that I'm sorry about, if they really do come up with a lawsuit, is that I didn't get a Blood Alcohol. Now I suppose they'll just say that it was all subjective, that I was prejudging, and that the slurred speech and unsteady gait were caused by the head injury rather than by the booze."

I must sound unhappy, because Anna moves to hug me more tightly, telling me not to worry, and before I know it we're really in an embrace. And then we look at each other, faces close, and some recognition is there, some spark of mutual emotion, a communication, two lonelinesses naked, and then we're kissing and I'm instantly hard. Anna seems glad, and I'm glad too. We're still being a bit like strangers, slightly formal in our tenderness, but soon after she's on me, and I'm inside her, where it's hot, the memory of past misunderstanding falls away, dissolves, and we know each other again, in long moments that seem neither fleeting nor unreal.

Later on, I'm drinking Jack Daniel's and Coke, out on the lovely terrace, listening to Fairchild talk, not uninterestingly, about inflation in Brazil. Other guests have arrived. I didn't really know this was going to be a party, but inasmuch as it is I don't mind.

For a little while I talked to Haziz, who had learned of my profession and wanted to know more, find out about my specialty and the like. He himself is studying engineering. I'm sure he is some rich man's son, but he really surprises me by his lack of arrogance or defensiveness. He starts talking then about technology in the movies, referring to what he calls "the resurrection of Walt Disney." I smile and agree.

I don't see Caroline. Mike is chatting with some men that I don't know. Anna's somewhere, I think, with Diane.

Brazil leads to Argentina, which leads to Latin America in general, and then Central America, ultimately Fidel. One of Fairchild's cronies says, "It's too bad, when the CIA was trying exploding cigars and all of that, they didn't manage to succeed. Even most of the Cubans would tell you that things were better under Batista; before Castro, Cuba had the highest standard of living in all of South America. There was some corruption, sure, but down there that's par for the course."

"Fidel didn't start out as a Communist," I put in. "In fact, the Communists disavowed him. They called him a gangster, they didn't want anything to do with him. He was just a nationalist rebel, up in the mountains, fighting for the usual things—like land reform. The Mafia and the United Fruit Company owned just about everything; I don't see how you can blame any Cuban for rebelling against that. We drove Fidel to the Soviets. After he took power, he came to America, and Eisenhower didn't even meet with him, he was off playing golf. Then, when he met Nixon, the first thing Nixon wanted to know was what Fidel was doing about cracking down on the Communists. It was ridiculous. Batista had gotten all kinds of weapons and money to fight Communism, so he called anyone who opposed him a Communist, and drove the actual Communists—who were mostly in the unions—toward support of Fidel only because they were persecuted, arrested and tortured and so on, whether they supported him or not. And then, of course, Fidel's suspicions of us were completely justified by the Bay of Pigs. And he knew, first-hand from Che Guevara, how we had overthrown a popularly elected government in Guatemala, in 1954, because the United Fruit Company was afraid they'd lose control—"

"You can't deny," the florid-faced man says, irritated by my discourse, "that Cuba has become completely dependent on the Soviet Union to survive. It's a much worse place to live than it once was, whoever might have owned what. The common man is worried about whether or not he can have some meat with his rice and beans."

I'm remembering my medium-radical past, when Cuba was nearly considered holy ground. It still is, I suppose, to some.

I have more reservations than I will express. Arguing is a symptom of my good mood.

"How much does the United States have to do with that?" I ask, amiably enough. If he was pro-Cuba I'd probably ask him about the official ill-treatment down there of gays. I've read a lot about Cuba. I also know the Russian and the French revolutions. I know very little about Mao or the People's Republic of China.

Fairchild leads us back to Central America, and then says that his own view is, "If you look at the history of the region, they've always been fighting. Same as in the Middle East. Continuous warfare, no matter the excuse."

He ticks off reasons: nationalism, religious or racial differences, and then more that I don't catch. Anna has returned to me. She's still happy, I can tell, but something has altered her mood.

"Oh, Diane's acting funny toward me," she admits, in a low voice. Then, realizing that I may follow this thought to Sam, she sends me a very honest look, and then sighs and gives a little shrug.

Having established myself as a leftist doctor, I'm ready to go home. The conversation has moved on, as one might have predicted, to China. The fellow who didn't like Cuba is, I note, rather more kind to the Chinese.

TWELVE

This is my third day shift in a row. I've been wearing ties, my lab coat, no scrubs. Taking refuge in the appearance of formal professionalism. Bearghost is dead; he died Monday morning. I had a talk about it with Matthew Vandermeyer later that day, in his office.

The crux of the matter is whether Bearghost acted the way he did because of alcohol or because of the head injury. I rather doubt that he would have submitted to a blood test in any case, but if we had the alcohol level we'd have an objective documentation of how much was in his system; as it is, there's only my and the nurses' subjective opinion, should the case ever in fact come to court.

Matthew's very sympathetic and supportive. There have been other deaths, in the past, resulting from errors of a much more direct nature; everything usually blows over in time. This Bearghost business is nothing special, nothing important.

Naturally I've contacted my insurance representative: there's a clause in the agreement which states that, if you don't contact them at the first hint of a malpractice suit, they can disclaim responsibility for your case.

"I don't think we've got too much to worry about," Matthew said, taking another sip of his coffee. "I checked Medical Records, and Bearghost was in twice earlier this year: once with abdominal pain and a Blood Alcohol of .337, the other time he had been in another fight—'multiple contusions and abrasions.' "

Matthew's been director of emergency services for the past six years. He's slightly chubby, with glasses and a manner that suggests he's anxious to please. He came here from Colorado, but he did his residency in Chicago, at Northwestern. He worked in Cook County, arguably the busiest ER, in terms of violent injuries, in the U.S.A. He's published lots of articles, and is in fact currently working on a book. His wife has the reputation of being kind of a bitch. They have three children, and Matthew dotes on them.

It was Matthew who hired me, and then he hired Steve Gold. Flanagan and Petibon are holdovers. Matthew would like to get rid of Petibon. The gossip about the new Chief Trauma Surgeon, Donald McIntyre, wanting to get rid of Matthew is probably an exaggeration: for, although it's sometimes now said that Matthew is ineffective, that the department runs itself and that he's uninterested and hardly ever here, nevertheless he does know how to cover his ass. By swimming in the waters of bureaucracy, he's picked up bureaucratic instincts. He's got a fairly easy, cushy job, and he wants to hold on to it for the foreseeable future. He and his wife have just bought a very expensive house. A veritable mansion. And he owns a big sailboat. He's a respectable member of the community, as solid as they come.

Now that Anna and I are sleeping together again, I feel pretty solid myself. I like the idea of the organized, unsecretive life. It's even crossed my mind again that I might want to get out of emergency medicine, go back and finish up my surgery residency. It would take two years, during which my income would be low, but then I'd be free to make a great deal of money and to control my schedule and the kinds of cases that I'd do. I don't look forward to being on call again, or to being under ego-crazed senior surgeons, but I suppose that I could stand it.

Anna would have to work full time again. And it's not unlikely that we'd have to sell the house. I don't know. I'll think about it some more before discussing it with Anna, I don't want to scare her without cause.

I wasn't impotent, during the months when we didn't have sex. I wasn't worried about that, either. Nonetheless, it's surprising, I guess, how good it feels, emotionally, to be having pleasurable sex again. I'm staying away from my private pharmacy—and at the moment this isn't hard to do. What's that old song? "Love is the Drug." Sure it is. Anna and I know each other so well, physically, that if we want to put forth some effort, we know each other's trigger points of sensation, the rhythm that works best—and if there's a potential for boredom in this knowledge, there is also the potential for great harmony.

I suppose I could spend time wondering about Anna's hypothetical orgasms with Sam; indeed, some more perverse than I might find such speculation exciting—as if Anna's vulva might be more attractive because someone else has been there. I'm not that way. I have to overcome a certain disgust, telling myself that others were there long before I even knew her, etc.

But I did ask her about him. I couldn't help it. After a session of affectionate lovemaking, as we were lying there comfortably, together in the dark, I said, in a matter-of-fact tone that became playful because of its context, "So, tell me about Sam. What was he like?"

Anna laughed. "Darrell, that was . . . well, you know. He's just young. Twenty-two. You can imagine what that means, I think."

"No. Tell me."

"All right." She thought for a moment, then: "Very passionate, not very subtle. Thinks he's wonderful. You know. Everybody does the same things. Even when he'd think he was being oh-so-sensitive, there was something crude about it, as though he was just being a certain way because he thought that was the way he ought to be. He's an actor: he performed. It was a performance for him."

"And you liked it?"

"Sure," she said, a certain brazen note indicating that she thought this might make me mad, or hurt me, but that she wasn't going to lie. "It was nice enough, at the time. It kind of, well, filled a void in my life, as you know. He was good-looking. It was okay."

"What did you talk about?"

"*He* talked, mostly, and I listened."

"What did he talk about? No, wait, I know. His plans for future glory."

"Right." Anna laughed, remembering, and I felt close to her again (having survived a little lapse). "Exactly. It seemed important to him that I *believe* in him. That was more important, maybe, than screwing me. He was only here a few days, you know. We only did it maybe three or four times."

"Where? Here?"

"No. A couple of times at Diane's . . . and once . . . out in the woods. Do you really want to know any more? It's sordid now. That's about all there was to it." She yawned, I could feel her jaw stretching on my shoulder.

"What about Christopher?"

"The preparator? Christopher Brown? Oh, he has some ideas, but I kind of let him know that I'm not interested. Besides, he lives with someone."

I could have said, "That doesn't mean anything," but didn't. Anna understood. She kissed me a few moments later, as though to seal our fates.

"I don't want a divorce," I said, and Anna understood. I let myself dissolve in the gentle warmth of her understanding, my only worry being that maybe I couldn't, wasn't capable of offering as much understanding in return.

I don't feel guilt about the Bearghost incident. I'm not possessed of supernatural powers: I couldn't see, with my naked eyes, through his skull into his bleed. There was no way I could have done other than I did.

I blame Joseph Bearghost for his own death. I resent him for it. Dislike him, or his memory, or ghost.

No doubt there's a certain amount of gossip, at least in ER and ICU. Not too much, though. It's not that interesting a case.

A white male, twenty-eight, comes in with his wife, claiming that he was "sexually assaulted" the night before. His wife has been allowed to come into the treatment room with him; and is holding his hand. He has a little mustache, and is slender and handsome, well-groomed, touchy and distraught.

"Tell me what happened to you," I say, with seeming concern.

"Okay. Well . . . yesterday, at about five-thirty, I was downtown, and these four guys came up on me and made me get into the back of this van. They blindfolded me, and tied me up, and then drove me someplace, to this house, where they shot me full of some kind of drug, and . . . raped me. In the ass," he says, casting down his eyes, as though both humiliated and enraged. "They kept me there all night. I don't know. . . . It was weird; I don't know what they shot me up with, but I was awake most of the time and yet I felt like I could hardly move."

"How do you feel now?"

"I'm sore. I feel dirty. My, uh, penis is real sore too, where those perverts were sucking on it."

The wife, who's younger than he is, or looks younger, with blond hair and an innocent use of makeup like a cheerleader, squeezes his hand to express, I suppose, her commiseration. She steps outside while I examine his rectum and genitalia. He continues his story to the effect that he escaped early this morning, walking for hours in a daze, until he finally fell asleep in a park. He slept until midafternoon, whereupon he found the presence of mind to make his way home.

I ask him if he's talked to the police. No, he hasn't, but he wants to. I tell him that we'll call them for him: they'll come down here to take his report. I leave him, and then, down in Room 6, I ask Patricia if she'll get the police. Before dialing, she asks me what I think.

"I don't believe him," I say, shrugging. "I think maybe he just got picked up in a bar or something, stayed out all night, and possibly it was his first time with a man. So he feels guilty, and confused, and the story's snowballed—so he's here. His rectum's normal; no signs of trauma, no scratches or tears."

In about ten minutes a cop named Haramoto comes in, and after he talks with the patient, David Twombly, he wants to ask me what I found. He's skeptical too. He keeps a straight face but I can tell that he's aching to laugh.

The next case I see is a dancer who probably has PID. While I'm doing the pelvic, I ask the typical question, "Do you experience any pain during sexual intercourse?"

She answers, "Only when I'm being whipped."

I'm too shocked, somehow, to say "Don't we all?" or anything else. In a moment she says it was just a joke. I think it's a good one. But I still can't give her an appropriate response. The patient-doctor relationship has been disturbed. Only when I'm down the hall do I start to laugh.

I go into the coffee room and open the refrigerator, though I have no intention of eating any of this food. The day shift nurses like to eat. Anything can serve as an excuse for a potluck at noontime. One nurse, a fat jolly one named Olivia, is a good cook—the others are really bad. Casseroles with cream of mushroom soup and frozen broccoli, crushed Fritos on the top. Horrible guacamole. Chocolate cake made from a mix. Everything bland, without anything to distinguish the dishes from the sort of food I imagine one still gets at bad church socials. Complete with paper plates. Some of these nurses, not just the fat ones, can really eat. Matthew, too, seems to enjoy these occasions; they call him in his office and he comes quickly to get his share of the "free food." Runny potato salad, overcooked, dry ham, cheese and crackers and those salads with mandarin oranges, coconut and little marshmallows: it's all the same to them, Matthew as well as the rest.

Today, at four o'clock the leftovers are in the refrigerator for the evening shift nurses, who will be delighted. I'm a snob, I know. The food is fine. And it's a nice impulse, certainly, that makes these workers want to share a meal together; some kind of solidarity is undoubtedly celebrated in this way.

"Have some of this," I say to Patricia and Judy. Patricia's always hungry. She doesn't get this kind of stuff at home, because Osborn thinks they should just eat vegetables out of their garden or from jars filled up the year before. And fish that he's caught, and game, ducks and pheasants and quail, up to and including deer. Venison. When Patricia comes to work, she's the first one who wants to send out for pizza or have the clerk drive over to Burger King or Taco Bell while she minds the desk.

An ambulance brings in a policewoman who was rear-ended by some fool while she was waiting at a red light. She doesn't seem too bad. Her pressure's okay. It's worrisome, though, that she's shivering: her main complaint is that she's cold.

The Trauma Surgeon, Gerald McKibbon, kind of a fat guy, severe-looking, authoritative in his black-framed glasses, in green scrubs, thinks that she'll be fine.

"You're probably right," I say, "but I don't like it that she's so cold. Remember the guy with the split liver? He came in like this, stable; the only thing was that he kept saying he was cold. Then, in about another twenty minutes, he went right down the tube."

"What do you suggest?"

"A scan. Or at least a belly tap."

"I don't feel like a scan is warranted," says McKibbon. "A belly tap, well, I wouldn't be opposed to that. I don't think I'd order it, but I wouldn't oppose it."

It's his case: he's rubbing that fact in. Fucking pig. I'm not going to try to change his mind, if that's what he wants. He certainly has the better chance of being right.

I go to look at a guy with back pain who came in by ambulance, allegedly unable to move. He's twenty-nine. He cries out in some kind of agony as he's moved from stretcher to bed. A little too histrionic for me to like him very much. Then I hear him say, when asked by the nurse which doctor he sees, that he goes to a chiropractor. He doesn't believe in M.D.'s, he says.

Nice touch, that. Then why is he here? He wants our drugs. Our narcotics. Yes, it seems that Demerol has helped him in the past. He volunteers this information, helpfully, just in case we can't think of what to do.

He's not getting shit from me.

They're doing a belly tap on the policewoman now; her hematocrit came back under 30, which may mean that she's bleeding internally.

I tell Anna about the case when she comes to pick me up. My Fiat's in the shop, something wrong with the carburetor. It seems like Fiats need a lot of work, though they handle wonderfully when they're on the road.

Usually I hate to be a passenger, but Anna's a sure, alert driver; while she steers and shifts I can be passive and relaxed, without suffering the urge to tell her where to turn.

We go to meet Paul and Julie at a northern Chinese restaurant downtown. I feel like having a drink. I'm still irritated at McKibbon. Anna, who also has dealt with him, agrees that he's a pig.

"Roger had another piano lesson today," she tells me, as she parks. "I like his teacher. She seems to be really patient, and I don't think that she's . . . overawing him. This was a good idea of yours. It's great to have him interested in something."

"Who knows?" I say. "Maybe he'll even learn how to play some music. Entertain us in our old age."

We go inside. Julie has a friend along with her. A dark, hot-eyed girl named Dawn. She's not really so pretty, but she looks passionate. Italian, perhaps, or Jewish. Prone as I sometimes am to instant assessments, I'd say that she's opinionated, given to sulks, with periods of being "impossible" for one reason or another. That's my printout on this Dawn.

Anna is gracious, without a trace of condescension or bemusement, and Paul's companions seem to take to her at once. Of course, Anna has met Julie before, a couple of months ago; and Anna knows and likes Paul, whose good heart and good intentions she can respect even if she sometimes wonders about the soundness of his thought.

Dawn tells us about her months in France. It seems to follow, inevitably, that she is critical of American tourists who did not speak French. Dawn thinks, also, that the run-of-the-mill French person lives with much more "style" in the execution of the simplest household rituals, such as having breakfast, than does the comparable American in the city or on the farm.

"It's just a different way of living," she says, seemingly aware that she may be oversimplifying, yet unapologetic, unwilling to qualify her remarks.

"You think they're hipper than we are?" I ask, with a reasonable semblance of good-natured curiosity.

" 'Hipper'?" she says. "I don't think I know what that means, or how you're using it."

"More culturally aware?"

The appetizers arrive. Smiling waitress. We start to eat. Julie, who has also been to France, says, "All of the Europeans have more of a sense of a tradition, and understand themselves better because of this—better than Americans understand themselves, I think. They know their history, while we forget ours immediately. That's why Americans don't have as much 'style.' "

Anna says genially, "Well, maybe it's just a different idea of what you might call style. And maybe the Europeans are so aware of their history because that's all that they have left. Their countries are too old. All they can do is watch America. That's the relationship now: we do and they watch."

"All the best new music and art comes from America," says Paul, amiably. The only one who doesn't seem especially amiable is Dawn.

"How come all the pop music comes from England, then?" she says.

"They're our colony," I say, and smile. "Also, usually they're just making our black music white. They launder it for the youth, to make it safe."

Dinner comes, a full vegetarian repast. I'd like to develop some additional remarks upon the subject of how American innocence is more jaded than European jadedness, which is innocent, and so on, but I get distracted by the food and eat.

Paul asks Anna about her exhibition, which prompts Julie to tell Dawn about some of Anna's photos that she's seen, and this leads us forward into an appreciation of Nature and famous sites and views.

"I think that when you're contemplating a landscape, in the forest or on a mountain or wherever," Paul says, "it's one of these few times you can still legitimately use the word 'beautiful' or speak of 'beauty,' without having some kind of price tag associated with your value judgment. In fashion, or in music or art, really, whenever something is called 'beautiful' that's really just a kind of cheerleading, and ultimately has to do with the subject's worth, which can be measured in dollars and cents."

"Usually," says Dawn in agreement, "I tend to cringe when someone says something is beautiful. The word—and the concept it represents—it's been so degraded, so debased . . . "

This leads us to Dawn's class in aesthetics. We are introduced (or reintroduced, as the case may be) to the principle of opposition. "Rightness of form." Dawn seems to like us all more the longer she holds forth. I give her my close attention for as long as I can; thereafter I just fake. We're drinking jasmine tea.

On the way home, I tell Anna about the guy who said he'd been abducted and raped. Anna laughs, and shakes her head. She, too, finds the scenario unlikely to have taken place.

"His wife believed him, though," I say.

"Oh, for now, maybe," says Anna. "Wait'll she thinks it over. Or wait'll he says, in a month or so, 'It happened again!' "

I like Anna's sense of humor. We talk about Paul. It's dark here on the road leading home. There could be all kinds of things going on in these woods. Witches' Sabbaths. Rapes and murders. Panthers tearing children limb from limb.

She tells me about her day. She says she'd like to take pictures in Alaska. Or New Zealand.

A strange car is in our driveway. I'm confused, and have a terrible moment when I think it's Bob and Sam.

"Shit, it's Richard," says Anna. "Damn, he's got no business here. Gretchen'll be upset."

Richard is Gretchen's former husband, the man in her life who did her harm. Who cheated on her, lied to her and generally put her down. Insulted her in public, criticized her looks and so forth. I've only had to meet him once or twice.

There aren't many lights on in the house: I hope we don't come in on Richard and Gretchen having sex on the couch. Richard is capable, at times, of talking Gretchen into anything.

He's been a woodworker, housepainter, banjo-player, guitarist, fiddler, carpenter, pottery and beeswax candle salesman—sometimes all at once. The last I heard he'd been involved with some friends of his who'd gotten busted for growing a crop of marijuana, which had been spotted from the air. However, Richard hasn't ever got himself arrested, as I understand it, though he's supposedly been questioned several times, at length, and has complained that the police are persecuting him, following him around, giving him nitpicking parking tickets and so on . . . generally "hassling" him.

A record is playing, a little more loudly than it should be, since it's after Roger's bedtime. Richard and Gretchen are in the living room. Richard stands up as we come in, smiling at us.

I'm watching Anna, to read her mood. She doesn't like Richard: she blames him for most of Gretchen's problems. At the same time, she doesn't want to interfere with Gretchen's autonomy too obviously.

"Hi," says Richard. "How was dinner?"

Gretchen is reclining on the couch. She looks like she's depressed. Or is she sulking? I can't tell if she's irked by Richard's presence or at the arrival here of Anna and myself.

"Dinner was fine," answers Anna. "Gretchen, did Roger get to sleep all right?"

"Yeah."

"Good."

"Richard needs someplace to stay," Gretchen says blandly, but I read into her affect that she doesn't want him here either. She hasn't been capable, I assume, of giving him a definitive no. He thinks he can manipulate her, as he has done in the past.

"Yeah," says Richard, "I've kind of run into a little problem."

I had to leave the place where I was staying, and I'm all out of money for the next couple of days. As soon as I get paid for this job I did, I'm going to head for Arizona. I've got some people I know there down in Tucson; I think the change will do me some good. I've had too much rain fall on my head around here, you know what I mean? I need to breathe some desert air."

"When are you getting paid for this job you did?" asks Anna.

"In a couple of days," he says, smiling again, as though she shouldn't press him but he will forgive her bad manners, as though he's long-suffering but still pure and sweet.

He's wearing a blue checked shirt, and has a brown beard and a good tan, slightly watery pale blue eyes. He isn't as tall as I am, even in his cowboy boots. The kind of guy who'd steal things out of the medicine cabinet of his best friend without a pang.

"You can't stay here," I tell him, not without some phony indication of sympathy for his plight—professional sympathy, like at the hospital. I don't mean it, in other words. And yet, in a way I do. I can see his position, see that he's only trying to further his cause, do what seems advantageous for himself, the same as anyone else.

"That's cold-blooded of you," he says, looking at me now. I feel like he doesn't really blame me: he blames Anna. "What if Gretchen wants me here? Doesn't she have any rights? Or is she, like, just your servant? Your slave? What if Gretchen wants me here? She's got her own room, doesn't she? Seems like she should be able to have a guest, you know, 'specially if he's in some kind of a spot."

"You're always in a spot," says Anna. "Always."

What's Gretchen thinking? It's funny, but it looks as though Richard's presence has possibly sexually aroused her, at least made her sexually aware of herself, conscious of her body, and she looks different, with everything, all the external details, remaining the same.

I think, meanwhile, that Richard is interested in Anna. That contributes to the tension whenever they meet.

"That's not very fair," he begins. "I know it's easy for you, with your nice house, your money and all that, to judge somebody who's kind of struggling, who's had his ups and downs—"

"Richard," I say, "come on. Why don't we go outside and talk? Let's leave the sisters alone here for a while."

I actually put my hand, with friendliness, on his shoulder. Docile, he comes with me out of doors.

The stars are out. The sky is very black, not blue, highlighting the stars. The air feels pleasant, not humid, and smells like the dark lawn.

"I realize," says Richard, "that I can't stay here. Anna doesn't want me. She thinks I fucked up Gretchen's head. You know?"

"You're right. That's what she thinks."

He's quiet. He takes the time to light a cigarette, as we walk out past the pool. "Yeah, well, it's true that I went out on her . . . but she had most of her problems way before I ever hit the scene. Really. I did the best I could, you know? Shit."

"Look, Richard," I say, "the way I understand it, you don't have anyplace to stay for a couple of days. And you don't have any money, either, right? That goes along with it, I suppose. In a few days you're getting paid, and then you plan to go to Tucson. That about sums it up, doesn't it?"

"You left out that I can't stay here."

"Right. You can't stay here."

"So you're telling me that I'm an asshole, aren't you, Doc?"

"No, I don't know you well enough to tell you that. I'm telling you something else. Here, look."

I take out my wallet. Somewhat surprisingly, perhaps, Richard seems embarrassed. I try not to affect any superiority, whether moral or social, and I sense that he knows I'm not trying to belittle or threaten him at this point.

"Do you want to say anything to Gretchen?" I ask, after I've given him several twenty-dollar bills.

"No," he says, opening the door to his car. "I think I'll just go."

In bed then, Anna tells me that we should get a watchdog. "A golden retriever," she says. "I've always liked those dogs."

THIRTEEN

Someone told me once that if the plane takes off without crashing, you as passenger have survived the major danger; that landings, even under adverse conditions, have nowhere near the same degree of risk. People survive emergency landings, even without landing gear, but if the plane has trouble during takeoff everyone on board has had it, the aircraft isn't yet under sufficient control for any backup maneuvers or contingency plans to be executed.

Still, it's the descent which tends to make me nervous. I don't like that feeling of deceleration, of floating, seemingly without power, as one approaches the waiting target airfield.

I can be happy in an airplane, for example, if I'm hungry and the food strikes me as good, which has happened, or a couple of times watching a movie, losing track of time. And sometimes, the initial thrust of the takeoff gives me kind of a thrill. It's nice to see that we, as humans, can make things that work. Big steel birds.

I wanted to bring something with me to read, something that would teach me something important, and I had an idea as to what general area I was interested in, but I couldn't find what I wanted. Maybe I'm too out of touch, and I don't know how to penetrate the intelligentsia any more (if I ever did); or maybe what I'm looking for is in fact too ambitious and broad.

What I'd like to see is a comprehensive survey of worldwide currents, searching for the interrelationship of developments of ideas in seemingly unconnected fields. What precipitates what, in other words. A move to the political right, for instance, results in certain changes in the kinds of movies that are made, or are popular. Do movies then, reciprocally, lay the groundwork for a further shift in attitudes and public will?

There are currents in politics, in philosophy, in medicine, religion, music, foods we eat, hairstyles and clothing, sexual conduct, colors, body shape, architecture, big families or small, pro- or anti-intellectualism, methods of intoxication, and on and on. Every facet of our life and thought, it seems, is subject to the tides of fashion. The idea that one can think for oneself under such conditions is, then, a palpable fallacy.

The control is elsewhere: I only wonder if anyone understands the origins of this control. One can look at grossly self-conscious countries and eras—Great Britain in the 1890s, Germany in the 1930s, France in the 1790s, the U.S.A. in the 1920s and 1960s—and, in looking at these "crises," what really does one see? A certain time, a certain place, when for a certain period a large variety of different forces were all somehow aligned.

But movement was continuous; things never stayed the same. Or perhaps, in China during some notable dynasties, or in ancient Egypt, they did. Or, at least, the attempt to keep everything the same, frozen in perfect harmony, was made. Usually, I believe, this is supposed to lead to what we call "decadence." Which can also, paradoxically, come about through too great an openness to change. An addiction to novelty. Everyone seems agreed that this can only, ultimately, lead the society astray.

Nothing stays the same. I hate to think that I am but one of many insects in a giant hive, yet this is true. What disparate elements lead to my selection of this or that philosophy, food-stuff or partner in life? Sometimes men like skinny, boyish-figured women; then big breasts make a comeback, and so forth. Long hair, short hair, generous or frugal makeup: all these variables, at any given time, combine to create the par-agon of what is, for each man, the attractive woman. Likewise, different types of men may be, in women's eyes, in or out of the current vogue. What was unthinkable yesterday may today be all the rage. Examples could be rattled off at length.

I don't know what ideal I might be after. For the most part, like everyone else, I enjoy the changes wrought by fashion. And certainly I have no wish to be at odds with the fashionable world in the sense of being an outcast, a pariah, or a crank.

But clothes and such are nothing. Obviously. In these and like matters, obeying the prevailing trend is a minor thing. What's more worrisome is what shapes one's thought, one's ideas, emotions, personality, regardless of or quite separate from one's deliberate will. This is what's important. And it's here that the power of the prevailing currents is most invisible and unannounced. It's the same problem again and again: one has no perspective; one can never properly contextualize things in their time. Even years later, great trends can only be gropingly described, and by then it is all *history,* and thus only indirectly relevant, if that, to what is transpiring at this present moment that is always lost.

The plane lands in Chicago. Then it lands in New York. La Guardia. I catch a taxi into Manhattan; I'm tired, but I enjoy the drive. I give the black, restless cabdriver a bigger tip than I need to, and go into the midtown hotel, where everyone at the conference gets a special rate.

I like New York. I like having all these people around.

It's not safe here, of course. My friend Stuart, whom I haven't seen in a few years, but whom I plan to see, got mugged pretty badly late last winter. He told me all about it on the phone. They broke his arm. Three sixteen-year-olds, Puerto Ricans. In broad daylight.

I take a shower and then get dressed again and go down the elevator and outside. Walking down Eighth Avenue, which is incredibly alive, cheers me up. Speaking of fashions—they're all here. Also black guys playing three-card monte; displays of watches; hucksters for sex shops and nude dancing (Girls! Girls! Girls!). Fruit and vegetable stands, flies, garbage, sunlight, cops crossing against the light. The sensory input somehow seems just what I need. I go on.

I buy a soda, because I'm thirsty and it's hot; drink half and then, sated, put the can into another of the many overflowing trash cans I see along the way. I walk all the way down to Washington Square.

Coming back, on Twenty-third Street a black woman and a blond white woman are having a fight. The black woman knocks the white woman down, flat on her back on the sidewalk. She yells at her fallen victim, calling her a no-good bitch.

The spectacle pleases me. I leave it behind. I'm hungry and I go into a Thai restaurant and eat. The coconut milk curry is very hot and I need a Coke. I like eating alone. It's not that I don't miss Anna. But being on my own again is different, and I enjoy it.

FOURTEEN

At the completion of this program, the participant supposedly will be able to:

- Demonstrate the proper management of behavioral emergencies
- Identify the threat to life posed by various neurologic disorders
- Perform a neurologic exam
- Explain the priorities in treating the poisoned patient
- Perform a rape exam

- Demonstrate the proper management of neonate and mother
- Identify factors associated with physician stress
- Discuss the key elements in establishing effective patient/physician interaction
- Demonstrate the proper management of OB/GYN emergencies

Will I actually learn anything here? Maybe. Some of the material pertaining to poisons may be new—though, in any case, we always look everything up in our (constantly updated) toxicology book. The seminars on physician stress and behavioral emergencies (subheaded "Dealing with the Hostile Patient," etc.) are unlikely to be terribly helpful or new.

Some of the neurology might be interesting. That's a strange, wide-open field. They know so little, really, about so many neurologic disorders. They don't know what causes them, and the treatment too is likely to be vaguely defined. It's an area of medicine in which one can still expect dramatic breakthroughs, "miracle" cures.

"I hope we get to see some good slides," says a guy with glasses, a southern accent, a smile like he means blood and guts. I murmur something, and am struck by how much this feels like medical school again. I can't help sizing everyone up, wondering how much they know, if they know more than I do, where they went to school. I shouldn't think like this, competitively. But I can't help it, even if I fight it down I'm just faking, or maybe competing, in some way, on a higher plane. Because to be cool, you must not show your teeth. In fact, the competition may even be in the matter of who shows the least evidence of having teeth at all, while still managing to bite off your leg.

I settle into my typical, semi-bored-seeming-attentive mode, waiting to see how alert I'll need to be. At least for the moment, since it's the first day, I'm listening very hard to what is said.

After the opening remarks, we move into "Dealing with the Hostile Patient." Speak in a calm, nonthreatening manner, and all of that.

I look at the material we've been handed out, and doodle a bit as though I might be taking notes, thinking about seeing my old friend Stuart tonight for dinner. I don't know if I'm really looking forward to seeing him again or not. We've grown apart.

Typically, there's someone literal-minded, who asks some dumb questions, unembarrassed, during the Q & A. He must not have worked in a big city ER.

While he talks, or is talked to, I begin watching with more interest the female doctors in the group. There are four, two of whom are somewhat attractive. One in particular, although not really stunning, catches my eye. She looks as bored with the current exchange as I am: I give her an expression that just may be a smirk. I'll have to read her name tag.

At lunch break, I'm close enough to see that this woman's name is Geller; however, she's engaged in conversation already with a couple of people, and I decide not to lunch with the others, on the prepaid plan in the hotel. Instead, I'll go out someplace. Even if just to walk around.

As long as I'm in New York, I want to feel like it. I sweat in the street with everyone else. All these faces, all these postures and bodies, affects and expressions. It strikes me suddenly, in a kind of euphoria, that all these people are more like me in their basic desires and needs than they are different. And I am like them. We're all so vulnerable. Life is so short, and our bodies and psyches are so fragile, at the mercy of so many thousands, even millions, of random destructive elements.

I'm mesmerized by the mutual animality we share. Animals in clothes, animals seeking animal warmth in whatever design. The hookers, black guys, hustlers, bums—all, however flawed, are so *alive*.

And here, in this most artificial yet weathered of cities, humankind's insouciance and will to master all reality, in spite of unforeseen side effects or plans gone awry, ending up quite differently than envisioned—I feel like I'm a part of this history, that these sidewalks and streets connect with my bones, perhaps as an American, perhaps as a simple "citizen of the world." In this, the most historical of all our cities, the past is the more fleeting and ignored. We go on, like some kind of crazed bacteria, individually pursuing what we dream we want and need.

All these creatures. What does one more or less matter, what difference does it make? If I'm here, and then I'm gone, everything continues as before. All I can do is do my job, perform my part, and find some logic in the form revealed thereof.

"How you doin', man?" says a tall black guy in a baseball cap and a blue U.S.A T-shirt, drawn in, evidently, by my expression.

"All right," I say, giving him a smile. That's all he wants. I go into a deli and get a sandwich, standing in line. Then I sentimentally eat my lunch out on the street.

The afternoon session deals with toxicology and overdoses. If you give too much Narcan to a heroin addict, he may go into withdrawal. I've never seen that happen, though I have had experience with OD's who, aroused by Narcan from their comas, have pulled out their I.V.'s and started out of the hospital, cursing us all, afraid we're going to get them busted or something, not exactly grateful for our saving their lives. The half-life of Narcan is only about sixty minutes, so the person could conceivably go back out on the street and have the heroin's effects come back, and then collapse again, as the heroin lasts four hours or more.

Nobody likes junkies—nobody who's ever tried to help them or deal with them. The junkie chemistry creates something that is not quite human, not quite up to the standards we are used to. If you save their lives, they will try to rob you in return.

I meet Stuart in a bar at seven. He has black hair and a mustache, and is a couple of inches shorter than me; what used to be an ironic, sometimes almost devilish turn to his lips and gleam in his eyes has become, over the years, a look of sadness and resignation. His smile has changed, too—it's not as aggressive, it's lost some of its bite.

A number of his enterprises have gone bad. Including both of his marriages. I knew his first wife, Hallie—this was in the time when Stuart and I were still best friends. His second wife, Mary, I met only once, when I was here in the city about three years ago. I don't know any of the details of their recent breakup, or even exactly what Stuart's been doing for a living in the recent past.

We have a drink, and he tells me that he's now in marketing for a firm called IMA.

"I'm making good money," he says, shrugging. "Business is good. It's kind of a grind, but nothing like when I was in sales. You know, I loaned Mary some money, so she could finish school. Shit, she'll never pay me back: I knew that when I gave it to her. But now Hallie's hitting me up for Steven to get braces—that woman hates me, Darrell, and she's training my kid to hate me too."

Stuart used to cheat on Hallie, as I knew at the time, though they went on together, with separations and reconciliations, for years. I liked her; I thought it was unfortunate they couldn't work things out. I suppose I think that it was Stuart's fault—his restlessness, his insatiability, his almost willed "despair." It used to be funny, how he would say, at the most absurd moments, "despair." It was also true that he made of his despair a bulwark against having sympathy for other people's problems. His father committed suicide, shooting himself, when Stuart was thirteen; and Stuart sometimes implied that he was doomed to repeat this act himself.

He dropped out of college (we became friends in high school), got a job selling oxygen products, flourished, then got into a personality conflict with his boss, quit, got a position in data processing at a low-skilled level, then moved up when he knew enough to get into sales . . . and so forth. Ups and downs. Things always seemed to go sour. Then he would bounce back.

It's taken its toll on him, I think, looking at him now. He's had two fast drinks while I haven't yet finished my first. But that in itself might not be such a telling sign. More to the point is his voice, which no longer seems eager to shock or amaze, to seize liveliness by its expressed disdain for the very stuff of life.

"How's Anna?" he asks, as if thinking he's talked enough of his business to me. Actually, I wasn't bored. Though I do feel a new detachment toward him, a distance that I sense he reciprocates. We're not quite on the same wavelength as before.

"Anna's fine," I say, feeling as I do so that I'm dissembling in the matter. "She's doing well with her photography; and, although we've had our troubles now and then, basically I guess we're a pretty solid couple. She'll be with me in Connecticut next week, with Roger, to see my folks."

"Well, that'll be nice," says Stuart, with a familiar smile that means it probably won't be as nice as all that. I show my

agreement—he knows very well how I feel about my parents—
and then he asks after my son.

"He's taking piano lessons now, but otherwise he's not interested in much. He plays with the usual space toys; maybe
too much, in fact, all by himself. I don't think it's so good for
him to be an only child, but ever since Anna miscarried, we
haven't thought much about trying it again. We probably will,
I suppose, because Anna thinks the same way. But it just hasn't
come up much for a while. Actually . . . well, there was a
period of a couple of months in which we just weren't, ah,
sleeping together at all. It was my fault. And it isn't as though
Anna has gotten fat, or drinks, or anything like that."

"Were you taking the temperature of some of the other
nurses at the hospital, then?"

"No. Maybe I should have been. I don't know. I was full
of 'despair.' "

"Oh yeah, Darrell, I know all about that little condition,"
says Stuart, whom the word seems to have cheered up. "What,
you got tired of the emergency room? Or just of life?"

"Or myself."

"Or yourself," he says. "I can relate to that. So can my ex-
wives. They got sick of me too—though I think I was the
leader here: I got sick of Stuart first. When they each still
thought he was a champion, I knew—and even told them—
that it wasn't true, that I was not a wonderful man."

We laugh, and he asks me to tell him more. I feel more
like we are old friends, picking up a conversation we left off.

Leaving the bar, we get a cab and go to a restaurant, to eat
what I rarely have anymore—that is, a steak. But first another
drink, as I fall into the hazard of telling ER stories. I don't
want to, but I do. I'm encouraged to do so by Stuart's amusement. Oh, they're entertaining enough little anecdotes, but
it's a weakness of sorts to relate them more than occasionally

(or, perhaps, on demand). And I forget so much. One incident blends into another, and another.

And I don't want to be a bore. I don't think I am; I don't think I talk about what goes on in ER that much, but I'm aware of the danger, the danger of becoming interested in nothing but one's little world, where one has control.

I put every kind of steak sauce on my steak. I'm used to so many spices—Anna likes things hot. She doesn't like Stuart, whose attitude toward women is rather suspect in her eyes. He in turn likes her, probably mostly because of the way she looks. And because she's mine. Or I'm hers. However that works anymore.

Stuart and I are somewhat drunk. He tells me about the last days of his second marriage, about how crazy Mary became.

"She was always really susceptible to anything about spirits, or the Devil, or God, but after her sister got cancer Mary started thinking that she was going to get it too, and worrying, and thinking she had it already, going to all these doctors who'd keep telling her she was okay. Then she decided she needed some help from above. I remember, after I got mugged, you know, when I came home from the hospital I saw that Mary had put salt crosses in all the rooms of our apartment. To protect us, she said."

"Sounds reasonable," I say.

"Yeah, sure, salt crosses, right—but then she started going to séances. I was still whacked-out on pain pills, and one evening I was asleep in front of the TV when I heard these weird noises—like a baby crying, and then someone talking in a little tiny voice like a four-year-old—they were having a séance right in the dining room, and Mary was in this trance. Well, you know, her cooking got real bad, and she started getting suspicious of me, and then I started wondering about what she was putting in the food. And I felt guilty, too, as you can imagine."

"Why'd you feel guilty?"

"Well, Darrell, I thought, Did I do this to her? Did I drive this woman crazy?"

He's being funny, and yet he's very earnest somehow.

"Did you get her to a shrink?"

"Her sister did, finally. He put her on some tranquilizers and told her she should go back to school. That was a good idea, and she got into it, but by this time she just wouldn't fuck me anymore. I don't know; I think I messed everything up when one night we came home from a party, did some more coke, smoked some more reefer, and I tied her up and fucked her in the ass. She had an old boyfriend named Kurt, who used to tie her up all the time, and I always wanted to do it." Stuart shrugs. "Then her sister got cancer of the uterus, and I got the shit beat out of me by some PR's. Also, I was doing this secretary, Linda, and I think Mary knew something about that. She never said anything, but I think she knew."

This seems to be a significant point, but there's a fatalism in Stuart's manner which suggests that one significant point equals another, and it all ends up the same. I see a disturbing pattern in there, somewhere, despite my drunken, blissful state, and I recognize the truth of Anna's feeling. Stuart does not like women.

I don't think I'm like that. For one thing, I don't think I differentiate the patients that I see by their sex, although there may be some problems peculiar to each. But a head laceration is a head laceration, asthma is asthma, a seizure disorder is a seizure disorder. Everyone suffers the same. Men are by no means more stoic, nor do women shy away from the sight of gory wounds. It's all flesh, all human, all animal.

I just don't think I hate women the way Stuart does. I have

never wanted to fuck Anna in the ass; I think such an act has too many unpleasant resonances of power relations, of master-slave, dominant-submissive, rapist-victim, and so on. It's "politically incorrect," in the broadest definition of politics; which is, to me, the relations between people, simultaneously between individuals and en masse.

Maybe I'm too self-righteous. Maybe I'm more like Stuart than I think: I know I have an affinity with him, that to a certain extent we instinctively understand each other. I can't say. Does he sense my pulling back? Yes, I'm sure of it.

After a wild, bouncing cab ride, I get out in front of the hotel. It's late. I'm overloaded with confidences and jumbled thought. I watch the television, though, instead of going to sleep. I wonder if I let Stuart down.

FIFTEEN

Talking with some of the others about their ER's across the land. Questions come up: "Do you have trouble getting plastic surgeons at night?"; "Do you ship head injuries out?"; "Do you have CAT scan?"; "How much trauma do you see?"

I end up talking to the woman I had noticed. She's friendly. Her name is Lindsey Geller. She's originally from Baltimore, went to college in Boston and med school in San Francisco, did a residency in internal medicine there, and now works at an Emergency Room in rural Texas.

"What's that like?" I ask. "Do you see a lot of cowboys, a lot of drunks?"

"MVA's," she says. "But it's not really very busy. Most of the time I can just read, or work on this book I've been doing with a friend of mine—a book on nutrition, dealing with regional and ethnic recipes from America and around the world."

She has dark brown hair, maybe kind of a big ass, probably Jewish, an intelligent, non-arrogant smile. Olive skin. She asks me if I like New York.

"Oh yes. I feel like I learn a lot every time I come here. I'm happy enough living in Seattle, though, at the moment. But I think I need to come here every so often, just to keep in touch with . . . the feeling I get here."

"Have you been to any of the museums? That's always a big part of New York for me."

"Not yet. I want to go to the Museum of Modern Art; in fact I was thinking about going tomorrow, since the schedule says we have a two-and-a-half-hour break for lunch."

"That's right, we do."

"Do you want to go with me? Or have you already seen it?"

"No, I haven't. Sure, why don't we do that? It'll be fun. We can get lunch somewhere nearby, on the way."

She reminds me of a resident I used to know, named Elizabeth Something—Beth—who also gave the impression of being fairly confident about everything except her physical attractiveness. Lindsey is more confident than Beth was. Still, I can see it in her eyes, even if she's well adjusted and relaxed. That vulnerability, based on having been disappointed or jilted in the past, shows through all her poise. Which makes me like her, and wish her well.

I don't think I'm going to try and have a quick affair, though I sense the opportunity is there. Just that fast. There are signals one decodes, at a preconscious level, easily enough. Especially when one is detached.

A part of me feels like I should, since Anna allowed her loins to be invaded by Sam, but I'm sure that's a petty impulse, and not fair to Lindsey either, even if she is as available to me as I suspect.

We watch a film on Disaster Management. We are told about Physician Stress and Patient/Physician Interaction.

I go out to dinner by myself, at Raga, an expensive Indian restaurant, where I have tandoori chicken. It's kind of funny to be here alone. I hear someone at the next table talking to another man who is evidently his agent, saying that he's never played in Italy before, but he's heard that it's nice. I don't recognize him; I have no idea what he does.

At nine-thirty I call Anna, but she's not there. I speak to Gretchen and Roger instead. I have nothing to say, they seem unreal, yet we talk for ten minutes or so. They seem so far away. Roger sounds so small and young. He's so vulnerable it depresses me. I don't know what to do for him. He's so wary of everything. I can't imagine what he's going to be like as a man. It confuses me.

Maybe he'll be a musician, I think, in simplistic parental dramatization; maybe he'll be a musician and be famous and blossom into someone who'll interest and delight me, so that Anna and I will sit out on our patio and discuss his innate worth, congratulating ourselves while his records shake the walls and echo through the woods.

Sometimes I speculate on the idea of adopting some kids, in case Anna can't have any more, both so as to impress my personality (and give Anna a chance to impress hers) on a few more creatures before we quit this earth, and to give us an opportunity to feel virtuous, unselfish and serene and grave. It would give us something to do.

It might be nice to have a black son, a Vietnamese daughter, an Indian, another white, all sitting together at dinner, having to eat whatever we gave them to eat. Stealing money from my wallet, getting loaded and falling into the swimming pool, running away and getting arrested, going to prison for Grand Theft Auto, getting pregnant and having an abortion, screaming back at Anna or me and then collapsing in helpless, stormy tears at the cruelty of it all.

After spending the next morning on Rape Exam and Pre-hospital Care, Lindsey Geller and I escape from the others and go to the Museum of Modern Art. It's terribly humid outside, close to one hundred degrees, but I feel all right. We're both perspiring on the busy, honking street. I'm more attracted to her today: she wears sandals, bare legs, and a nice print summer dress.

She tells me that, at the end of the week, she's taking a plane from here to the Bahamas, where she'll meet a friend.

"Oh, you're lucky," I say. "I'm crazy about the Caribbean. We might go there again this winter—I'd like to get back to Antigua for a couple of weeks, just to vegetate. It's a different feeling, really, don't you think, to have the weather and the scenery be such a big positive every day? Maybe it gets boring after a while, if you live there, but I think I could be pretty serene as a hotel-keeper or having a restaurant, just watching the days go by."

"Why don't you get a job down there? It wouldn't pay as much, but you see in the journals that they need people here and there once in a while."

"And do my own X rays, run my own labs? No. I'm too spoiled. I don't like little hospitals."

She accepts this. I'm not very curious about her. We look at some Picassos, and then at some Jackson Pollocks, which I like rather better. I don't know why. Usually I'm conservative, and tend to rely on the appreciation of palpable skill—but some of these Pollocks (however he wielded his paint) speak to me, make me reflective, seeming to illustrate some process of Nature—illustrating the unillustratable, the "mess of thought," pattern and emotion, color and weight. Lindsey and I spend a long time looking at them. I regret that she's not Anna: if she were Anna I'd be interested in knowing what Anna thought, and in communicating to Anna some of what I feel. She would want to know, I'm sure. Maybe we can come here sometime next week.

Fifteen minutes later, as I'm coming back from abstraction to the here and now, wondering at my presence at this particular time with this particular person in this particular place, Lindsey asks me in a kind of low, sincere tone of voice to tell her about my wife.

She is especially interested, it develops, in the fact that Anna is a nurse; she also wants, for some reason, a close physical description. I tell her about Anna's photography.

Then Lindsey says, "My divorce just went through about a month ago, though we hadn't lived together for almost a year. He's a radiologist. Doesn't like people, so he didn't want to have to deal with patients." She pauses, then adds: "Terminally stuck on himself. Jogs, lifts weights a little, always worried about his tan. Smart, but read too much Nietzsche or something, and thinks it applies to his life. He likes to go mountain climbing, you know, get up there and feel like he's Master of All Creation."

"The *Übermensch*," I say, and she seems surprised for a second that I know the word; then she smiles, releases some of her bitterness, and says, "That's right. That's his vision."

I see a Franz Kline that I like very much. We go back to the hotel for the afternoon, making plans to have dinner tonight, since we've hit it off and neither of us has other plans.

I'm not thinking far in advance. I just want to enjoy dinner, and we do, going to a Greek restaurant, having kalamari and drinking retsina, all of which pleases us both a good deal. Comfortably, we talk about ER medicine, shaking our heads at all the ignorance-related disorders and concocted illnesses, commiserating, comparing horrible cases, getting high on the retsina, and it's after ten o'clock when we get back to the hotel. By this time I feel that we understand each other very well. The warm light in her eyes matches mine.

I accompany her to her room, on the fifteenth floor (I am on the sixteenth), and ask her if I may come in.

In a moment, I ask Lindsey if it's all right if I lie down on the bed. Then I say, "Why don't you lie down here with me?"

"Okay," she says. "Only—and I shouldn't ask this—but what about your wife?"

"Oh, it's all right: we have an open marriage. Really. It was her idea. Now come here."

Anna seems like a bitch to me now, and I experience a curious desire to hurt her, if only *in absentia*. Lindsey is much more understanding. I will myself to respond to her body against mine. It's easy. She melts, and I'm seized by the passion of vengeance, which translates into a brand of lust.

The next day, as I'm walking down Eighth Avenue, I am accosted by a skinny young girl, sixteen or seventeen, who asks me if I want a date. "Do you want to go someplace and party?" she asks me, not very hopefully, shyly, even with some fear. For a whore she's not dressed very sexily, nor is she very pretty—she looks pale and thin and stoned. A junkie this young?

"No thank you," I say automatically, politely, and then feel badly that I did not give her any money. She looked like she needed it. Just think, she's somebody's daughter.

I continue on, ruminating on all the pain and unhappiness

in the world, wondering at it, dodging the crowd. When the light changes, turns green, every car except the first begins honking its horn. Other hookers I see are more what you'd expect—dead souls. I should have given that poor girl twenty dollars and something to eat. I could go back to look for her—but I don't think I will, and I don't.

SIXTEEN

The food is bad. It doesn't seem like it always used to be this way, that my mother would overcook everything, depending only on salt and pepper or maybe a bay leaf, in lieu of more exotic spices—it seems like, when I was young, the food used to taste pretty good. Maybe I was just very hungry, but I always thought of my mother, back then, as being a good cook. I can't believe that the change is exclusively in me, that my taste buds have become so jaded that I can no longer appreciate plain food properly cooked. No, I think the problem is my mother's; her cooking has gone downhill.

Roast beef: it's dry and gray. The mashed potatoes and gravy would be okay, but the gravy's too salty. That doesn't stop my father from automatically sprinkling salt all over everything on his plate. Forget about high blood pressure, all of that. I'm not going to say anything; there's nothing he likes better than being nagged. No approach is more sure to make him stick to a course of action, whatever it might be. My mother knows all about that.

Roy and Joyce. Roy, my father, is shorter than either of his sons, but he hasn't put on much belly—in fact, for a man in his sixties, he seems rather admirably fit. He doesn't look like me. My brother Jack and my sister Eileen resemble him, but my face comes from my mother's side. I look like my mother's long-dead older brother, Edgar. I've seen a photograph, and the only thing that's really different is the eyes. His are dreamy, blurry, otherworldly in a way that mine are not.

Roy looks like a drinker, though he does have one of those faces with a lot of "character": women have found him attractive, the more so because of his flip, unself-conscious manner. Every waitress is "honey" or "babe" to him (Jack has inherited this too). He's at ease with them, and with other working men—what he's not at ease with, and never has been, are those in positions of authority or putative superiority over him (like policemen, or doctors, or lawyers). That's when his charm starts to go false. He'll still talk, may even talk more than usual, but his air of decision deserts him.

I remember once when I was thirteen, and my father took Jack and me out to eat in a Chinese restaurant where he knew one of the waitresses (not Chinese; a tall, tough blond, kind of pleasant, with a bit of a horse face—Roy may have been to bed with her, I don't know), Jack and I each tasted Manhattans and got a little high, then on the way home my father got us into a wreck. More or less a fender-bender, but ambulances came (my brother had a deep cut that needed stitches)—

and I'll never forget how Roy acted, trying to gain favor with the police. The policeman was cool and detached, above it all, while my father's attempts at humor and camaraderie just seemed graceless and drunk. And yet, somehow, he did not get arrested for drunken driving—so perhaps his efforts worked much better than I knew.

His hair is gray now, finally, and he has succumbed, in recent years, to the need for both glasses and a hearing aid. He resisted the hearing aid for a long time; conversations with him were, for several years, tedious affairs rife with repetition and the suspicion that he could hear whenever he cared to, that the infirmity was half-faked.

My mother, Joyce, does most of the talking tonight, chattering about this and that. Everything mentioned brings to mind some article she's read or some program she's seen, but she can never quite get all her data straight. I think she was fuzzy-headed, to a lesser degree, even when I was young. She would lose things, and insist on our making a thorough search for them, while she wondered more and more dramatically and perplexedly how this item could be missing, who could have taken it, until it would eventually turn up in some ordinary place where it had been originally overlooked. It was a maddening habit, which served no useful purpose and which several times aroused ugly feelings—normally mild-mannered, a pushover, Joyce could come out with some wild accusations at times, and in such a manner that it was not easy to forgive her, later, when she was sorry.

She has changed a great deal in the last twenty years, thickening and losing shape, her face losing definition, hair going thin and white. She's old now, and more like a child, in her assumed innocence, than like an adult. She chatters inanely, she can't follow anything: if you attempt to talk with her adult to adult you'll find that she's operating from a premise that has left out some elementary fact.

It will come as a big surprise to her, say, that Richard Nixon was a Republican and not a Democrat, or that Robert Kennedy was shot and didn't drown. It's almost like someone trying to imitate one of those clichéd bubbleheaded blondes. I dislike it; my father seems to secretly enjoy it. He likes to correct her, fulminating as he does so: it's like some infantile game that they're playing just for show, symbolizing something else. It isn't simply that Joyce plays the child, or clown, and Roy plays the parent; it's also, somehow, often the other way around. She feels like she's wise in her "innocence," her "gentle ignorance," while he becomes the know-it-all son, who can tell you the capital of Denmark but remains eternally, essentially, unwise—yet is not to be contradicted no matter how wrong he may be.

I watch Anna as she eats. She's doing all right, eating enough mashed potatoes and gravy to be polite. Of course my mother tries to press extra helpings on all of us—to the point where I wonder whether Roger may be in danger of eating himself sick.

It's a strain on me to be here, but it's much worse having Anna here, to see my family and judge them, or refrain from judging them: I don't like feeling this vulnerable and defensive, it's a kind of nakedness that I can barely stand.

At least the little dog isn't yipping right at the moment. During my childhood we had dogs, several dogs, but they were reasonably big dogs, beagles up through Labs, real dogs—not like this puny, overbred little white poodle. I like cats, it's not that I don't like effeminate animals, but this dog, Fritzie, is something else. I suppose it's the way they treat it, talking baby-talk and so on, because they haven't any more real children in the house.

When it's time to go to bed, and Roger is asleep, the strange bed opened up, I'm so relieved when Anna just says, in a low voice, "God, they're pretty bad, aren't they?"

Smiling, almost laughing, I embrace her, grateful that she hasn't offered up some banality that neither of us feels. She's capable of perverse reactions at times, I suppose I am too . . . but tonight she's after solidarity, she's not in the mood to say, "Oh, they're okay," or "They're not so boring as all that." In return, I won't ask if she's sorry we agreed to do this.

I was unreasonably annoyed earlier when I saw that Anna had brought along our tennis rackets. I didn't say anything, but Anna could tell. Naturally.

In bed, she tells me more about the trip, and I tell her about New York. I leave out the Lindsey Geller business—I'll tell her tomorrow sometime. I think she can sense that I have a secret, but she's too tired to dig. Or else she doesn't feel comfortable, feeling that now I may have a right to secrets, or think I do, bigger secrets than before.

We make love, and I'm asking her questions, silently, with little pauses or changes of momentum, wondering about her, trying to get her to tell me something, I don't know what— but it's nice, the message she's giving me is highly affectionate and warm. I can't help but briefly compare this with what I did with Lindsey Geller: this, while without the strangeness of a new body's responses, is familiar and rich. There's something reminiscent of nocturnal masturbation, that discovery and hidden joy, in being inside Anna's vagina under my parents' roof, and the whole fact of sex seems fresh and terribly interesting, something I'm so curious about, a mystery I'm finally able to explore.

Maybe it's false, I think, even as I'm seemingly lost in the truth. I *was* lost; now I'm not, not quite. Do I trust Anna?

How can I? How close are we? All these questions pang me, agonizingly, even as I'm about to very pleasurably come.

I find her mouth with mine, kiss her, connect tongues, an earnest look on my brow in the dark. It's just the two of us, I want to say. I wonder if she knows; I try to guess. Do we really *need* each other to continue our lives?

I tell myself that we're okay, and say to her, "We're not going to be like them, are we?" as we lie together, no longer moving, in the humid night.

Understandably, I dream that I'm a child again, maybe eight years old, thinking about playing with my friend Kenny. In the backyard, in the dirt, we built a network of canals, lookout towers and battlements, red and blue and yellow plastic men, to be buried and drowned (they would float) when we turned on the hose and slowly filled up the canals. It was war. It was always war. Sometimes we shot rubber bands (indoors), threw dirt clods, or, on rare occasions, burned them up with gasoline (melting their limbs), or blew them into the air with firecrackers we weren't supposed to have.

Lost in intricate, methodical scenarios, we'd play for hours, working, digging, setting something up. Whole, imaginary, funny worlds, seen in simple terms, interrupted by our mothers calling us in for dinner or something, so that every time we returned to the play it was different, altered by a TV show seen or just the passage of outwardly unreflective time.

At eight-thirty, breakfast is heavy Bisquik pancakes and syrup and link sausage and fried eggs, sunny-side up, the yolks still runny and bright orangy yellow, bleeding slowly into the clear sweet syrup on pale blue plates. It tastes okay to me. Even the coffee, standard grocery store coffee on sale, tastes all right.

Joyce is happy, humming a song to herself as she bustles about. Roy reads the paper, is cheerful enough in a gruff way, and asks Roger if he's sure he can eat all those pancakes on his plate.

Anna gives me a private smile, her eyes sending me intelligence that, in this case, I can easily decode. I think both of us are still a bit out of focus from the good fucking last night.

"If the Yankees get hot, get some pitching, I think they can still make a run," says my father, staring at the folded, unfolded newspaper. I think this remark is directed toward me; I can't remember if the Yankees are in second or fifth.

After I venture something appropriate, he gets more specific, complaining about a certain pitcher, left-handed, whom he thinks they ought to have traded "a long time ago." He muses then about the infield, and surprises me by saying, "You know, if Jack would've kept on playing, I can't help thinking he would've been some kind of player. He was a real athlete, a natural—it's too bad he didn't stick with it."

I can't believe this.

"*I* was the one who was the baseball player, Dad. Jack couldn't hit a curveball, and he certainly couldn't pitch. I was the one with the arm."

"Yeah, well, it seems to me I remember you getting banged around pretty good one Saturday out at Oak Park. How many runs they tag you for, anyway? Eight? Ten?"

"I had to pitch Saturday at noon after I threw a shutout Thursday night, because Dick Frazier got thrown in the Juvenile Home for some trouble with his folks. We still won, eight to seven, and three of those runs came when Mickey Daley dropped a pop fly with the bases loaded and two out."

"Seems like I can recall some big lug knocking one out of the park, just about the longest ball I've ever seen anyone hit . . . might have lost the ball in Yankee Stadium, he hit it so far." And he laughs, shaking his head. I'm not sure if he's deliberately trying to annoy me or not; if he's not, then nevertheless he's revealing, in his obtuseness, some unfriendly sentiments that I'd think he'd have the tact to cover up.

It's childish, I know, but I'm angry. The home run he's referring to *was* a tremendous shot, but I'm pretty sure that every other time I faced that guy, Tom Puterbaugh, I struck him out. Probably, over a couple of years, twenty to twenty-five times. One bases-empty fluke homer hardly changes all of that.

I leave it alone. Let him think what he wants. I know I shouldn't care.

When Roger is installed in the den, playing with his space war toys, and my father has gone out back to work on an outboard motor, I ask Anna, who's trying to help my mother with the dishes, if she wants to go play tennis somewhere.

"Help burn off some of those pancakes," I say, and Anna lets me know that she accepts my apology for having been critical, wordlessly or not, of her decision to bring along the tennis stuff.

Joyce says that Roger will be fine here, of course, and lets me have her car keys, saying, "Now, don't be driving it too hard. You always used to drive too fast and then jam on the brakes: this old car needs to be treated gently, like your old mother."

"Do you want to bring along your camera?" I ask Anna, because I think she does, and she gets it, we're changed and out the door, into my mother's car.

We go by my old high school, then by my old girlfriend's house, and, taking a little detour, by Stuart's house, where his parents, I think, still live.

Things are different. There's a Vietnamese grocery store, a singles' apartment complex, a boarded-up massage parlor where there once was a little record store, and so on. The streets are familiar, but not the same. I start to click into my childhood consciousness and then I click back out, the cassette won't fit.

"I've got a bunch of new photographs," Anna tells me, diffidently, as we drive up a shady street. "I wanted to do a series on department stores, and supermarkets, showing some of the goods but mostly featuring the customers, the expressions on their faces as they examine the merchandise or interact with the salespeople. I spent a couple of days in Safeway and the Bon Marché; I'll have to be there some more when we go back. I think they want to hire me as a store detective at the Bon Marché—the manager really likes me."

She amuses me with this, and I ask her when can I see the new shots? Anytime, she says. She never believes me when I say I like her photography. Maybe it's true that I wasn't particularly impressed at first, but I never discouraged her, and now, as she achieves a larger vocabulary, I'm as interested as anyone in what she catches on film. I suppose there are limits to my fascination, but I wish she wouldn't doubt my good intentions and good faith. She should believe me when I say things to her.

"You should believe me," I tell her. "You always think I'm insincere when I'm not, when I'm being perfectly straight with you."

"People can take you as pretty sincere, and I'm sure patients never think there's any possible irony in your manner; but I think you hardly know anymore when you're insincere and when you're not. I'm not trying to give you a hard time, Darrell, really—I just think you're too philosophically uncommitted or something."

"No I'm not. Jesus, Anna."

"It's not just cynicism," she says. "It's on more levels, it's more complicated than that."

We reach the park. We hit balls back and forth, losing our

grip on the subject of my sincerity as we exert ourselves, running and lunging, having a kind of fun. I'm a little preoccupied, in an indefinite way, by the charge that Anna made.
I think she's wrong—maybe she didn't even really mean it,
but was just talking, speaking carelessly, trying to see if I'd
react.

My backhand is worthless today. Anna's probably going to
win: this will please her. She supposedly deplores naked competition, but she likes to win. Sure. She's cool about it, though.

In the afternoon it gets hotter than I'd thought it would, the
last of a whitish haze burning off, and I'm sitting in my parents'
backyard watching my father play catch with Roger when my
brother Jack arrives.

The first thing he says to me, all in apparent heartiness and
fun, is, "Well, if it isn't my brother the quack." He doesn't
care if this goes over well or not. I give a smile that might as
well be a grimace and attend to the introductions of these other
family members whom I don't know or have forgotten.

Jack is about my height, an inch or so taller, more muscular,
with the beginning of a hard beer belly. He's deeply tanned
and ruddy, with short, curly, light brown hair. He looks like
me, otherwise, with some important differences. No one would
ever mistake me for Jack or the other way around.

His wife, Shelley, may once have had a nice figure but,
though still sexy in a way, she's put on some significant weight.
She's wearing a lot of makeup, however, and her red hair is
dazzlingly frizzy; as she hugs me, ostensibly glad to see me,
her big breasts press against me through the tight crimson top.
I smell her floral perfume.

In comparison, Anna is a fashion model, an ice princess,
slender and tall. But she's pleasant, she smiles, and I admire
her composure and determine to hold up my end of our team.

Jack and Shelley have two sons, nine and eight, and a younger daughter, six, who is deaf. Roger greets the boys shyly and agrees to go and play.

Roy brings out some cold beer, and I take one, in a can, and drink, not planning on getting drunk. Later there'll be steaks cooked over charcoal.

"So how's business?" I ask Jack, and he drops his joviality for a moment, just a moment, and says in a subdued and measured, serious voice, "Well, the whole economy in the state is down, you know. Things are a little tough everywhere, I suppose." Then, back into his manner, he says, "You know, driving over here, we saw the damnedest thing. A guy on a bicycle was going across the intersection when a car turned into him, and hit the front of his bike. The guy wasn't hurt, he was hardly even knocked down, but when the driver got out, this guy from the bicycle started kung fu-ing him—they got in a big fight right there on the sidewalk, it was funny as hell." Then he makes an aggressive move toward his wife, exclaiming, "Kung fu!" and laughing, laughing in a way that seems menacing, especially insofar as I recall how much he liked to fight.

"You know Jay McGowan?" he says to my father, who nods. "I heard he got caught selling scrap metal off the back lot at Hadley Aluminum."

"Really? What happened? He get arrested?"

"No, they just fired his ass. Told him to clean out his desk and get out, get off the premises before noon."

"Shit. Old Jay."

"Yeah, he worked there what—twenty years?"

"About that," says my father, shaking his head, drinking his beer, both of them united in this temporary sadness, like a funeral oration over the fate of this fellow Jay.

I try to get serious too, to seem as though I share in their feelings, though it sounds to me like the guy was a crook. Maybe they're saddened by his moral "fall," though somehow I don't think so: what they're saddened by, not too intensely, is that he got caught. Whatever the ethics of the situation, however, it's clear that they're communicating, that they're in basic agreement, that my father and my brother here have an understanding, a sympathy, in which I have no part—and never did, never could (and perhaps never really wanted to, as I do not even now).

The little dog is barking inside the house. Anna is doing something in the kitchen, with Shelley and Joyce. (And with little Kelly, who follows her mother all around, wearing a hearing aid that doesn't seem to really help.)

"How's the doctoring business?" Jack asks with a sly look as though, in the presence of our father, he's making a show of placating me by taking some interest in my affairs.

Roy snorts, and says, "Still charging two hundred bucks for a cold, two hundred bucks to say there's not a damn thing he can do."

"Well," says Jack, "what is he supposed to do? People get a little cold and run to the emergency room, what is he supposed to do, take out their appendix? People on welfare, too lazy or ignorant to take care of themselves—but then you've got to see them, don't you? Doesn't the law say you can't turn them away?"

"That's right," I admit. "We see everyone who wanders in, no matter how ridiculous the problem. A lot of people with runny noses, or bruises, or pimples—and a lot of fakers, or people after drugs."

Jack wants to hear more about this. Roy goes in the screen door, and comes out with more beer. Shelley is laughing very unselfconsciously at something someone said. The coals are started, a pleasant smell. We're getting along.

Our little sister, Eileen, is in Atlanta, with her husband and four kids. She couldn't make it up here for the reunion. I talked to her on the phone. She's a Christian, sweet-natured, unassuming and plump, sure of herself somehow. I like her, but I can't say that I miss her.

The women come out of the house. Anna has evidently been utilizing more of her skill at making others comfortable, which she's practiced as a nurse. She looks very nice to me, in my warm, benevolent, slightly drunken state; I wonder if Jack is jealous. He's not unintelligent. He's capable of dissembling, perhaps even better than I can. I don't know, though— I'm a pretty good liar. I can keep an awfully straight face.

It looks like, I'm pleased to note, Roger isn't being bullied or anything by the other boys. They seem absorbed enough in friendly play.

We talk about politics as the steaks sear on the grill. Hot dogs for the kids. Potato salad, which isn't as good as my mother thinks it is. She's always taken pride in her rudimentary version of the dish. I think it needs some dill, or some vinegar, something to make it less bland.

We talk politics. Or rather, Anna and I mostly listen. Roy gets going on welfare and how those who won't work deserve to starve; moves on to criminals and capital punishment, whereupon Jack enters the discussion and registers his support. By nodding and murmuring, I seem to agree with all that's said. Who knows? Maybe I do. I know I use the same technique in a gathering of conservative doctors, but maybe it's no longer a disguise. I surely have come to have my reservations about the poor, and after seeing so many victims of violence I know I have very little sympathy for the perpetrators—or for thieves. I want my property intact.

Anna says, blithely but knowingly, "What about handguns,

then? If you look at the murder rate in Britain or Japan, or any other country where they've banned them, it's amazingly low compared to America. Darrell can tell you, it's really hard to kill someone with a knife. You can stab them ten or twelve times and they still might live."

Jack grins. "I'm not going to get in a big argument about Japan or Sweden, but I need my guns for protecting my household, and I'm not exactly inclined to give them up. Things are different here in America; it's too big a country to keep track of everybody the way they can on those islands."

Anna shrugs lightly, and says mildly, "Well, it would just be nice if people weren't shooting each other so much. It's kind of hard, you know, to stick up a bank with a butcher knife—or to conceal a rifle in the pocket of your coat."

Jack looks, for the first time, a bit drunk: he just says "yeah," and leaves it at that, seeming to enjoy Anna's comment without having it mean anything or have any real value—"Hey, look at those steaks! I'm about ready to eat the whole damn cow!"

An anecdote is related by my mother, about how she once made a coconut cream pie and made the mistake of using orange food color to dye some shredded coconut—and Jack mistook it for grated carrot and wouldn't eat it, thought it was a trick when urged to taste it and see, and succeeded in getting me to adhere to his position, disdaining the coconut pie.

My steak tastes fine. The charcoal helps, as does eating it outdoors. There's also corn on the cob.

Afternoon merges into evening, and there is apple pie with vanilla ice cream, melting off one's fork. One of Jack's boys gets crotchety and starts talking unpleasantly, in a loud voice, whereupon Shelley spanks him and takes him inside. He cries noisily, like a brat.

During the course of a slow conversation it comes up that

my father has had a recurrence of his old back trouble, and he says, "Yeah, it's about time I went in for another adjustment."

"You go to a chiropractor?" I ask. "Adjustments" are what chiropractors say they do when they crack the back.

"Sure do. He knows a lot more than you guys do—all you guys do is tell me to rest and give me some pills. That doesn't do the trick."

I'm tired, and this irritates me more than it should, considering the source. Anna knows my feelings about chiropractors; I gather, at a glance, that she is following the exchange. I just shrug.

A while later, Jack and Shelley finally leave, about ten o'clock. In the kitchen, while I'm getting a drink of water, Joyce asks me if I liked the dinner. I say yes, I did; but she's determined to disagree.

"I know it wasn't fancy, like all those weird Chinese things you like to eat. Actually, I don't think you really like that sort of food; I think you just want to be different. I don't know why you can't just be satisfied with regular food, regular living, regular people. Don't you think you could have been a little more friendly to Jack? He was trying, but you just looked bored at everything he said."

"So what? He was drunk."

"He was not!"

"Who was not?" says Roy, coming in from some nameless task outside.

"Oh, never mind," says Joyce. "We were just talking about Jack."

"What about him?"

"I don't know," I say. "I don't understand this whole conversation."

Joyce is tight-lipped, rinsing dishes, smacking them together dangerously. She won't talk in front of Roy, but he's sensed the thread, or mood, and means to tell me what's on his mind.

"I know you boys aren't close," he says, "but if you didn't have to act like such a big shot. Just 'cause you went to medical school. Well, if we hadn't put you through school, you know, where do you think you'd be now? You might have had to get your hands dirty for once in your life."

"Now, Roy, I don't know," begins my mother, trying at once to seal over the real rift with her jelly of hypocrisy, going for a sweetness that, as far as I'm concerned, is empty form.

"No," says Roy, as if now annoyed with Joyce, and drunk, "it's time I said something about gratitude. You know, Darrell, your mother and I don't ask for much, but we struggled to put you through school so you could be a doctor, and in all these years do you think we've ever heard a word of thanks?"

"Sure you have," I say.

"No we haven't. You're ungrateful, and you've always been ungrateful. It's the way you are, and maybe there's not much we can do about it now, but that doesn't excuse your acting high and mighty around your brother, your *older* brother, remember? Who, tonight, well . . . he wouldn't mention it, and he wouldn't like it if he knew I was, but he's got some bad debts right now, he's in a little temporary trouble—"

"If he wants to borrow some money from me, why didn't he say so? How much does he need?"

"I don't know, exactly," says Roy, disconcerted by my offer, not wholly trusting it, yet not wishing, either, to throw away his victory, even if he might get pleasure out of bitching at me a little more, seeing how much of it I'll take. We've been through similar scenes before. At the moment, perhaps he wants me to be angry: my lack of reaction throws him off.

He tries to be more pleasant, asking me if I want a nightcap. I say no, I think I'll go to bed.

"Now, Darrell," begins my mother, with a kind of slippery sugar, but I'm ostensibly very tired, I don't wait to hear the rest. The apologies are worse than the attacks.

I don't feel like telling Anna very much, because I don't want her to be indignant on my behalf, not now: I do, however, tell her the story of how my brother supposedly needs this loan, couldn't bring himself to mention it, out of delicacy I guess, so now my parents are twisting my arm.

"What did you think of him?" I ask.

"Jack? Oh, you two aren't very similar, it's no surprise you're not friends. Still, even though he's sort of a creep, he isn't totally without charm."

"I didn't realize. Tell me, then, what you found so charming about him."

Anna smiles, not sure if I'm going to be temperamental now or not. In either case, she thinks I'm funny. Even if I'm trying to pick a fight.

SEVENTEEN

Leaving Roger at my parents', Anna and I journey into New York for the day, taking the train. I like showing her around. Everything that we see or experience, a little part of me feels like I'm responsible, I can somehow take credit for it, and, perhaps generously, Anna plays the part of a good audience, so that I feel masterful and unusually urbane.

The cab ride is an adventure; the streets are full of notable specimens. We go shopping—that is, Anna does, and I accompany her. It's all right. I enjoy it. Looking at my wife in many mirrors. What a nice couple. Right.

"Remember when you read that book, a couple of years

ago," says Anna, "that changed your mind about everything?"

"No," I say. "I never read a book like that in my life."

"Come on," she says. "What was it called?"

"I don't know. That seems like a long time ago."

We go into a record store. Anna wants to get some new music, she says she's bored with the records we have at home. I say fine, and abandon myself to curiosity and the thrill of new acquisition, the search for something truly new.

We buy ten new records, charging them on the MasterCard, and arrange to have them sent to us in Seattle. The record store guy is very helpful and pleased.

In the Museum of Modern Art, retracing my steps of a week ago, because I want to see the Pollocks, I'm stuck when she asks me if I came here before alone. No, I say, someone from the conference came along. "Lindsey Geller," I offer. "She works down in Texas, out in the sticks."

"Oh? And is that where she's from?"

"No. Actually, she's from Baltimore."

Anna's suspicious—it's as though, just like that, she can read my mind. Talking now will just be an imprecise formality, something to be gone through to settle details such as affect and specific tone of voice.

"What else did you do together?"

"Went to dinner."

"Yeah? Where'd you go?"

"Didn't I tell you already?"

"I don't know. Tell me again. What else did you guys do? Did you go to bed with her? You did, didn't you?"

"Yes," I say, nodding, as we walk by some other art lovers, big pictures on the wall, possibly being overheard—we're hardly keeping our voices down.

Anna's more emotional than I thought she'd be (more emotional, perhaps, than I hoped for); although she's cool, collected, I can pick up on her signals, I'm tremendously alert to all her frequencies right now.

I touch her and she jerks away; I say, "Anna, come on," and put my arm around her shoulder, pulling her next to me, and she doesn't resist too hard, although her frame does remain stiff.

"How could you?" she says, when we're once again outside on the sunny street.

"What do you mean?" I reply. "You're the one who inaugurated this open marriage shit. This was nothing compared to you and Sam."

"Oh, that's a bunch of shit. You planned this: you did it just to get back at me."

"How can you say that?" All injured innocence.

"Cut it out, Darrell. I know you. Shit."

"She was just available, and I'd had a few drinks, and it seemed easier to do it than not to. It wasn't very good, if that makes any—"

"You fucker."

There's nothing I can say, so I shut up and accept it. Maybe it's shameful, or shameless, but at the same time that I feel bad I feel all right, I feel like I've accomplished something, that I wanted to hurt and I have and now I'm pleased with myself. I guess I was afraid she'd be indifferent, even as I'm concerned, walking next to her, feeling like I've done something wrong, that I've made a mistake and maybe messed everything up. I feel sorry for myself, then, and kind of enjoy this too.

Here we are, walking down the street in New York City, perspiring a little, warm, the concrete soaking up and reflecting the humid ancient sun, and we're in love in a way, modern, complicated, stupid love, not without spite and a tiny bit of hate. Self-hate which encompasses also, I guess, whoever's intimately connected, flesh of one's flesh or something less eternal, something maybe temporary, just how temporary we don't know.

A guy's playing a bass guitar and singing, led on by a simplistic rhythm machine. He looks like an old, wasted, dirty junkie, but I like his song. I find myself smiling, and then think I ought to be morose, but I catch Anna's eye and she's almost smiling too. Though not quite.

We're supposed to meet Stuart later on for dinner. There are a couple more hours to kill before that. I'm not sure that I know what is Anna's complete reaction to our situation together: she looks as though I attacked her but she has survived, and we have a strange rapport now as fellow tourists on the loose. I like being an unfaithful husband much better than being a stick-at-home husband with an unfaithful wife. Why sex should be such a decisive matter, as irreversible somehow as murder, is beyond my powers of analysis—and yet, in this culture, and seemingly every other, this business of genitalia and who has access to what is a critical, killing question time and again. Look at the Moslem world. I would have had Anna stoned to death or beheaded a month or so ago, and done God knows what with Sam.

It's different (and it should be) here in the U.S.A.

Stuart's eyes glow attentively as he greets Anna, hugging her, and I shake his girlfriend's hand. Her name is Michelle. She's blond, as blond as Anna, shorter, with bigger breasts.

Alcohol. Cold drinks.

There was a big crime the day before, a multiple murder, and Michelle brings this up, so we talk about crime and criminals for a while.

Then somehow we get onto the topic of the apartment Michelle is subletting for the summer, and then her job (which she says she hates) as a copywriter, and she goes on, acknowledging my own occupation, to tell me in a way that's meant to be amusingly aggressive how much trouble she has had with doctors and the medical establishment in general.

"I know," I say. "It's terrible. Dehumanizing. I don't look forward to ever being a patient myself."

Stuart interposes, asking me if I recall Pete Livingston, who was one of our mutual friends in school. Sure I do, I say. Why? What's he doing these days?

"I ran into him the other day, and we had lunch together—you wouldn't recognize him now, I swear."

"Oh? Why's that?"

"You know how he was always kind of fat? Well, he's a vegetarian now, and he's lost an incredible amount of weight. And he's wearing glasses; and he's shaved his head. He recognized me, and started talking to me, or I never would have known him. He's very outgoing now, which is different—he gives seminars on self-improvement techniques, like how to give up smoking, lose weight, or, especially, I guess, how to relax."

"Pete's teaching people how to relax? That's a little, uh . . ." I laugh.

"Yeah, I know. But he's also, now get this: a professional hypnotist, a yoga instructor, and an editor of some poetry magazine, that's called—let me think . . . *Spike*."

"*Spike*."

"Right. But once we got talking it was still the same old Pete. Said that he got into yoga because he thought it would be a good way to meet girls."

Michelle really starts laughing at this.

Films. Movies we've seen or not seen, like or dislike. Anna defends Wim Wenders and attacks Godard. No one can refute her.

We eat dinner, and talk turns to living in New York, and then to Seattle and the whole question of the West. Michelle hates California, which she's visited, and has only the vaguest image of the Pacific Northwest. A lot of rain, she thinks. Everything's green. Water. Kind of provincial: nothing is open all night long.

"That's true," says Anna. "It's not like this."

"I have an old boyfriend who moved to Montana," Michelle says. "He's a teacher, and he got a job in Butte, I think. Every so often I still get a letter from him."

But when she vacations, she likes to go to Florida, where her sister lives.

EIGHTEEN

I t's late, and Anna and I are exhausted and perspiring, so hot where our flesh touches, after a long session of push-and-pull half-hostile lovemaking. We got home too late the night before, after Stuart, to do more than just go to sleep—tonight I wanted to redefine our bond, and Anna made a show of not wanting to, but in a provocative manner that said she didn't really want to be left alone. "What do you think you're doing?" she said, but I persevered, saying, "Nothing," and going forward with my intimate caress.

At a strange moment when we were locked together, I was on top, floating in friction on her liquid core, she squeezed me especially tight, almost violently, her arms around me, and asked, "Do you love me?"—something we rarely, anymore, directly discuss. "Yes," I said, "I really do." "You're sure?" she asked, and I said yes and then kissed her seriously, feeling like this was a truly meaningful ritual for us to go through.

Now, as we lie sated, rubbed a little raw in tender places, I become gradually aware of the phone ringing, persistently, downstairs. I look at my watch, in the dark, and see that it's two forty-five. A wrong number or a crank call, I'm guessing; though then, for a moment, I seem to hear my mother's voice talking, and then when I'm about to drift away indifferently I hear her voice, much closer now, in the doorway to this room.

"Darrell?"

"Yes," I say, suppressing a very momentary, playful impulse to feign sleep, to make her wake me up like when I was a child. She sounds rattled and afraid.

"Darrell, your brother's been in a car wreck. That was the hospital calling. He's not hurt seriously . . . but they need someone to go pick him up."

I sit up, and then Anna, who's been dozing, sits up too, reflexively hanging onto my arm, listening, yawning.

"All right, I don't mind. But what about Dad?"

"I don't want to wake him up." She whispers, though he is nowhere near. "He was sick tonight, before he went to bed. You didn't hear him? Oh God, I thought he'd never stop; it just went on and on."

"Okay," I say, after a pause. "Give me a minute to get dressed. What hospital is he at?"

"Do you want me to come with you?" asks Anna, after Joyce has left the room. Anna stretches, arms up, and I kiss her and say, "No, go back to sleep. You know how it is. I'm liable to be there half the night. You get some rest; you can stick up for Roger tomorrow while I take a nap."

"All right," she says, and then, as she's lying back down, "what happened, anyway? I didn't really hear."

"I'm not sure. Jack supposedly got in an MVA, but she said he wasn't badly hurt. I guess I'll find out pretty soon. Go to sleep."

Downstairs, my mother has made me a cup of instant coffee— something I never drink. I'm such a fucking snob. I take a sip, just to be polite, since she's gone to the trouble. She's trying to keep from weeping now in front of me. I pat her perfunctorily on the back, and she hugs me, then seems to calm down. I accept instructions to the hospital, though I think I remember where it is. I'm sleepy and warm.

For dinner we had overcooked ham with a pineapple glaze, dry and salty, canned yams baked with marshmallows, green beans, and then lemon meringue pie. Did Roy have more beers than usual, or was it just the combination of ingredients that made him ill? I think it was the beer, and feel justified in saying now, to Joyce, "It seems like he's drinking an awful lot—is this his usual amount, has he been going on like this for some time?"

"You sound like a doctor," my mother replies, inanely, and seems pleased with herself (or with me), and then goes on to say, "oh, he's always liked his beer, you know. That's your father. It does seem like it doesn't agree with him quite as much as it used to. His stomach can't handle it anymore. And, well, you know, he's nervous about your being here, and so he probably drinks a little more than usual, and then, the other day with you and Jack . . ."

"Is there ever any blood when he vomits like this?"

She doesn't know, or doesn't want to tell me, and I'm not sure I want to find out. It's not my business; in a very real way it's just none of my affair. My mother looks fragile and old, and she gives me another hug after handing me the car keys, telling me to be careful and not be too hard on the brakes.

The hospital is way across town. It's windy out, and I roll down the windows in the car. There's little traffic, and I vaguely recall driving down these same streets years ago, in a less detached frame of mind, I suppose, coming home from a date.

Only after I have parked and am walking toward the emergency entrance does it occur to me to wonder what I may be in for. Where is Jack's wife, Shelley, or his other friends? I don't understand. I'm wary now, awake, somewhat consoled by the fact that I'm in a hospital, that here I know the parameters of what to expect.

"Hi; I'm here for Jack Patterson, who's supposed to have been in an MVA."

"Oh yes," says the clerk, who was reading a book, studying. "They're still stitching him up. Let me go check, and I'll find out how long it's going to be."

"Sure."

When he comes back, he says, "It should be just another five minutes or so, and then you can join him."

"What happened exactly? Do you know?"

"All I know is that there were two cars involved, and we got Mr. Patterson and his friend, uh . . . Joanne Welsh."

"Oh. How is she?"

"Well, right now she's in Surgery. Mr. Patterson's been very concerned about her."

"He was the driver?"

"Yes."

I go down to the waiting room, where there's a TV set near the ceiling, showing a rerun of some series nobody ever missed when it went off. A couple in their late fifties, the man looking at a magazine while the woman digs in her purse. I can see, very quickly, why people get restless in these rooms.

I'm relieved when a nurse comes and fetches me, taking

me back to where Jack sits on a stretcher, a bandage wrapped around his head. I can smell the alcohol on his breath from ten feet away. The nurse, who's of the tough, no-nonsense variety, begins to give me head injury instructions.

"It's important that somebody wake him up every two hours, just to make sure."

"He knows all this shit," says Jack, who I had thought was feeling subdued. "What about it, Darrell? Why don't you tell this bag where she can get off? Start throwing your weight around, man! I want to know what's happening to Joanne and they won't tell me; they haven't even goddamned let me see her. You find out what the big cover-up is, okay, and get me in so I can see that she's all right."

He's risen up off the stretcher and approached us; the nurse has taken a few steps back to stay out of his way. A security guard appears, out of nowhere, in the hall. One of Jack's eyes is swollen nearly shut; he wears other bandages that presumably hide other lacerations, his shirt, which he still wears, is ripped and soaked with drying blood. I take it that his face and scalp are cut, in addition to his arm.

"You're a physician?" asks the nurse, falling into a tentative deference, and I nod.

"In Washington," I say, and then think that I should have specified "the state" so she won't think "D.C.," but it doesn't matter; it's sinking in that possibly this Joanne Welsh is my brother's lover and that he's concerned because he messed her up. Maybe she's married too. Maybe, on the other hand, she's someone young, a babysitter or something.

The ER doc comes to talk to me, as a courtesy, and I learn that this Joanne is suffering mostly from lacerations, and a plastic surgeon has been called in to attend to her face.

"Who is she, Jack?" I ask, as he comes out of the bathroom, walking slowly, in some pain.

"What difference does it make?" he says, and suddenly I'm fed up, I'm sickened by him. I don't think his acting tough is covering up any sensitivity he dare not display, that he's anywhere close at all to going to pieces—he's just another drunken clown. I haven't liked him for years, anyway—and what affection has he ever given me? It all comes through me, and I hate it—he expects me to take him seriously, to be impressed with him, just because he's my big brother.

"No difference," I say. "Let's go. I'll give you a ride home."

"I thought you were going to get me in to see Joanne. How do I know what the hell they might be doing to her?"

"I don't think," I say, "that you need to be worried about the plastic surgeon doing his job. You should have maybe been a little more concerned when you were driving around drunk in your fucking car."

"You bastard, I'm not drunk. You shut your fucking mouth! Where's Joanne? I want to see what these butchers are doing to her, and you can't stop me! I'd like to see you try!"

"Let's go, Jack. I'll drive you home to Shelley and the kids. You want a ride, I'll give you a ride. I'm not going to hang around here all night while you act like an asshole."

"You think you know so fucking much, don't you? Well, let me tell you . . . let me tell you—you don't know a goddamned thing, I don't give a shit about your medical school, your degree, your M.D.—'cause you don't know the first thing about life, real life—I wasn't so banged up, I'd kick your ass."

"You never could, Jack, you never could."

He's stronger than me, I suppose, and yet I mean it, and he knows it. He never could. Not like that. He waves at the security guard, who hovers near again, as if, in exasperation now, to tell him there's not going to be a scene.

"Just tell me how Joanne is going to be," he says now,

appealing to me, glazed, going through the motions of something I don't need to understand.

"What does it sound like? She's going to live, but she's going to have some trouble with her face. She probably won't look quite the same as before."

"Jesus!" he exclaims, sucking in his breath, turning his head away from me as though he's going to cry. If I'm supposed to be embarrassed by his emotion, I'm not. Rather, I feel like I might hit him—and I ought not, as he's in a weakened condition and all that.

But it would feel so good to knock him down. I shudder. He's oblivious to my hatred; he's thinking about his guilt in relation to the sorry state of this Joanne.

"Do you want a ride home?" I offer, one last time, and he shakes his head, looking at me then, and it's all there, a very clear message passes between us, and there's no need for anything more to be said.

He's in the waiting room, using the telephone, when I leave. There's nothing left—we're strangers. I'm disturbed, but there's nothing I can do. On the drive back to my parents' house I remember that he needs money, that they think I'm rich and should give him a loan. Maybe I'll write my mother a check, and she can give it to him. Or maybe I won't. I don't know. I'm glad that tomorrow we're taking a plane home.

My mother's awake, trembly, wanting to know what happened. I give her the car keys and say, "I don't want to talk now; I'm going back to bed. He wouldn't come with me."

When I take off my clothes and get into bed Anna wakes up, and asks me how I am. She senses my tension. She's tender and cool, and claims not to have slept while I was gone. Her skin feels so smooth.

NINETEEN

I thought that it might be strange to come back to work but it's easy, it's even somehow a sort of relief. I come in a little early, in the morning, to talk with Peter Flanagan and find out if anything's new.

Flanagan is tall, with a closely trimmed brown beard, and, although I know he's politically and culturally liberal, lives with a local actress, and has a lot of stained glass in his house, I've never been able to figure out exactly how smart he is. I know that, medically, Peter's sound; but his specific variety of intelligence isn't one to which, perhaps, I particularly resonate. He gives one the impression that he listens hard to what one

says, and he talks slowly, seeming to weigh his words, yet he
seldom says anything original or remarkable. At times he has
a certain dry wit, more in his manner than in what he actually
says.

He asks me if I know a patient named Teena Overstreet.
Yes, I say.

"Oh, well, she's been in a few times, asking for you. You're
the only one here she likes."

"What, does she want more Valium?"

"I guess so. I was going to give her some Vistaril one night,
but she wouldn't take it. She made kind of a fuss, and had to
be escorted off the premises." Peter thinks this is amusing,
though one can't really call his expression a smile.

"Oh, Bob Lockhart got fired," he says.

"Really?" Bob Lockhart is (was) one of the vice presidents,
pleasant enough, from what I saw of him; to all outward ap-
pearances an upwardly mobile young administrator.

"There's some kind of a shakeup in the works," says Peter,
"but no one seems to know who's behind it or where it's going
to lead."

"What does Matthew think?" Matthew was close to Bob
Lockhart.

"I'm not sure. He's not saying much—he's taken over the
Flexible Residents now, I guess you know."

"Yeah, but that doesn't mean much."

"No," says Peter, as though I've said something bright. It's
as if we're in agreement, but I don't know exactly what point
was in dispute.

He tells me that in the last two weeks we've received three
separate individuals who have poured gasoline over their heads
and set themselves alight.

"So, if this is some kind of a trend—" He smiles benignly.
"I don't know. Otherwise, there hasn't been much trauma.

Steve was on a couple of days ago when somebody lost their legs under a train. There've been a lot of heroin overdoses, it seems like, but only one that I know of was very serious; and I think she's still up in ICU, on a ventilator."

In a little while Peter is gone, and I begin seeing patients. My professional persona, not really a mask, but a manifestation of my social self, comes back to me like an amiable friend.

I feel benevolent toward most of these people, like a chimpanzee predisposed to like other chimpanzees. If I meet a chimpanzee who's a sociopath, or psychotic, or who tries to manipulate me, then I react accordingly, exercising the prerogatives of my profession, and fend this person off. I do not "help" them in the same way I help the others, who are more sincere in their need.

I see a black kid, fifteen, wearing a baseball cap on backward, a white mock-airline-mechanic's jumpsuit, old tennis shoes, a red jacket, black leather fingerless gloves. I like him. He's okay. There's nothing really wrong with him, but I express no disapproval, I'm neither aloof nor overly friendly: I don't say "Hey man" or call him "Champ," like Steve Gold might. I'm straight with him, I don't treat him like a fool.

A thirty-two-year-old white guy wants Workmen's Comp for eating a cookie. Toni, the nurse, tells me this before I've seen him, rolling her eyes. I don't think I understand. I go into Room 4 and introduce myself, then ask, "What happened to you?"

"There was something in this cookie, and it did something to my throat."

"And this is a work injury?"

"That's right. I was at work, at Nabisco, and there was something in that cookie."

He's humorless, even a bit mad. A dour, mustached, red-cheeked face.

"What are you, a cookie-taster? I mean, is eating cookies something that's part of your job?"

I think the whole business is funny, and I don't care if he does not. I'm playing to Toni, who smiles discreetly.

"Listen," says the guy, "I was on the premises, and it was their cookie, and so it's an on-the-job injury. There was something in that fucking cookie that ripped my throat. It feels like it's still in there."

In a moment he'll be even more dramatic: I ask Toni to fetch the laryngoscope. Of course there's nothing there. The patient does not tolerate the (uncomfortable) procedure very well, in spite of the viscous Xylocaine anesthetic.

A woman and her husband want to talk to me about their medication. I observe them closely as the woman speaks. She's twenty-six, by the chart, but looks older, yet kind of attractive. She has honey-colored hair and a full, maybe slightly overweight figure, shabbily dressed. Her husband is Hispanic or Native American, and he too looks older than (his listed) twenty-nine. He is impassive, but does not look insensitive, really, on a second glance. He may know English very well, probably does, in fact, but seems to prefer not to speak. There are two children with them, sitting with great patience and docility. The older boy, about nine or ten, is blond. The younger, black-haired and brown-skinned, is only maybe four.

"We're on the methadone program in Salt Lake City, and we ran out. We're traveling up to see Henry's aunt, in Bellingham, who's going to take the kids for a while. Look, we're not trying to jive you, but we need something. We'll take *anything*." She sounds quietly, despairingly desperate. There's something remorseless about her, and I'm curious, momentarily, about them both.

"Look," she says, "we can prove we're on the program. We've got the papers and everything."

"Okay," I say. "Let me see."

I take the papers back to Room 6, looking through them; when Janet (one of our older, more officious nurses) asks me what I'm going to do, I shrug and say I'll call Salt Lake City. Why not? We can get methadone from the hospital pharmacy; one time I remember admitting a junkie with a broken leg, who then supplemented the meth with heroin his friends brought to him in his room.

I'm put on hold for a while, but I get through. I talk to a Dr. Van Buren, who has a lazy accent that I like. He says yes, he can confirm they missed their fix.

Who can imagine what urgent interpersonal or familial crises these people may have, or how their minds work, what madness there is to their logic? I can't. Or won't. The methadone is ordered: Janet will administer it. I don't talk to them again.

With tweezers, I extract a live, wriggling cockroach from the auditory canal of a dirty, white twenty-year-old girl, who I think is retarded. "Something's in there" was all she'd say before, holding her head cocked to one side, listening to it move around. Now she grins, with bad teeth, and I don't know what to do with the ugly insect, I can't slack my grip for a second or I'll let it fall.

"What have you got there?" asks Christine, the day admitting clerk, and I say, "You don't want to know," as the automatic doors open and I go outside, into the big turnaround, drop the insect on the ground and then smash it with my foot. I think it deserves this execution. One has to draw the line.

Matthew Vandermeyer stops by, on his way from one meeting to the next (or at least giving that impression), asking me about my trip back East, whether I had a good time.

"How was the conference?"

"Not bad," I say, stuck for a meaningful reply. There's always something slightly ill-at-ease about relations with Matthew, I'm not sure why. We're cordial—I suppose I kiss his ass, in effect, since he's my boss—but we'll never be great friends.

I try to say something a little more substantive about the conference, and then he asks me if I've heard yet about Bob Lockhart. When I'm noncommittal, he says, "He's accepted a position at Mercy Hospital in Kansas City; it sounds like a good opportunity for him—though we'll all be sorry to see him leave. His wife's expecting, too, so . . ."

"Hi, Matthew," interjects David Harrison, one of the neurosurgeons, coming down the hallway with authority, in his suit. "Hey, Darrell, haven't seen you for a while. Listen, Matthew, I need to talk to you about our protocol for cervical spine injuries. There was a case the other day—"

I listen, interested, then edge away, wondering if any new patients have come in. Yes, there are two fresh charts in the rack.

In the coffee room are posted notices of forthcoming lectures:

—Why Do Trauma Patients Die?
—Why Keep Comatose Patients Alive?
—What's New in Burns?

For lunch, I accept the offer of Toni to bring me back a tray from the cafeteria; I order a cheeseburger and a Coke. Junk food. The guy who shot the mayor of San Francisco a few years back successfully copped a plea for manslaughter by saying that he'd been influenced by eating too much junk food. It's true. I use several of these little packets of catsup, which squeeze out and get on my fingers. Ice melts in my Coke.

Some lacerations to sew. An old, white-haired woman with a broken hip. Turn her over to the orthopods. A pelvic on a fat black woman who says no, she hasn't had any discharge; opens her legs and two pounds of cottage cheese fall out of her gaping hole. I don't like bad smells.

The helicopter brings in a twenty-four-year-old white male from a rural MVA. This guy's in bad, bad shape. A closed head injury. Fractured pelvis. Bleeding in his belly. He goes up to Surgery: I doubt he'll ever get off the table. Later on, a state trooper comes in, from the scene, and a nurse leads him to me. I ask him how it happened.

"As near as we can reconstruct it, he was coming around a turn when this pickup, speeding, came around right at him, in the wrong lane—and our guy swerved and lost control, went into a tree. There was a witness, but we don't have too good a description of the pickup—he just kept on going, apparently: he may not even have seen the accident occur." He smiles, somewhat grimly. "More likely, though, he just thinks he can get away."

The state trooper shows me the driver's license of our patient. I study the face, which is smiling and not unsensible, dramatically different of course from the shattered visage I saw, only in passing really, in the Trauma Room a short while ago.

"It's too bad," I say. There's never anything to say. Because I have nothing better to add, I ask if his relatives have been notified. Back to routine.

At about five-thirty Tom, the security officer, comes by and asks me how I liked New York. I'm a little uncomfortable with him: I don't really want to be friends, partially because I feel that he likes me mainly because I'm a doctor, I feel that deference, which I only need so much of. So I'm wary. I don't want to be used.

To distance him a bit, perhaps, I ask, "How's your knee?" The question seems to embarrass him; at any rate, he does not have a prepared response.

"Oh, I don't know, better, I suppose, though it still bothers me some. But"—he's thinking about something else—"Patricia's leaving in just a couple of weeks now, you know. What is it, winter down there, if it's summer up here? Do they really have winter in Australia? Maybe it just rains."

He shrugs, and smiles. I can't wholly read his affect; he may be sad, he may be enjoying his sadness, he may have convinced himself that the grapes would not taste as good as he once thought. Also, there well may have been developments I'm unaware of, conversations and whatnot, the gist of which I'll never hear. That is, if I maintain my reserve.

"You know that guy who lit himself on fire the other night? The human torch?"

"Yeah?" I say, not knowing where this is all going.

"Well," says Tom, "he had somebody come in yesterday, wanting to talk to him. Said he had something *very important* to tell him, and he threw kind of a tantrum, down in the lobby, when Lee told him he couldn't go up. This guy was wearing a big white hat, see, with 'SATAN' written on the front of it. Lee said the guy scared the shit out of him. He was about fifty, and Lee said, 'Man, if this dude's into Satan, he been into him for a long time.' Lee didn't want anything to do with him—neither did I. Jesus."

"What happened to the guy?"

"We were just about ready to call the police when he ran out. Just ran off down the street. I tell you, though, the rest of the night—we kept thinking he was going to jump out of the bushes or something. You should have seen this guy."

I'm amused. Tom gets a call on his walkie-talkie and goes off. I feel like I may have misjudged him, somehow, and I feel kind of bad.

When I get home, Gretchen reheats some vegetable curry for me. She's on a diet, swimming laps and cutting out sweets.

I tell her about the guy who wanted Workmen's Comp for eating a cookie, and she's appropriately entertained. Anna is out with Diane. The exhibition of her photographs opens this weekend, and she's anxious. I am too, for her sake. I don't want her feelings to be hurt, and I have no real basis for imagining whether things will go well or ill.

What did Gretchen do while we were away? I interrogate her, gently, and she tells me, with some elusiveness, while we watch TV.

Roger says, "Do you want to see a trick?" and when I say yes, he shows me something with his toy.

TWENTY

Anna says she has just been "very lucky" with her photography, but I think there's more to it than that. She has the best camera, the best darkroom equipment, but others have this too, and many more years of practice.

Among the newer shots in this exhibition are two swimming pool shots featuring Sam, which I knew about but which still irritate me. He's extremely good-looking: wouldn't you know that Anna, the photographer, had fucked him? This strikes me as sordid, as though I live in a sordid world.

Anna is nervous, drinking white wine out of a little plastic glass, her poise shaky, something maybe slightly vulgar in her affect. She's not sure how to handle herself here.

There's a certain kind of middlebrow critic or fan who may not take her seriously, because of her looks. Though she's far from appearing to be, by any stretch of the imagination, a "dumb blond," neither does she have that special homely but intense air of ungainly, neurotic intellect—which perhaps would be, for maximum impact, the air she ought to affect.

She was worried, all yesterday and today, that no one would show up, but her friend Christopher, the preparator, has taken care of that, inviting several of his friends, who are musicians or actors, it seems. Other people also have come, and a lot of this Liebfraumilch is being drunk, a lot of voices being heard.

When I see Paul Swanstrom, I'm pleased, and move toward him, curious as to why he's not with Julie. Maybe she's at gamelan gong practice instead. He seems preoccupied, excessively gentle even for Paul, a gentleness that means something else. He likes some of the photographs, he says, and shows me just which ones. I wait for him to complete his inspection. Respectfully, though on the lookout for nuance, I gaze at this or that photo yet again.

"How's Roger?" he asks, bending forward to study a detail of some cloud.

"He's being a brat lately, as a matter of fact."

"Oh really? What's old Rog up to? Maybe he's just sticking up for his rights."

"Could be," I admit. "But he threw a major tantrum the other day after his piano lesson."

"I thought he liked them."

"He did, but—something happened between him and the teacher, we're positive, but we haven't been able to get her on the phone. We left a message with her service." I shrug, and sigh. "As soon as we talk to her, I'm sure we'll be able to straighten it all out."

"Or maybe not."

"Right. Or maybe not."

"Is that it? That's just one problem, probably some kind of a little misunderstanding—that's not enough, believe me, Darrell, to make Roger a brat."

"Well, he's also been bitching about what we give him for dinner."

"That's because you want him to eat that weird Indian shit. Roger just wants some good, plain old American food. Take him to McDonald's; he'll be happy as a clam."

And, having said this, Paul laughs uproariously at himself. I join in, though it wasn't that funny, even if it did go against all of Paul's dietary codes.

Then, to finish off the recital of Roger's erstwhile brattiness, I add that he's been giving us a hard time about when he's supposed to go to bed. Paul's pediatric curiosity is aroused; he wants details. "A very early case of teenage rebellion, maybe," he says, and then, ostensibly blasé, he lets drop, "Julie and I split up. She moved most of her stuff out last weekend; even as we speak, she's getting the last of it, picking up her, you know, records and books. It just didn't work out."

"How come? Whose idea was it to make the break?"

"It just wasn't right, Darrell. I couldn't live like that."

I'm not sure if I'll ever get through to the real reasons or not; but, to demonstrate my sincerity, I persist. I didn't even know they had problems, I say ingenuously, giving Paul the opportunity to come back with, "Everyone has problems. Whenever people live together, there's friction, just in the ordinary process of day-to-day life. Julie and I got on each other's nerves, just like I'm sure you and Anna do sometimes. It's inevitable."

"You're crazy," I say. "Anna and I live in perfect harmony . . . without ever a ripple to disturb our pond. That's how *we* live."

My mild tease here breaks his thread, but he finds it again in a moment, even as I see that Anna's mother, June, has arrived. June is tough, not unhandsome for a woman in her mid-fifties, wearing maybe a little too much turquoise jewelry. She's always got a tan, and wears eye makeup to set off the stones of her necklace or something. I don't really want to talk to her. I hope she's not a vision of the future Anna, though it's true one could do worse.

Gretchen talks to her, and to her mother's tall, white-haired escort, and soon Anna leaves some strangers and joins her relatives near the wine. I see Diane, talking to a darkly bearded man; I wonder if he's one of her lovers. Anna's let it out that Diane has strayed a few times, that she's on the loose, and from Mike's manner it's easy to assume that he for his part does a secretary or a junior file clerk once in a while.

Does he know Paul? I can't remember, so I introduce them again, and when he indicates that he knows Paul is an M.D., asking if we were "talking shop," I say, "Actually, I was just telling Paul that I think I should go back into surgery—Ear Nose & Throat. There's one ENT at the hospital, who sometimes does as many as twelve or thirteen myringotomies a day. Putting tubes in kids' ears. It's probably necessary only about twenty percent of the time, but it doesn't hurt the kids any, and the parents feel satisfied that they're doing everything possible, they enjoy themselves in a way; and for this simple, low-risk procedure you can make about a five-hundred-dollar surgeon's fee."

"Jesus." Mike is impressed.

"The only problem," says Paul, picking up my line, "is getting all those referrals. You need to be on pretty good terms with quite a few pediatricians in order to generate the kind of volume we're projecting here. So the pediatrician has to be interested, or else he can just say the child has a recurrent ear infection, needs more antibiotics, and tell the parents it'll probably go away in less than a week."

Mike is getting the picture, I think. You can almost see "kickback" go on like a little light in his brain. He's not too troubled by ethical considerations, but now he's probably beginning to wonder about the hernia operation he had last year.

"In ENT," I say, "you hardly ever have to come in at night when you're on call, and nobody dies, and really your malpractice liability isn't too bad. Who's going to take you to court over a tonsillectomy?"

"Right," says Paul, who might now be taking me seriously, despite the wine we've had to drink. "Long-term, it's a good specialty. Low stress, high return. And you were good with the knife, as I recall. You just didn't like doing bowel resections very much."

He laughs, again loudly. He told me once that he doesn't like the way he laughs, hates the sound of his own voice. I like mine, though I guess it would be nice to have a really deep one like some of the black guys I've seen, or Dennis the cop. But as an instrument, my voice is okay. I think Paul believes his voice makes him sound like a lightweight, which goes over well with children and parents but does not sufficiently impress women or other adults. He sounds like a nice guy, and he'd like to be less so. Tougher, more worldly, somewhat of a bastard . . . that certain edge some people have, and which makes them no less likable as a result. More likable, perhaps.

In the close quarters of the car, later, Anna laughs and says, "It went okay, didn't it? I'm glad that's over—God, listening to all those people flatter me, I kept thinking that I was even worse than I'd thought I was. I kept wanting to correct them, to say, 'But I'm not really very good. Please forgive me.' "

She laughs, and I do too, driving the car. I have a clear twilight view of the surrounding hills, green vegetation, neutral hard cement and crisscrossed dark telegraph wires beneath the pink-lit sky. I hug Anna with my free arm, holding her shoulder, and she leans over and kisses my neck. She's kind of drunk. I feel protective, and sexually aroused. I suppose I'm excited by the idea of fucking her when her defenses are down— taking advantage of her in a way that's not often possible. This I intend to do and enjoy. I accelerate, knifing around someone who's turning left, shooting out through a little corridor into open, clean road.

Anna turns on the radio and says, "This is one of our new records."

I don't recognize it yet.

TWENTY-ONE

Wendy tells me that there's a call for me from West Plains Pharmacy. The pharmacist asks me if I wrote a prescription for a Michael Harris, for some Talwins. No, I didn't, I say. I'd remember. I very rarely give Talwins, perhaps because I'm not all that clear myself as to exactly how strong they are.

So somebody's using my number. I don't think the cops pursue this kind of crime with much manpower or anything, but it doesn't seem so petty to me. I'm angry. This might be the only time this person's done it, or it might be merely the first time a pharmacist's looked askance. The prescription blanks here in the Emergency Room are pretty easy to get hold of;

just about anyone who works here, really, could get some off a pad with a minimum of guile or stealth.

A junkie comes in with a fairly original scam. He claims to have trigeminal neuralgia, an excruciatingly painful, transient condition which afflicts the nerves of the face. The only known treatment is narcotic pain medicine. The nurse says, "At first, I felt sorry for him, you know, because he acts like he's really in pain. But then he didn't want to roll up his sleeve so I could take his blood pressure; then, when I insisted, he tried to turn his arm so I wouldn't see his tracks."

The patient's name is Ronald Shaw. He's white, about thirty, sort of tough-looking, not completely unattractive, not the kind of guy you'd hire to do your taxes or whom you'd want to take your daughter out on a date. Not a biker exactly, and not noticeably dirty, though his clothes have seen better days.

"Are you a neurologist?" he asks me, guarding the right side of his face with his hand, a deep voice with some rage.

"No," I say, not yielding anything to his stare.

"Do you know what trigeminal neuralgia is?" he says, after I've waited him out.

"Yes, I know what it is."

"I've had it for the last ten years," he says, and I do notice that he's holding his mouth kind of funny, as if to keep his lips in a straight horizontal line. This would go along with the ailment he advertises. If he's faking, having read about this in a book, his acting isn't bad: I'm inclined to give points for inspired conception, and think I'll give him what he wants.

"Don't you have a neurologist here in town, then?" I ask, and he slowly shakes his head.

"I'm just visiting here, up from San Francisco."

I look on the chart; naturally he's said that he's allergic to codeine. I put out my hand as if to touch his cheek. He flinches; I desist.

"How wide can you open your mouth?"

"I can't," he says. "It hurts too much."

Something tells me that he's acting. Maybe I've just seen too many scams, but I don't buy the idea that this guy is real and sincere.

Nevertheless, quietly, I write down on the chart an order for 100 mg Demerol; Vistaril 25. Then I go to Room 4, where a lesbian with one of those haircuts is being very dramatic with her stomachache. Supposedly she's been vomiting blood, and her friends (the nurse informs me) carried her in. At least her pain is epigastric rather than pelvic. She gags a little, producing nothing. Her color's good, I note. She's overtender everywhere when I try to examine her abdomen.

I order some blood drawn: a CBC, amylase, 6-60. I don't give much credence to the story that she vomited blood. The CBC will clear this matter up; if I wanted to be cruel, I could take her at her word and have an NG-tube stuck down her nose into her stomach, and we'd see immediately if there was any blood down there or not. But I'm not cruel.

A sixty-three-year-old white male comes in, somewhat embarrassed, saying that he's been having difficulty for the last several days motivating his left arm. It feels numb and tingly, he says, and tonight his face feels numb as well. He has full, white hair, and from his affect I conclude that he is really concerned. Yes, he has a history of high blood pressure. Right now his pressure is 160/110.

What medication does he take for this? Has he been taking it lately?

Slurred speech?

Yes, but it went away.

It's eleven-thirty at night. I call this guy's doctor, at home, and he isn't pleased to be woken up.

"Now wait a minute," he says, "are you sure you've got the right Dr. Thompson?"

"He said Green Lake Clinic, and that's where you practice, isn't it?"

Dr. Thompson doesn't appreciate my pointing this out. He also holds it against me that he didn't recognize his patient's name. So he tries to give me a quiz, hoping to make me look bad.

"Is there any anatomic numbness? Any *objective* signs?"

I hate this. My function, really, is simply to determine: Are they sick or are they well? Is the present condition significant or nonsignificant? If intervention seems indicated, then I pass the case along. I don't need this patronizing, deep voice on the phone trying to find out how thorough my examination has been.

"His reflexes are okay; grip a little decreased on the left side . . ."

"How do you put that together pathophysiologically?" asks Dr. Thompson. "Since the speech center, you know, is in the left hemisphere."

He's referring to the crisscross: the speech center is in the left half of the brain, therefore it should be the right hand's grip that is decreased.

"He could have suffered a loss of proprioception of his tongue," I improvise, "and that could account for the slurred speech."

Eventually, with ill grace, Thompson agrees to have the guy admitted. I don't know Thompson; I can't recall ever seeing him or hearing much about him, but now I'll have to look around for him, see who he is.

I go down the hall to get a Coke out of the machine. Tonight Anna told me, before dinner, that she wants us to buy a painting.

"I'm crazy about it," she said. "I want you to come with me tomorrow and see it."

"What does it look like?"

"Oh, it's kind of abstract," she said, "and it's a large canvas, I think seventy-two by fifty-four. You have to see it."

"Okay, let's go look at it tomorrow, then," I said, feeling that I was only blessing what might already be a fait accompli.

I played ball with Roger today. Out of a sense of duty, he has become more adept, so that we can now have a reasonable game of catch. I still think this is an important childhood skill.

The piano-lesson controversy has been resolved, though not without one more unseemly demonstration of crying by Roger— I never cried like that as a child, never. I don't like to be unsympathetic, but I really feel a chill run through me when he gets like that. I don't know what to do. Anna doesn't like it either, but she's better, she can hide her feelings more productively at such times: she can be warm, and try to connect emotionally.

Anna and I are talking about getting Roger a computer. He played a game on one recently, over at the house of his only friend, Davey Stark.

An ambulance brings us a girl who jumped out of the balcony at a heavy metal concert and broke her leg. The leg's already in traction, and she's terribly drunk. Her makeup is all smeared; she's not a pretty sight. Alcohol plus maybe some unknown drugs. I don't know what the kids are taking these days, other than booze.

This girl's name is Cheryl. Two friends of hers arrive shortly, also intoxicated, impossible to talk to, looking for her with a certain edge of desperation, both wearing T-shirts they evidently bought at the concert. Black. Never before worn. I can't make out the band's name, though there's some kind of a skull either bleeding or on fire in the frightening logo.

"Cheryl!" the boy yells, and then the girl, even more loudly, calls, "Cheryl, where are you?" They come right down the hall. Security's not sure what to do.

"Let go of me, you fuckers," Cheryl says, struggling with Lucy and Gail. "Andy! Bill! I'm in here!"

Andy must be the girl, who's pretty high, with long, wild blond hair and glazed, crazy eyes.

"What are you doing to her?"

"Get me out of here! These assholes are *hurting* me!" screams Cheryl.

"Hey," I say to Norm, the Christian security guard, "they can't be in here. We need them out, now."

Norm starts to talk with them, ineffectually, trying to be reasonable, but Cheryl keeps yelling, tears now pouring down her face, and the situation has gotten ridiculous. I'm being called names, which I don't like. Norm looks at his black walkie-talkie and calls for backup.

Since Gail is trying to hold Cheryl down, Andy goes after Gail, who's Japanese, short, and stronger than she looks.

"Get that off me!" shrieks Cheryl, very ugly now, referring to the traction device that straightens out her ankle and foot.

I've been passive, thinking about nothing much, but this has all gotten out of hand.

"All right, come on," I say, and pull Andy away from Gail, roughly, by the upper arm, when she resists, and push her out into the hall. Bill comes out too, saying "Hey, man, you can't do this kind of shit." I close the door behind us; Norm decides now is the time for aggressive action and starts to shove Bill down the hall, whereupon Bill takes a wild swing at Norm's bespectacled head. Bill is taller, but skinny, rangy, and very stoned.

Norm, still trying to use his radio, seems off-balance and embarrassed after the punch knocks his glasses off. Andy then tries to kick him in the balls, but I stop her, grabbing her hard by the wrist and throwing her over against the opposite wall.

"Get out of here!" I say, loudly. "Cheryl's broken her leg, it's got to be in traction, and you guys are just getting in the way, getting her excited." Nobody hears me, I think.

Lee and Mel arrive, running, and as he grapples with Norm, Bill now wants to surrender, saying, "Okay, okay, okay."

Lee gives me a big smile. Andy is crying. She's a beautiful girl. I think I hurt her wrist. She really looks drunk. Behind closed doors, Cheryl is still hollering, "You fucking bitch, you got no right; let me out of here!"

Her friends are taken away, down to the waiting area to call their folks. Butch Hardy, the orthopedic resident, arrives. He'll hurt Cheryl some more, without a doubt. Lucy is trying to get her to tell us her phone number, so that her parents can be called, but now she shuts up and closes her eyes.

"She's peaking," I say, and Butch Hardy thinks this is a pretty funny remark.

About ten minutes later some black people carry in a young woman who they claim has been shot in the chest.

"Get up off your ass, man, she been *shot!*" (Nobody's sitting down.)

"This is an *emergency*, motherfucker!"

In the Trauma Room, it's hard to get all these friends out, and they look very threatening, dressed all in black leather, with silvery studs and chains. Our patient is hysterical, and drunk, and has a ring through one nostril.

When I've got her blouse cut off, I don't see any wound. There's one little laceration on her neck, and blood has been drawn down by gravity to soak the space between her breasts, but I don't see any evidence at all of a bullet.

"He shot at . . . shot out the . . . windshield," she sobs, when I press her as to what actually happened. It seems she was hit by shards of shattered glass. Boyce, the surgery resident, doesn't find any bullet holes either, anywhere, so I go out to tell her friends.

They're gathered in the foyer, by the admitting desk, where poor Charlotte is trying to find out our patient's name and where she lives. They're angry, belligerent, and when I tell them she's all right, that she wasn't shot, several are disappointed and incredulous, asking me if I'm sure, as if they think this is some trick.

"She's just hysterical," I say. "She got cut by some flying glass. A couple of stitches and she'll be fine."

I think most of them believe me; I'm not going to try to sell them anymore. Security's here, of course—and Lee, at least, is good. Sometimes, because he's black, black people will cooperate with him more readily than they would with whites. Other times, occasionally, they pick on him precisely because he *is* black, and call him Tap Dance or Tom. The unruly whites call him a nigger, thinking they can get away with it since he's in a uniform and is supposed to be restrained.

A car squeals very loudly to a stop just outside the double doors and a blond girl comes running in, saying, "You've got to help him, he's been shot!" and repeating herself; close behind her enters a very tall black guy in a blood-soaked gray suit and vest, ebony-black skin and at least two hundred and fifty pounds, strong-looking. I go to him; he's been shot in the left eye.

The others, in their black leather—I hear the same bad-tempered woman's voice say, "That's *him!* That's the mother-fucker—hey, Ben, Jamal, come *here!*" calling to others down the hall, milling around, on and off the phone.

I have my arm around this big guy's shoulder; he's a little unsteady. We'll have to go to Room 6 instead of the Trauma

Room, and I'm trying to reassure him, he seems hostile, uncertain—and then we're pushed, and his girlfriend screams,
and Lee and Mel and Norm are shoving back at this crowd
that's trying to get at our new entries. The plump blond's hair
is pulled, face is slapped—I detach myself from my man and
push some people back, surging adrenaline, knocking over one
skinny young woman and seeing one guy square off like he's
going to do karate on me. I yell, at the top of my voice, "Now,
just *get back*, get out of here, this is a *hospital!*" The people
seem to temporarily disperse, and I get my patient down to
Room 6. He doesn't seem grateful or anything, but I like him
anyway. I feel a great affection for him. I realize that I'm
covered with blood.

"The police should be here any second," says Gail, and I
nod and begin to look at the damage done to Earl Love's eye.
That's his name: Earl Love.

"Man, they shot right through my windshield," he says. "I
was just gonna get out of my car. Cindy? Cindy, honey, where
are you?"

"I'm right here."

I've allowed her, in her fur, to sit here on a black-seated
adjustable stool, in the corner, out of our way. It seems like
a good idea to keep an eye on her, since she seems to be in
some danger. Boyce comes in, followed now by the just-awak-
ened, still-yawning, fat Trauma Surgeon, Larry Stevens, whom
I don't especially like but who's said to be quite good.

In a little while, when I'm sure that Earl's being properly
looked after, I go to wash up. Down the hall, I see eight or
nine policemen, sergeant's stripes on one arm (which means
they're serious). I'll probably have to check each security guard
for little injuries, since they were involved in some rough
action. They're sure to discover some bumps and bruises,

maybe a pulled muscle, so they can miss work, ask for pain pills, whatever—just as I would do, I guess, were I in their place.

I ask Dennis, the only cop here at the moment with whom I'm very familiar, "Have you figured out yet who shot who?"

He glances around for his sergeant, then says with a smile, sipping from a Styrofoam cup of our coffee, "No, but it looks like you sure got both sides of the dispute here at the same time. The spillover from B.J.'s, I guess."

"Is that where this started, then?"

"In the parking lot there, from what I gather. Not my call." He smiles, wider now. "Thank God. No, it was six-twenty's, and now"—he gestures down the hall—"they're taking statements from everyone. How's our man? This one *is* shot, I take it?"

"Oh, yes. I think we'll want to CAT scan him right away to see where that bullet is. Anyone say anything about what caliber it might be?"

"Not yet. From what I was hearing, nobody's admitting anything, you know how it goes. Thirty-five people in the bathroom when it happened—as usual, nobody knows a thing."

"They sure seemed to know a fucking lot when they brought that girl in. Bunch of assholes."

"Yeah, well, we already got three of them in cuffs, and there's a bench warrant out for one of them, so we'll be keeping him for a little while."

In Room 6 Dr. Stevens has established some rapport with Earl Love, and is being nice to Cindy, mainly, I think, on my behalf; they're going to CAT scan as soon as the tech gets here.

I sew up the neck laceration of the girl who usurped the Trauma Room (and who now is, very sullenly, in Room 4).

When things settle down, I take a Percodan, calculating

that it will cheer me up just enough to make the night worthwhile. By the time it starts to wear off, I'll go home. In the meantime, it won't interfere with what I have to do.

And I deserve it. I deserve the unambiguous positive feeling it gives me, that portion of short-lived confidence and joy. Fuck anyone who wouldn't understand.

Impervious to all we have undergone since, in her absence, the lesbian lover of our earlier patient with the epigastric pain comes back in, wishing to talk to me about Gen's case. This is a rather forbidding-looking woman, dressed in a blue denim cap and sleeveless denim vest, with brown hair, faint pale mustache, tattooed arms. Definitely lifts weights. Blocky, stocky frame.

And yet she's very pleasant, once we get talking, and not aggressive toward me at all. When I hint that Gen might have been faking, explaining that we checked her orthostatic pressures and so forth, this woman nods and understands. Yes, she says, lately Gen has been under a great deal of emotional stress.

"Stomach troubles," I say, "can cause one a lot of true discomfort, especially when one's under stress, or uses alcohol, or eats the wrong things, smokes cigarettes or drinks coffee— and the person is likely to be more uncomfortable at night. And yet, if there's no ulcer or other organ involvement, it's difficult for us to do much here in the Emergency Room, other than offer antacids, you know. It's a long-term type of problem, and diet and stress-reduction are just two of the things that have to be looked at."

"What about the emotional stress, Doctor? We have no money, no insurance, no welfare."

"Well, then it's harder to make appointments, even in the sliding scale agencies." I'm speaking in such a soothing manner—no question we're getting along very well, even though

I didn't see much value in Gen. "Maybe you should try to see what resources are available through the Crisis Center, or the Woman's Hotline."

"I should try the Hotline. I bet you're right. If there's anyone around who can help, they'll know who it is."

"I think so," I say. "And she should also follow up on the medical end of things, you know, and see her regular doctor. She did have a prescription for Librax, so he's aware to some extent of her problem, and the Librax means that he understands there's some stress involved—there are other tests that we can't do here in Emergency, like an endoscopy, where they put a tube down and look at the inside of your stomach—and that may be necessary, if she keeps having trouble."

I am copiously thanked, and after this woman leaves I'm pleased with myself, as though I've gone "where no man has gone before," though that's probably not true. She was a tough-looking dyke, though, one of the toughest-looking ones I've ever seen.

A manic-depressive comes in, by ambulance, in full bloom of mania, saying that he has started up twenty-five companies to support every aspect of his revolutionary water-purification scheme, and he opens up his briefcase and shows me the certificates of incorporation, with the state seal on each, to prove he means it. I ask him if he's ever taken lithium, and he says yes, but recently he stopped, he didn't think he needed it anymore. He's a good specimen, even charming; he had the ambulance bring him in with a cut on his finger, which Lucy disinfects and puts a Band-Aid on. Then I ask the EMT's to redirect him to the local hospital with a psych unit, to which our fellow agrees to go, saying that he has some "old business I need to get straightened out."

I sew the deep leg laceration of a blackened, inappropriately irritable steelworker, putting in place a four-inch plastic tube, like a drinking straw, as a drain. I do a careful, craftsman's job on the meat of his calf.

Earl Love is in Surgery. The bullet is lodged in his brain. Luckily for him, Dr. Albert Scherer, the best neurosurgeon in town, is doing the case. So maybe Love will have a chance to wake up.

TWENTY-TWO

I felt bad a couple of days ago; one of the cases affected me and I found myself unwillingly filled with pity and terror and hopelessness, hopeless rage. A whore beat up by her pimp, at least that's how we figured it out afterward. Face down on the sidewalk, face rubbed back and forth, pressed into the cement. She was quite stoic, she held back the tears as best she could, she was brave, and that made it worse.

Today, as I'm lolling here in this boat, sitting in the back, hearing the steady lapping of the blue waters, a glass of Asti Spumante in my hand, I'm recalling the whole scene. I tried to tell Anna about it, and she tried to listen, she wanted to understand, but I felt as though I was just telling her in order to torture her, because all I wanted to convey was the sight of that young girl's face, and what was that? More brutality. Viciousness. And did I have any moral I could draw, any lesson I could teach?

It's the colors that stick in my mind. The bright red of the blood—brighter than raspberries—struck one first, as her nose was completely abrased, and then she had a cut on one brow, and that was bleeding freely, and her lips were mashed: her skin was pale, her hair was palest blond, and she had on a lot of blue eye makeup, and clear blue eyes, and was wearing a cheap black fur stole. I think I just wasn't ready, for some reason, and I could hardly look at her, I wasn't interested, I didn't want to evaluate anything, and of course she wouldn't say what had happened and she didn't want to talk to the police.

"I fell down. That's all. I fell down on the cement."

She was being brave. At a certain point a "Steve" showed up; the clerk announced that he was here to give her a ride home and our patient then reached into her pink sequined sock to get out her money, to see if it was all there. I sewed up her brow but could do nothing for her skinned nose. Her little flinches, her determination not to show us much, we who ostensibly had her at such a disadvantage—but then she had her pride, pride that had something to do with going back to Steve.

Maybe he didn't do it. Maybe he had nothing to do with it. Maybe I completely misunderstood the situation.

Percodan doesn't just kill pain. It also gives one, as a side effect, a feeling of well-being and good cheer. I don't know if I could read with comprehension for any length of time after having taken Percodan, but I can do a lot of other things well; and, when it's time to go to sleep, one is ready, one has a predisposition, and sleep is pleasant and not an abrupt or forbidding change.

Anna is wearing an emerald green one-piece bathing suit, cut high on the sides the way they are now; Diane is in a terribly scanty black bikini. She has a very dark tan. Her skin gleams with oil. Mike drives the boat.

He's lost weight this summer. Playing tennis and swimming, jogging: on the go. Diane runs him around. She has three abortions in her past, now can't get pregnant, they've been trying for nearly two years. It's a problem. Mike is good-natured, feels responsible, even though his sperm counts are all right. Sometimes I think Diane secretly hates him, though Anna says I am wrong. She knows that I consider Diane to be a bitch. Ever since the Sam business, I haven't trusted her, I don't like the way she regards me; I save a special irony for her and never let down my guard.

Asti Spumante. It tastes perfect to me today. Not too sweet. I have a little buzz, a little blur. If you let chimpanzees try alcohol, after they get past the burning, they want it all the time. It's a natural urge. Our brains come equipped with special receptors sensitive to specific substances, not only our biochemically produced endorphins and the like.

Tom, the security guard, made me a curious offer. He wanted to know if I'd be interested in buying a gun. He was smiling, but didn't seem really to be joking.

"Protection. You live out there in the sticks, you never know. One of these days the Hell's Angels might come up your driveway, looking for some fun."

"So I blow them away," I said. "What kind of a gun are we talking about, an M-sixteen?"

"M-sixteen's are shit. I have a nice nine-millimeter automatic, fires off fifteen rounds per clip. Just the thing."

"That's what it sounds like," I said, the conclusion arriving in my mind that Tom was the one who'd been using my name and number on forged prescriptions. "Just the thing."

Tom said, "Well, anyway it's a thought." Yes, definitely. Talwins or Tylenol 3's. Maybe Vicodins. Not Percodan: that's too elite. To do it right, he'd have to minimize risk, make the prescriptions as innocuous as possible, each time for small amounts. Looking at him, he looked as though he might be putting on weight, lying around all the time, losing some of his muscle tone and tan.

"One thing about Reagan," says Mike, turning the wheel, concluding some thought, "he can take a body count."

I agree, and take another sip of the sparkling white wine. Is Mike more complicated than I've previously imagined? How much does he know? He's suffered, in his own way he's known pain. I can see that in him. But does anyone really learn anything from suffering? That's an old myth that dies hard: I'm not too sure it ever happens. If you're ignorant and something bad happens to you, how often do you become less ignorant? It's more likely that you then just walk around, blinking, wondering what hit you; with no new insight of any sort.

"Yeah, you're right, he can take a body count all right," I say, suddenly finding this so funny that I laugh and laugh. Anna thinks I'm drunk, but she knows I'm capable of observation, so she tries to appreciate what I think is so funny. She looks nice in her swimsuit, turning thirty hasn't hurt her looks at all, she's a lot more appealing than Diane, who's practically naked. We're floating around in sight of land, on the Sound; the wind's starting to blow now and it's not so warm anymore, a cloud has crossed in front of the sun.

The other day I started talking about leaving emergency medicine, going back and finishing up my last two years of surgery or maybe going into something else, neurology or

nuclear medicine or even ENT, give a good deal on tonsillectomies or something—and Anna just looked at me. She
didn't know if I was serious or not. If this was a test.

Then she said the usual sort of thing one ought to say,
whatever was best for me was best for her, she could stand a
change, all of that, and I thought of how little money we'd
have coming in during a residency—even if she worked full
time again—and the thought of losing the house, for instance,
depressed me.

"I don't know," I said. "I just don't think that I was meant
to go on doing this forever."

Then we were interrupted by Gretchen, and talked about
her new boyfriend with her. He's a contractor named Jim,
once divorced, much more settled and seemingly "bourgeois,"
in the good sense, than any of the other guys Gretchen usually
likes (or who like her). She met him at Anna's opening. He
had some connection with a friend of a friend; anyhow, he
asked her if she'd like to go have a drink.

From there it has blossomed. I almost dread its working
out, I'm so used to having Gretchen about the house. Somehow, even though she doesn't say much of any substance, I
count her as some kind of an ally. I'm not sure why.

But later on, in bed in fact, Anna brought up what I'd said
about quitting ER. But then I didn't want to talk about it, I
didn't want to think about it, I wanted to do something else
instead. And we did.

Although I wasn't on Percodan at the time, Percodan can
make one feel like having sex—a paradoxical effect, as it can
also make it difficult to grow hard. I haven't been taking a lot
of them lately, by the way—but I have been taking some.

I'm not sure if Anna knows about this or not. Sometimes
a humorous languor will inflect my voice—a giveaway; or I'll
be unnaturally still and calm. She talks to me as though I am

there, all of me, and I'm touched by what may be her trust, her simple trust. I get sentimental, and think how much I love her, pure animal affection, and I touch her all the time.

The next day, Sunday, is the annual Emergency barbecue at Matthew Vandermeyer's house, for the doctors and their wives—and children, too. No nurses or other minions are included in this particular event. Substitute doctors work the ER today and tonight, so we're all here, Flanagan and Petibon and Patterson and Gold, under the benign eye of our leader, Vandermeyer, who's barbecuing salmon steaks.

It's another windy day. August still, but it's not as hot as it was. There are thin white clouds in the high blue sky, moving slowly in the wind. The sun is blurry and bright white, the big star of our sky.

Matthew isn't the most naturally charming or gregarious guy you'll ever meet, but I always give him points for trying. He means well, I think, in his way. He wants to be liked, and I guess I like him for it. He's modest, despite being our boss (though he knows he is the boss). His wife, Sue, is commonly thought to be a bitch.

And if she's not, she gives a good imitation of one. The other wives, for the most part, I understand, don't like her. Neither do the nurses in the department. It's true that she often gives one the impression of being impatient and peremptory, not to mention seldom satisfied, so that one imagines Matthew endlessly catering to her moods, trying to please her, but Anna, after initially disliking her, has come to the conclusion that Sue is just shy and socially maladroit, uncertain of her position and afraid of being snubbed. As a consequence of this insight, Anna attempts to be nice to Sue, nicer than she might usually be, hoping to put her at her ease once and for all.

A brave attempt, but I think it only makes Sue suspicious. And there's no question, as a further reflection of something, that the little Vandermeyers are spoiled brats. Craving attention, cranky, lacking charm. Matthew indulges them to a fault. They climb all over him, giggle and whine, do in general just exactly what they want. Which might make them happy, if they were self-directed enough to know what to do.

"Daddy, why do we have to have salmon? I hate fish. Chrissie hates fish too, don't you, Chrissie?" says Jeffrey, the eldest at nine. Chrissie assents, making up for not being the first to speak by being more vociferous and repetitive. Matthew patiently explains to them again that they don't have to eat any fish, nobody's asking them to do that; there are hot dogs being broiled inside the house. This isn't enough, they're hungry *now*.

Roger smiles at me, with—dare I say it about a seven-and-a-half-year-old?—at least a hint of irony, as if to say, "Look what a good boy I am in comparison, and you don't even appreciate it," something like that. I smile back. He *is* a good boy. I think I can see now that he's going to be a person someday, a real person of his own devising, a separate individual from either Anna or myself. We've been reading to him lately at night, either Anna or myself, whoever's available on a given night, one picking up where the other has left off. T. H. White's *The Once and Future King*. Roger likes it. He's an attentive listener, rarely interrupting with a question unless he's really puzzled, so puzzled that he cannot, for the moment, follow the text.

Peter Flanagan's wife is named Susan, as distinct from Sue; there is never any doubt about whether, here or in this circle, one is referring to Susan or Sue. Susan has red hair and freckles, a sunny kind of face, and *opinions*. She's pleasant and cheerful, ordinarily kind of putting up with us medical folk, definitely not in awe of us or our fabled powers of healing. She's likable, with an infectious smile, yet there's a seriousness to her, just under the surface, which seems all the more potent because of her obvious well-being, mental and physical, her optimism and air of general health. She belongs to some organizations of a New Age liberal bent; accordingly she's against South Africa, pro–Third World, antinuclear, and so on.

She doesn't like Sue at all, and doesn't make any great secret of it, despite all her smiles. Susan just doesn't find Sue very interesting to talk to, listen to, or be around. She likes Matthew, though, and Matthew's a bit seduced by her, I think, so he doesn't even notice, or scarcely notices, at any rate, the fact that Susan will more or less ignore and avoid mingling with Sue. Susan likes Anna; they've had coffee together and lunch a few times. Anna keeps saying that we ought to see them more, she and Susan might have the possibility of becoming closer friends, but the issue is muddied some by the point that I've got no great desire to see much more of Peter than I already do, coming and going at meetings and at work. I've got nothing against him, but I'm not excited, usually, by the prospect of talking to him. Perhaps he feels the same way about me; his enthusiasms are often somehow tepid, at least as seen from the outside. He's crazy about Susan, though, and delighted, evidently, by the prospect of becoming a father. Susan is now six months along. Big with child, as they say, and she is indeed, attractively so.

The one wife who's unattractive is Nancy Petibon. I always think of this when I see the way Dan flirts with the nurses, touching their bottoms or hugging them or kissing them on the cheek every possible chance that he gets, cracking jokes in his southern accent, flattering the women, telling even the plainest ones that they look cute today, or he likes their hair, or haven't they lost weight . . . good old Dan Petibon, the worst doctor and nicest guy among us, on the level that is of lowest common denominator.

His voice has gotten positively melting at times when he's spoken to me of Anna, praising her looks to me, as though to please me by this, I suppose, by inflating my pride in my woman. Nancy wasn't very pretty, I remember, a few years back; the change has all been for the worse, principally in the matter of an alarming weight gain after their second child, Frazier, who has acute and chronic asthma. In the last three years he's been admitted to the hospital, in respiratory distress, ten or fifteen times. The older boy, Dan, Junior, has some kind of learning disorder and can't, at eight, spell or read or write. He seems like an okay boy otherwise, gentle and quiet, and he and Roger get along. But Dan certainly needs this job, and it doesn't help any that he misdiagnosed a tension pneumothorax last week, thinking the patient had COPD instead, with the result that the fifty-six-year-old went bad and coded and died. Basically, he didn't listen attentively enough to the breath sounds with his stethoscope. In intubating the patient, an X ray is always taken to check the placement of the endotracheal tube; it was in viewing this that the "tension" was discovered.

Steve Gold, when he told me about it, was exultant. He dislikes Petibon, thinks he's a disgrace to the department; Steve figures that if Dan "fucks up *one more case—phhht—*he's out the door." It's suspected that Matthew also has a rather low regard for Dan's abilities, though he respects him for his "compassion" and ability to give patients the impression that he cares. When patients have to spend two hours in the waiting room, they ought to know that this is because Dr. Petibon is writing copious notes and giving copious instructions to some fool with a cold or a mildly twisted ankle, or ordering goddamned acute abdomen X rays on some girl with PID. Acute abdomen films tell you very little, unless someone's got a bowel obstruction. Gas patterns—that's all you see. Petibon orders them all the time. And anyone with a cold, it seems, gets a chest X ray and a CBC. So, while I can feel sorry for the man, who's trapped in his marriage and has two very ill-omened sons, heartless as it may be, I side with Steve Gold, who'd like to see him gone.

Steve is the only single male in the department, and today he shows up in a Hawaiian shirt, pineapples on flaming scarlet, with his very latest girlfriend, who must be barely twenty, with an aggressive, punk haircut and garish eye makeup—thank goodness she's not someone from the hospital: I know Matthew wouldn't appreciate some lab tech crashing our party. A nurse would be acceptable, particularly if she worked in a critical care unit, and a secretary might pass muster, if she was especially stunning and bright, but otherwise the social hierarchy in the hospital is rather firm.

This girl is outrageous, of course, but somehow she strikes one as rich, and soon this interpretation of raw data is borne out: she's the daughter of a local university president, and has just returned from a trip abroad. She's actually soft-spoken and seemingly a bit shy, despite her fashionably threatening façade. Her name is Roz.

"I wonder what drugs Steve's got her on," says Anna privately, before we all start to eat, and I laugh—the girl does seem a little too placid and calm. So does Steve, who's usually so animated, even manic. He's being very nice to Dan, and Dan responds warmly, making his down-home jokes; I think this is all serving some hidden purpose of Steve's, to amuse Roz—or just himself.

"Tell me again about the time the alligator chased you," he says, as though it's just such an irresistible story, and Dan seizes at the bait.

The told and retold 'gator story is thence performed, with relish, by Dan. It's funny. We all laugh. Dan exaggerates his accent at such times to good effect.

We're eating salmon, baked potatoes, green salad vinaigrette, corn on the cob. Drinking chablis. The food is really good, and I'm enjoying it much more, simply *noticing* it much more than I have any meal for several weeks. I don't know why, since it's pretty simple fare. My biorhythms, I suppose.

Talk turns, after a while, after touching on recipes and films and children's habits and toys, to tales of medical derring-do. Shop talk, among the men. It's what we have in common, and it's what we do.

Steve bitches about a resident who keeps forgetting to order Beta Hcg on women with low abdominal or pelvic pain of uncertain etiology (a Beta Hcg is necessary to rule out ectopic pregnancy, as should be obvious to our young Dr. Marsh); Peter tells an anecdote about an orthopod, commenting that the only antibiotic orthopods ever use or seem to know about is Keflex, and Keflex just doesn't happen to kill every single bacterium known to man; Matthew, who also, as evidenced by quantity consumed, seems to be greatly enjoying his meal, laughs about how everything went wrong in a trauma they were trying to videotape the other day: the autotransfuser was set up wrong, wrong end of the tubing hooked up to the patient's end, a monitor fell and hit a nurse (Toni) on the head, three times—Matthew holds up his fingers—three times he asked for a luer-lok and was handed a luer-slip instead. Add that the patient was combative (they soon paralyzed him with Pavilon), his relatives were frantic, the anesthesiologist was inept—"I told them: don't even develop that film! Get rid of it; burn it! We don't want to have that lying around—it could be used against us one of these days!"

Steve Gold recently had something happen that upset him:

it seems like the kind of thing that could happen to anyone but ends up only happening to Steve Gold. A misunderstanding with one of our prominent cardiologists, whose mother came in to be treated after a fall in a nursing home. Just one of those things.

As I drive us home, Anna asks me if I was attracted to Steve's Roz. I laugh. Roger is asleep, or pretending to be asleep, in the back seat.

"Is this a loaded question? Yes, it is, isn't it?"

"Kind of. Maybe."

"Well, I didn't think she was very pretty, really, but . . ."

"But you'd like to go to bed with her, wouldn't you?"

"Kind of," I admit. "Maybe."

"Why? I mean: what attracts you to her?"

"I think you're waiting for me to say her youth, aren't you? Okay, her youth. Young new skin. But I wouldn't want to spend much time with her. After you've satisfied your curiosity, what's there to talk about? I'm sure Steve thinks of something, but that's Steve. He's not exactly the most mature and sensitive person, so it doesn't make any difference to him. He doesn't notice."

"No, I don't suppose he does." Anna is pensive, looking out the window of the moving car. "Well," she says, as we pull into the long driveway, "I had a good time."

TWENTY-THREE

"Go ahead," I encourage Roger. "Throw the ball for him."
Danny, the six-month-old golden retriever, enthusiastically chases it down and brings it back. He's a pretty dog. Patricia smiles. She's serene. If we were to change our minds and back out of the deal, it wouldn't bother her. I think Tom sees her as an enigma, a woman of mystery, whatever. I can't really speak for what might go on in his mind, what fantasies he might entertain. But she's cool, sure of herself in a way that Anna is too, perhaps without Anna's awareness of the limits to her powers. I don't know. Mr. Excitement isn't here. They're leaving for Australia next Monday morning. Today is Thurs-

day. Some other couple is taking over this farm, livestock included, cow and goats and geese, chickens and ducks and cats in the barn.

It's hilly and green. They have a huge garden, five times as big as ours (though a lot of it is taken up with corn. I've had sample loaves of Patricia's cornbread in the past: it's one of Osborn's particular loves.) Patricia wears bib overalls and a faded red flannel checkered shirt. Hair back in her customary austere long braid. She's quite appealing in her way.

I pay her for the dog.

It takes nearly an hour to drive home; when we arrive, and Anna sees Danny, much to my surprise she doesn't seem very pleased.

"This is just like the piano," she says, as soon as Roger's out of earshot. "You just go and do these things, without talking to me, and then there's nothing to be said—it's done. The dog is here."

"We talked about it. You knew that I had to get him from Patricia before they left, and I told you the other day that I'd probably go today or tomorrow, so I don't see, you know, exactly what the problem is."

"You didn't say anything last night."

"I forgot. I was tired. And then, this morning, you were out doing your nature studies or something, so I thought we could just go do it, and you'd be happy to see us when we got back."

If she had an accusatory tone to her voice, now, softly, I have one as well. I feel unjustly, unfairly attacked. Yesterday we had some kind of inane, petty dispute over the issue of who broke the Cuisinart. I didn't help things much by asking her if she was on her period, when I knew full well she was not. She hates that kind of generalization about her moods, for which I don't blame her—I only do it out of purposeful spite, expressly to annoy, when we're already on bad terms. I have many weapons of this sort, and Anna and I have known each other long enough so that we share a common language: the most oblique reference will usually be understood.

Sometimes, in fact, it seems that we understand each other better in our malice than in our joy: communication is never so swift, so certain and unambiguous, as though we are wired up to one circuit and share the same subtle electricity of the will.

"I'm sorry," says Anna, sighing, "you're right. I didn't realize they were leaving so soon, that's all. He does look like a nice dog; I'm sure it'll be good for Roger to have him around."

"I hope so," I say, mechanically, wondering what's on her mind. Maybe it's something about the exhibition. I'm still irritated at her, though, for her manners, and decide that I'll forgive her later: for now I'll take a nap. I've been having trouble getting my sleeping straightened out, switching back and forth as I do from days to nights.

Oh well, I'm not going to worry about the changing weather of Anna's moods. I've once or twice been accused of being too up-and-down myself. It's warm, and I remove clothing and lie down on our bed, I can hear the buzzing of a bee . . . and then I'm back pitching baseball, I can feel it in my shoulder as I release each fastball, I'm throwing hard and then striking them out with my change-up, a floating knuckleball that drops onto the plate. It feels good to be pitching: the mound is high and I feel like a king, throwing straight overhand, muscles smoothly functioning for maximum power and thrust.

When I wake up, I'm disappointed; I was enjoying being in my dream. How long did I sleep? Maybe an hour and a half. I yawn, but I don't think I can go back to sleep and finish pitching that game. Besides, my mouth is dry. I brush my teeth and go downstairs to get a Coke.

Nobody's around. I get the Coke and go out by the pool,

where I find Gretchen sunning herself. Since she now has a boyfriend, she's developed an interest in her appearance, and it's surprising how attractive she actually can be. And she doesn't look enough like Anna to give me the willies or anything, so it's nice to see her improve.

"Where's Anna? You look hot."

She does. Suntan oil gleams on her stomach, in her navel, and on her thighs.

"Oh, it feels nice." She smiles. "I'm having a pretty good afternoon." There is a science fiction paperback at her side, next to a glass of iced tea, the tea diluted and paled from melted ice. "Anna went somewhere up in the woods. Roger ran around with the dog for a while and then got sleepy, so he's in his room taking a nap."

Danny comes out of the shade, tail wagging, tongue hanging out. I think dogs smile. I pet him and tell him he's a good boy, trying not to use too absurd a voice.

Gretchen says, "He seems like an awfully well-trained dog."

"He's a good boy, all right," I say, and then: "I think we'll go look for Anna, see if she's found some woodpeckers or something."

"In a few minutes I'm going to go in, and then I thought maybe I'd go to the store."

"Do we need anything?"

"Oh, you know, there's always something. I thought we might have scallops, and a lemon cucumber salad, some rice. But I thought that for dessert I'd get some papayas or some mangoes—does that sound good to you? I guess this weather makes me think about tropical fruit."

"Mango sounds good to me," I say, and remember an old joke that I used to have with Anna, in which I would refer to the "mighty banana." That's all I'd have to say, after a while, and Anna would start to laugh. I feel like saying it again.

I'm in a good mood. My nap refreshed me. I don't dwell much on my old baseball memories, but these memories remain pleasant to me, and it's nice to have had it all seem, temporarily, so vivid and real.

The dog follows and then leads me, seeming to realize which path I'm going to take, as we go up the hill, walking on dry pine cones and leaf scum and twigs and browning moss. The only sounds are those of my feet on the ground, the dog's progress and his breathing, and the twittering of a few birds, the meanderings of some flies.

We travel around the top of the hill, looking all over for Anna, and then start down the other side, toward the creek. I'm a little bothered by the fact that we haven't found her by now. Maybe Danny will track her down. Or else, I suppose it's possible that she took some other route and is back at home by now, wondering when I will return. I pick up a rock and throw it, hitting the trunk of a tree.

I go after the dog, down past some rather dense underbrush, and then he barks, just a couple of barks, and stands there, and I advance to see what he has found.

I literally can't believe my eyes: I spend a few seconds totally unable to process the data I am presented with. Here is Anna, and she's gazing at me, unhappily, and evidently she has been visiting Sam, whom I recognize at once, who sits on a log outside a tent. They see me and I see them. Nobody knows what to do, how to react.

Sam starts to smile then, as though all can be explained, and I just don't want to discuss anything with him right now.

"I don't know what's going on," I say, shaking my head, finding out quickly that speaking's a mistake. I turn and go back the way I came, walking quickly, and Danny barks and follows, runs ahead, happy to show me the way.

Behind me, I hear Anna's voice, kind of raised, and I can't

understand her, also I have no idea if she's talking to me or to Sam—probably to Sam. I'm gone. I'm unable to theorize or think. It's such bad news.

The idea of Anna fucking him again, of him penetrating her, much less her enjoyment of this act—all this disgusts me beyond words. I feel hurt, and insulted: I never would have imagined Anna hated me like this. She should have just asked for a divorce. This kind of betrayal seems so unnecessary. Why fool me, make a fool of me? What kind of relationship are you preserving if you have to use big lies to keep it intact? Anna's depraved. This is so beyond anything that I deserve, however fucked up I may ever have been.

I'm not sure what I'm going to do. I could break all the windows in the house, for instance, though that would inconvenience and frighten Gretchen and Roger. I could go back to that clearing and beat up Sam, or give it a good try. I think I could beat him up, even though he's young and strong. Indomitable will. Like walking through a wall. I should have jumped on him immediately. I can just hear Anna saying, "Stop it! Stop it!" Fuck her, this is her problem. She didn't want me to find out. I hate her. If I had a gun I'd kill them both. I wish I had taken Tom up on his offer of a 9-millimeter automatic. I'd use every bullet, even if I missed and hit the sky.

I'm really in pain. I guess anything bad seems like a dream, but this seems like a dream. Jesus, this is a terrible thing to happen. Maybe it would have been better if I had not found them out. Maybe, though, Anna is planning to run away. Then what about Roger? Maybe I should take Roger and drive away in my car. I have credit cards; I could drive a long way.

I get back to the house and give Danny some water. He noisily laps it up. Gretchen and Roger are nowhere to be found. I assume they went to the store. If this was the movies

I'd pour myself a drink, but I don't feel like that at all. Nor do I want to take a pill.

Anna shows up in a while, not too long really—she can't have been too far behind. Even if she ran.

"I don't understand," I say, standing there. "It's just beyond me—I'm totally in the dark. Explain things to me, will you, Anna? Tell me why this is going on."

"Darrell, it's not like it looks—or it's not as bad as it looks, it's really not. I'm stupid, and I fucked up, but . . . this doesn't mean anything, and it certainly doesn't mean—I don't know," she says, almost starting to cry for a moment, breathing tragically. "It's all a big mistake. My mistake."

"Okay. I'm ready to listen to anything you tell me."

"Well, Sunday he showed up, and I guess he was spying on us, because when I walked into the woods he was right there, waiting for me—he just about scared me to death. He was all upset, and said that he couldn't stay with Diane, they'd had a falling out, and his parents were threatening to cut off all his money for school, and he wanted nothing more than to stay there in his tent for a day or two, and talk to me a couple of times . . . he said that he valued my advice."

"Where did he come from?" I ask. "How did he get here?"

"He's been on the road all summer, all across the U.S., hitchhiking and taking the bus or the train, sometimes getting rides from friends. I'm not sure, I mean, by this point—I'm not sure how much of what he told me was really true, but he told me about some terrible experiences he'd had, things like male friends of his father coming on to him sexually, or being seduced by some college buddy's girlfriend and then getting beat up by this buddy and some of his friends, getting ripped off and stranded in Alabama, being arrested and strip-searched—all kinds of terrible things. He was so emotional,

saying that I was the only person he trusted, so on and so
forth, and I guess I believed him, so I finally, you know, with
a lot of misgivings, said that he could stay there, in his tent,
until Tuesday."

Today's Thursday. Sunday was the day of the barbecue.

"Wait a minute," I say. "Is that why you were asking me
if I was attracted to Roz?"

"I suppose so. I told him, you see, that you and I were
happy now, and that there was no way he and I were going
to have sex; and he seemed to accept this without any problem.
He asked me not to say anything to you, he pleaded with me,
he said he was really scared of you, and I—I don't know, I
was confused. He seemed like he was just on the edge of really
cracking up, and I didn't want to push him, and I was afraid
that if I told you, I guess, that he'd be able to tell."

"So you thought it was okay, then, to leave me in the dark?"

"I don't *like* having secrets," she says. "I thought he'd be
gone soon, and then I'd tell you, and it wouldn't be any big
thing."

"Things didn't work out, though, did they? You ended up
fucking him after all, whatever your intentions were supposed
to be at the start."

"Darrell . . ." She puts her arms around me; I resist; she
anticipates my resistance and hugs me more tightly, hanging
on. "I kept thinking that he'd go, and that I was being put
upon, but that I was being a friend. I thought I could straighten
him out. Monday we talked and talked, and I heard all about
his problems with his parents, and it seemed like he was being
really honest, not trying to put himself in a good light or
anything. You know, I've only heard his side of it, but his
parents sound like they're awful: selfish and neurotic, just the
worst kind of examples of California dog-eat-dog pleasure
seekers.

"Anyway, all of that's fine, and I'd like to think it did some good to talk about it, but now I wonder. I wonder, I don't know—if it might not be some kind of a ploy . . . confess to someone, you know, as a way of gaining intimacy, so that you're afraid to hurt him when he . . . comes on to you."

We sit on the couch and drink iced tea, sharing a glass.

"I went over there on Tuesday," she says, "to see if he was going: it was then that he tried to get me to have sex. I mean, he didn't try, he succeeded. I didn't want to fight him. I stopped trying to get away, at a certain point, because it seemed easier to just let him. Then afterward, he started crying, and when I didn't respond he beat his head against this tree, saying that he was just bad, fucked up, he spoiled everything he ever touched. So then later on I let him, trying to be nice, like a goodbye sort of fuck . . . but it still wasn't any good. And when he started asking me to go with him down to L.A. I just thought he was crazy. The situation was out of control. I couldn't tell you he was here and wouldn't leave, not after letting myself sleep with him, and I couldn't seem to get him to actually go, he kept putting it off, saying that he had a plane ticket for Friday. It was just impossible, I was going crazy. And then you came home with that dog, and for some reason I just *knew* that dog would find him, I just knew it. God. And he did. I was telling Sam he absolutely had to leave and that I didn't have much good feeling left for him anymore; and then there you were."

"Yeah. Well."

"He's gone now."

"Oh? How did he leave?"

"He's got a motorcycle."

This makes me mad. I'm not sure why, but it does, and I grab Anna by the shoulders and look at her and think about slapping her or beating her up.

WITHIN NORMAL LIMITS 241

"A fucking motorcycle!"

"Go ahead and hit me," she says, reading my face. "I deserve it. He's a jerk, and I . . . messed things up. I can't believe I was so stupid, I should have told you."

"Why'd you fuck him the second time? The first time, you said he kind of forced you, but then the second time was for fun."

"It wasn't fun."

"It doesn't *matter* if it didn't turn out to be fun; the point is that you thought it would be."

"You're right. Okay. I thought it might be fun. Up close . . . he . . . I guess I still found him attractive. I'm sorry. I'm trying not to lie about this to you, Darrell, even if it makes me look bad."

"Worse, you mean."

"Worse."

"You know," I start to say, after a moment, after a long sigh, "you know, what's tragic, in a way, is that you can do this, and it's awful, and I hate it, but—it's not fatal. It doesn't just end it."

"We're beyond all that," Anna says, "I think. I could never, I would never want to leave you—and it's not because of Roger, or anything like that. Remember when I was in the hospital, in the Delivery Room, and it hurt, and you were there with me, holding me, talking to me. . . . We're tied together, I thought then, and I still feel like that, it's like we can't help it, no matter what either of us do. I'm sure there's a point of no return, but . . . you could murder somebody and I'd stick with you: I'd help you cover it up. All of this other stuff, even if it's terrible mistakes, it's so trivial, kind of."

"That doesn't mean I like it, either. But I guess we're stuck together, at least for a while. I don't know why. It's just chance, in a way, I don't see it as so inevitable or anything."

"I can imagine us being together when we're fifty. And I don't mean," says Anna, "ten lovers down the road. I don't think that's how we're going to live. You shouldn't have fucked that doctor in New York, you know? That really pissed me off."

"Well, at least I told you about it."

"You only did it to get at me, though, and that's what really made me mad. I don't think you even really wanted her, it was just the idea; you wanted to get even with me."

"How do you know if I really wanted her or not? Don't be such an egomaniac."

"Well . . . it's true," she says, and I know what she means, we're flirting now, amusing each other like a prelude to good sex. I'm a little uneasy about it, and I'm relieved when Gretchen and Roger come back from the store.

Then there's the distraction of dinner.

This is my life, I think, imperfect as it is. To change things abruptly would be crude. Pointless. I'm where I am, in my own unique path, like a salmon swimming upstream. Somehow I'll go on until I wear out. Anna looks different to me as we eat, and I'm trying to adjust my vision, but it's hard.

After dinner I leave the dog behind, playing with Roger, and go off into the woods. I'm not going to believe Sam is gone until I see that campsite again. I don't know how much of what Anna said is the truth. She was wearing an attractive outfit today, for instance, in which to go tell Sam to hit the road. Red tube top and tan shorts. You could really see her breasts, as if her legs were not enough.

Oh, she has her wiles. Probably most of what she told me was true, and I think she does want to stick with me, she doesn't want to part, but I can't help but feel there are matters she's glossed over, important details that she's suppressed.

I have a scalpel in my pocket. I'm not planning on stabbing

Sam if he's still here, I'd rather have a conversation, see what he says, but you never know what might come up. And if I stab him I'll have to kill him, finish him off, because you can't wound somebody and expect him to say thanks. No, I'd go for the carotid artery, at the side of the neck; he'd bleed to death in short order—this blade is fantastically sharp. Then we'd see if Anna meant what she said about staying with me if I was a murderer. We'd have to bury the body, and I'd make her give me some help. It might be smarter to wrap him in plastic, transport him someplace else, and then bury him there, deep, out on the Olympic Peninsula maybe, someplace really out of the way. And then stonewall it. Maybe read up on criminology to know what other traces of his presence we could remove. Of course, even if, in the end, they could somehow prove he camped out here, without a corpse they could never be sure that he was dead. It could turn out to be a pretty good crime.

Anna has been swimming, in her emerald-green swimsuit; when she sees me she comes up out of the pool. She's all wet, and I love her, and I want her to kiss me and soak me to the skin.

"Ow," she says, as she hugs me and then holds up her hand. A ruby-red glare of blood has stained her palm. I kiss it, bring it up to my mouth. It's not a bad cut, I see, and suck it for her to ease the pain. She sees that it's okay.

TWENTY-FOUR

I have to stay on, after working all day; there's a Green Alert because some plane is having trouble in the sky. Landing gear won't come down, something like that. A lot of extra people are called in, just in case we really do end up with some sort of crisis on our hands.

Meanwhile, we get a fifty-five-year-old judge who's having a myocardial infarction; he was attending a dinner where he was being named Legal Citizen of the Year. His well-dressed, attractive wife and other lawyers and judges and friends all hang around. Kind of as a joke, I'm extra, extra nice to them. No perceptible irony in my affect.

The word is, Matthew has told me, that the Bearghost suit

may never come to trial. The guy had such a history of violence, jail time, alcoholism and concussions; the little bop on the head that I was supposed to be so impressed with was really nothing new. Who could know? It all comes back to that.

Today Teena Overstreet was in, complaining of abdominal pain, and I did a pelvic and I couldn't find anything wrong. She was histrionic, moaning and groaning, and I let her have a shot for pain; but I'm getting tired of her, next time I don't think I'll be so kind.

Two black guys showed up, one with a lacerated hand, and he explained how it happened, saying, "I was trying to hit the motherfuckin' rat with the motherfuckin' bottle, and I missed him and it broke." And his friend said, "That wasn't no rat. That was just some itty-bitty mouse."

I call Anna, tell her I'll be late, we don't know if it's going to turn out to be anything or not.

"Okay," she says, "I'll keep the television on, see if there's anything on the news. I'll save you some dinner. Roger's practicing his piano. And Gretchen's out at a movie. It's really raining, isn't it? Does that make it any more difficult for the plane?"

"I don't know. I suppose so. Anything in the mail?"

"We got another brochure about Antigua. God, won't it be great to get down there? Only a couple more weeks. Oh, Paul called. He didn't know you were working. He said he'd call back later on."

"Well, I guess I'll see you in a while. If they land the damn thing I'll be home pretty soon."

But then they don't. The plane crashes in a field, catches fire and falls apart. The helicopter flies us some patients, and then more are brought by ambulances; others go to other hospitals all around. Matthew is here, Peter is here, Petibon is here—only Steve Gold can't be found.

I take care of a woman with a broken arm and a head laceration, from Florida, who's in pretty good spirits, thanking God she's still alive. The Burn Doctors, I know, are treating a couple of really fucked-up-looking young burns. Some kids are screaming and crying. The department is totally jam-packed. It's orderly, but it looks incredibly confused.

There's a part of me that wishes it could always be like this, or even more intense, more wild—like in a war. All that's missing is some gunfire and explosions, a few more patients, and we'd be there.

A fifteen-year-old boy has a bump on his head and a sprained ankle; his thirteen-year-old sister has broken her wrist and possibly some ribs. I examine them and order X rays. Then I go into the Trauma Room to see if I can help.

"Will you talk to the media?" asks Matthew, through his mask. "I'm all tied up in here for now. Tell them . . . four critical, five fair, and, what is it, seven or eight that are just a little bounced around? Make sure you get the numbers right. Names withheld until families are notified. Four critical, all right?"

And so I go out to meet the press. Big bright lights, big cameras, carefully made-up TV people I've seen on the screen. I try to be grave and concerned.

At home, later, Anna and I eat popcorn and watch me talk on Channel 5.

"We have four patients in critical condition at this time."

"You look good," Anna says. "You're good. You should be on TV all the time."

I take a handful of popcorn and watch myself looking serious; Anna changes the channel so we can see me again. There is some dark footage of blinking red lights around the wreck. Then some patients being rushed into the hospital, with voice-over, and then I see my face. I say those words.

ABOUT THE AUTHOR

TODD GRIMSON was born in Seattle, Washington, and grew up in Portland, Oregon, where he still resides. He has worked at a variety of jobs, including time spent as a flogger, grinder, emergency room interviewer, intensive care unit clerk, warehouseman, and musician. In 1980 he began sending stories out, and these have appeared in *Impulse*, *Minnesota Review*, *Gargoyle*, *Mississippi Mud*, and several others. His first novel, *Within Normal Limits*, is derived from some of his medical experiences.

VINTAGE
CONTEMPORARIES

"Today's novels for the readers of today."

—VANITY FAIR

"Real literature—originals and important reprints—in attractive, inexpensive paperbacks."

—THE LOS ANGELES TIMES

"Prestigious."

—THE CHICAGO TRIBUNE

"A very fine collection."

—THE CHRISTIAN SCIENCE MONITOR

"Adventurous and worthy."

—SATURDAY REVIEW

"If you want to know what's on the cutting edge of American fiction, then these are the books you should be reading."

—UNITED PRESS INTERNATIONAL

On sale at bookstores everywhere, but if otherwise unavailable, may be ordered from us. You can use this coupon, or phone (800) 638-6460.

Please send me the Vintage Contemporaries books I have checked on the reverse. I am enclosing $_____ (add $1.00 per copy to cover postage and handling). Send check or money order—no cash or COD please. Prices are subject to change without notice.

NAME_____

ADDRESS_____

CITY _____ STATE_____ ZIP_____

Send coupons to:

RANDOM HOUSE, INC., 400 Hahn Road, Westminster, MD 21157

ATTN: ORDER ENTRY DEPARTMENT

Allow at least 4 weeks for delivery.

V I N T A G E
CONTEMPORARIES

___ LOVE ALWAYS by Ann Beattie	$5.95	74418-7
___ FIRST LOVE AND OTHER SORROWS by Harold Brodkey	$5.95	72970-6
___ THE DEBUT by Anita Brookner	$5.95	72856-4
___ CATHEDRAL by Raymond Carver	$4.95	71281-1
___ DANCING BEAR by James Crumley	$5.95	72576-X
___ ONE TO COUNT CADENCE by James Crumley	$5.95	73559-5
___ THE WRONG CASE by James Crumley	$5.95	73558-7
___ THE LAST ELECTION by Pete Davies	$6.95	74702-X
___ DAYS BETWEEN STATIONS by Steve Erickson	$6.95	74685-6
___ A FAN'S NOTES by Frederick Exley	$5.95	72915-3
___ A PIECE OF MY HEART by Richard Ford	$5.95	72914-5
___ THE SPORTSWRITER by Richard Ford	$6.95	74325-3
___ THE ULTIMATE GOOD LUCK by Richard Ford	$5.95	75089-6
___ FAT CITY by Leonard Gardner	$5.95	74316-4
___ WITHIN NORMAL LIMITS by Todd Grimson	$5.95	74617-1
___ AIRSHIPS by Barry Hannah	$5.95	72913-7
___ DANCING IN THE DARK by Janet Hobhouse	$5.95	72588-3
___ NOVEMBER by Janet Hobhouse	$6.95	74665-1
___ FISKADORO by Denis Johnson	$5.95	74367-9
___ ASA, AS I KNEW HIM by Susanna Kaysen	$4.95	74985-5
___ A HANDBOOK FOR VISITORS FROM OUTER SPACE by Kathryn Kramer	$5.95	72989-7
___ THE CHOSEN PLACE, THE TIMELESS PEOPLE by Paule Marshall	$6.95	72633-2
___ SUTTREE by Cormac McCarthy	$6.95	74145-5
___ THE BUSHWHACKED PIANO by Thomas McGuane	$5.95	72642-1
___ NOBODY'S ANGEL by Thomas McGuane	$6.95	74738-0
___ SOMETHING TO BE DESIRED by Thomas McGuane	$4.95	73156-5
___ BRIGHT LIGHTS, BIG CITY by Jay McInerney	$5.95	72641-3
___ RANSOM by Jay McInerney	$5.95	74118-8
___ RIVER DOGS by Robert Olmstead	$6.95	74684-8
___ NORWOOD by Charles Portis	$5.95	72931-5
___ MOHAWK by Richard Russo	$6.95	74409-8
___ CARNIVAL FOR THE GODS by Gladys Swan	$6.95	74330-X
___ THE CAR THIEF by Theodore Weesner	$6.95	74097-1
___ TAKING CARE by Joy Williams	$5.95	72912-9